TIMELESS BEGINNINGS

TIME ✈ FLIES
BOOK ONE

Jill Wallace

TSOTSI
PUBLICATIONS

TIMELESS BEGINNINGS

by Jill Wallace

Copyright © 2023 by Jill Wallace

Paperback ISBN: 978-0-9997768-8-9

Second edition

Published by Tsotsi Publications

www.jillwallace.com

With Sincere Thanks

It is with great thanks that I acknowledge these wonderful souls, all of whom graciously supported *Timeless Beginnings* in her infancy, showing your faith in me by backing my Kickstarter campaign. It's important to me that your name lives on in this book forever.

~Scott Casey
~Debbie Sekula
~Susan S.E. Smith
~Frankie & Dawn Giaramita (Sponsored Dawn - the young midwife)
~Diane Vaccaro
~Narelle Todd (Sponsored Donald Cox – the heinous villan)
~Isabella Jo Baines
~Eliza Sinclair
~Natalie Palmadesso
~Stephanie Harrell
~Mike Williams
~Cassandra Chandler

~Lucy Lakestone
~June Long-Schuman
~Kerry Evelyn
~Debbie Shannon
~Becki Svare
~Barbara Kroon
~Crystal Donak
~Melanie B.
~Lila Ferrari
~Ann McIntosh
~Carlos Fuentes

*This book is dedicated to
my besties for over five decades,
Alana McIntosh and Kitty Low.
Your love and unconditional support
have followed me over oceans.
I am the luckiest girl in the world to be
one of the ever-changing
Faith, Hope & Charity.
I love you forever.*

xx

CHAPTER 1

I was one who knew how to entertain herself.

I found my own company quite scintillating, thank you very much.

Who needed people when you have the ability to see the dead, can easily slip into past lives, and have the marvelous company of a faithful, intuitive dog?

I stroked the fluffy back of my mottle-coated Aussie shepherd, Tula, as I picked up the steaming coffee mug. It was glazed black with a pair of white clock hands showing six o'clock emblazoned during its time in the kiln.

Remembering the gruff sheriff from Indiana made me smile. We'd just cracked and wrapped a tough case. He thrust this cup with the odd time in my direction and said: "Got this for you, Lucky. Never believed in psychics and all that bullshit before I met you. But you're straight up and down like six o'clock and damned if you haven't made me a believer in things I will never understand."

Later, I wondered if the six o'clock also alluded to my being straight up and down physically, because the crusty old dog made no bones about an over-the-top appreciation for every set of hefty boobs in sight. And if the woman was blond, he'd practically be drooling.

Very different from how he looked at me the first time we met. And who could blame him? A flat-chested, auburn-haired woman sporting a large nose definitely wouldn't be on his dream list.

Bright red Ruby Woo lipstick notwithstanding.

But then it wasn't a beauty competition, and he was not one of the judges. Nevertheless, we'd made an impression on each other in the end. And, since then, every cuppa joe I partook of from the two-tone vessel, I thought of that tenacious lawman, the dead middle-aged woman in the sewage tank, and my flat chest.

Each morning I looked forward to Dunkin Donut Original brew teasing my olfactory glands. And without fail, with my twitching nose leading the way, Arabica coffee took me somewhere different.

Memories of this life and vignettes of past lives in equally splendid technicolor, along with all the feels, smells, sounds, tastes and touches, confirmed that as far as our souls are concerned, there are no timelines.

I reckon that through the centuries of time, in every life we come back to live on earth, we wear a different body, but keep the same soul.

And that heavy old soul hauls with its past-life memories which, inevitably, make the present life more...complicated.

I willed myself to concentrate on the aromatic coffee. The acidic bouquet alluded to bitterness with a nutty-smoky-sweet fragrance and infused every molecule of my body, magically conjuring up delicious visions.

FLASH!

In a midnight café where a colorful silk scarf thrown haphazardly over a lampshade adds to the mystique. I lunge backward, languid and secure in a dark, interesting man's arms. Roy! I run my long fingers through his thick black hair and his intense gaze burns into mine. His generous mouth is slightly parted as our knees entangle tightly and our thighs ache for more...

Riiiiiiiiiiiiiiiiiiiiiiiiiiiiiiiiiiing.

BACK!

Bugger!

I released a low groan and shook my head. "Just as well, Tula. If I dipped into a backbend, I would surely have dislocated a hip. The old bod isn't as supple as she used to be. Even a ruptured disc would be worth it for more time with my soulmate.

Riiiiiiiiiiiiiiiiiiiiiiiiiiiiiiiiiiing.

"Okay, okay! Hello?"

I recognized the FBI agent's voice.

"Jim! I always like to hear from you, but it means somebody's in trouble."

"Andy and I were just talking about you. Long time no see, but we heard you and Tula did an amazing job in Arkansas with that missing boy."

"It was rough how it turned out." An involuntary shudder accompanied visions of a broken young body amidst a green field dotted with corn, high as my armpit, waving in the wind. The distinct aroma of fresh-cut grass was as intoxicating as moonshine. I'd heard somewhere that corn plants increase their fecund smell when chums growing around them are in danger. This hapless human form crushing their fellow stalks and precious yellow ears could easily have amped up the tang that drew me to the pitiful victim.

"Our success is another's undoing when we give the victims' families tangible proof that their loved one is dead. Makes you wonder why we do what do, doesn't it Jim?" Boy! Even to my own ears I sounded morose.

"We do it for the closure we can deliver, Lucky. Not knowing is a lot worse than knowing, no matter how awful the truth. And at least we can give them something real to weep over as they give their loved ones a personal farewell."

All I managed was a hmphhh!

Enjoying but half a tango with her dream man can make a girl decidedly grumpy.

"And don't forget. We don't stop there. We make it our mission to find the bastards responsible." Jim was giving me the hard sell.

Tula's nose brushed against my hand to let me know he was near.

"We do that," I admitted, "but it would be nice to deal in *life* sometimes, Jim, don't you think?"

"But we do. We help the living to keep living and not wishing they were dead from the not-knowing."

"Ok, you cheered me up. So, how can Tula and I help the living this time?"

"It's complicated. Can you come down to Springfield?" Jim asked.

"I hope that's Springfield, Massachusetts and not Springfield, Missouri."

"What? Just a second, Lucky, Andy's saying something in my other ear."

While I waited, I took another sip from my six-o'clock mug

and distant syncopated tango rhythms tempted me in four-four time. Damn the untimeliness of this call. That vision reeked of serious potential and time with my long-lost love.

"Andy says he wants to see where you live. How do you feel about us high tailing it up to Hull? We can be there by lunchtime."

I didn't do home huddles.

"Jim, I don't like visitors. You know that. I'm a hermit."

Andy's voice with its slight Latino inflection came on the line. "Hi Lucky," he said, as if we were planning a party.

Heaven help me.

"Listen, we won't stay over or anything. No evidence boxes are available for this puzzle yet. We're waiting on the local yokels to give them up, so if we come to you, well, we can discuss what's coming down the pike, you can give it some thought 'til we can attack the case full-on when the boxes are released. Plus, Jim and I can check out your hermit pad you're always so anxious to return to."

Tula nudged my leg. I glanced down at him, but his eyes held mine. *Chill.*

He was often much smarter than me.

"Okay but don't expect me to entertain you. I don't do that. And bring lunch. I'll be even hungrier when you get here."

"Yes." His voice was chipper, and I could imagine him doing a fist pump like he'd just won twenty bucks on a scratch and win. Not a big payday, but something.

Jim's voice, "So the good news is, today we'll deal in life and not the other thing."

He got me. "Soon," I said and clicked off the phone.

Suck it up, Lucky. Your psychic gifts not only pay the bills, they're also your penance. Find those who need to be found, for

Alana's sake. Even if it means you have to (shiver) *entertain the FBI.*

"But having them in my own house?" I asked Tula, Alana, God, The Universe.

Tula gave me a look. He was right. I shouldn't be so uptight about so little. They were just visitors, not poltergeists.

"Damn it! My nose gets me into so much trouble." My body convulsed with an icy shiver so violent it wracked my body. My all too-quick-to-remind-me conscience played back just a smidgeon of the unbearable pain from years before, when I'd trained myself to mentally block out the smells and the touches that spawned psychic experiences and past-life regressions, just to save my airline career.

What a travesty that my hyperosmia couldn't help me to find my best friend...

Not now, Lucky! Don't go there! I shook my head like a dog emerging from a river to rid myself of life-shattering memories.

Sometimes time, distance, and the unfamiliarity of a new continent helped.

But only sometimes.

A vision of my bestie Alana, who saved me at thirteen, flashed before me. She smiled, but that didn't ease my conscience.

Instead, I studied my dream house objectively to regain my composure—or was it to confirm my worth?

2757 Reunion Street was the address.

My soulmate Roy Moreno-Reyes was born on the twenty-seventh day of the seventh month in 1957.

It was the perfect house for me.

Reunion Street.

I'd been searching for Roy for too many years to count, and

when you're desperate, you look for all sorts of clues the universe might be leaving you.

Tidbits of hope.

I needed those optimistic scraps like a hyena needs the lion's discarded bones of her kill.

Sure, I was drawn to the number and the name. 2757 Reunion Street might be a sign I'd find Roy. That it was a contemporary home on stilts in the midst of saltboxes and Victorians originally built by seventeenth-century settlers, made it the only one worth my contemplation as a buyer.

There were enough dead people in my head to populate a small village. I didn't need to take on a house with guests who'd been trapped in it for centuries. 'Contemporary' was my preferred style *and* promised the least number of ghosts I might inherit.

It was an enormous gift to myself, this home with its twenty-foot-high ceilings a short seagull's flight from the ocean.

Upstairs, naked windows, and sliders let in brightness from day to night. Boston's lights glimmered and flickered across the bay. And for divine backup, I had the moon and the stars keeping my sanctuary aglow.

For a girl afraid of the dark, who became a woman with the same fears, this house, Tula and Opium—the Yves Saint Laurent perfume that I wore to dull all unwanted smells—were my saving graces.

I consoled myself that Jim and Andy would come and go in a few hours. I'd have a chance to show off my home, which happened more rarely than a hen having a tooth extracted, and soon I'd have my palace to myself again (and Tula, naturally,) and blessed peace would reign.

CHAPTER 2

On the computer in the guest bedroom with the window open to let in the sea breeze, I looked up murders in Springfield from the last 20 years. There were surprisingly few. My immersion was interrupted by the sound of the big SUV's tires crunching the shale of my driveway.

Tula's ears went up, and he dashed to the front door. A few long minutes later, the doorbell rang and he let them have it in his gruffest, most threatening timbre.

I'm vain enough to have applied my Ruby Woo red lipstick in advance, but not in anticipation, you understand. It was more like what was expected from an old air hostess. It was part of my DNA, as was the spritz of Opium between my lack-of-boobs others might call a cleavage. Opium had been my protection since my South African Airways years.

One couldn't be too careful, I told myself. One never knew, in their line of work, what darkness FBI agents had attached to their spirits that they might unintentionally schlep into my sanctuary. And it was so fabulous, which spirit wouldn't like to stay?

I opened the door and Jim's hand was already out to shake mine. I faced him, clasping my fingers around his. His grip was strong and dry, and I surveyed the tall, lean Black man whose smile could brighten a cloudy day. Jim kept his finest visible asset for long absences and rare occasions. It was a smile worth waiting for.

"I see you, Special Agent Jim Massey. This must be serious."

"It always is when we see you, Lucky." Jim heaved a sigh. As I inhaled, a few of his past lives I'd never seen before flashed in front of me like a PowerPoint presentation on speed.

This quick summary of lives over thousands of years happens sometimes when I meet someone who's an empath. Jim was a helper in all its connotations over many centuries. His past demeanors were that of someone soft and cuddly who blurted out on-the-spot, self-constructed platitudes that took your blues away. Nothing at all what you'd expect from the driven, detail-oriented FBI agent I knew him to be.

Deep gratitude for my gifts enveloped me. Every time I touched Jim's hand and glimpsed a few of his many life journeys, I respected his elected profession even more profoundly. It took a strong soul to unravel humanity's darkest deeds.

And then, if I'm honest, the real reason for the careful lipstick application and the up-do I'd spent too long on, stepped into the foreground.

Special Agent Andy Martinez.

If indeed there were past lives to assess by Andy's handshake, they were entirely upstaged by his plain-as-the-nose-on-your-face sex appeal. Those bedroom eyes looked directly into mine and his slow "I'd-love-to-show-you-the-way-to-heaven" smile spread wide.

Damn that little somersault in my solar plexus.

Careful. Your heart – nay your soul – belongs to another.

"Special Agent" I said formally, though in spite of myself my grin shone through. "Come on in. Tula and I are thrilled you brought lunch." Despite his sniffing like a bloodhound, my dog diligently escorted them inside.

"Wise Guys burgers and one for Tula without the carbs." Andy said.

"By George, Special Agent, you'd swear you knew a way to a girl and her dog's heart." I threw my best impersonation of a Southern drawl over my shoulder as I led them up to the bedroom-level landing.

Another curled flight up and we were in the living space of my modern pad.

"Your house stands out in the street like...well not a sore thumb, but a diamond encrusted ring finger in the middle of New England's refurbished colonialism," Jim said.

"Well, at least you didn't get the impression my pad was giving the seventeenth century homes the middle finger," I smiled.

Andy's face was the easiest to read but he didn't hold back vocally either. "Man-about-town! This place is amazing, Lucky. No wonder you're a hermit. I could live here forever."

"You *are* just here for lunch, right?" I asked in mock concern.

"Promise." Jim grinned. "It really is something, Lucky. The ceilings. The windows. The views."

"Fukinnuts. Check out the deck, the hot tub, the widow's

walk!" Andy had opened one of the floor-to-ceiling triple glass sliders and was yelling back to us against the ocean breeze. He was accompanied by a strutting Tula who was taking all the credit for his pad. I didn't mind.

Andy was still whistling his amazement when he came inside and I took my 'best' plates down from the top shelf and dusted them off.

"What to drink, boys?" I opened the fridge. "Sorry, let's reverse this. I have iced water. A half bottle of Amarula..." I saw their brows furrow. "South African liqueur made from the marula fruit that falls off the tree and ferments. Monkeys, elephants, and other bush inhabitants get smashed out of their minds on the marula. Some genius threw in a hefty dollop of cream and made it deliciously fit for human consumption."

"We'll have some of that," said Andy shooting up his hand like a grade school student.

"Slow down, sailor," said Jim, patting his shoulder. "We're here on FBI business, remember."

"Oh, coffee. I have great coffee," I announced proudly.

We sat at my dining room table, off the open kitchen. The living room was only a step below. Tula lay with his head on my feet, happy as a lark with his Wise Guy's cheese burger, sans bread or pickles.

We hungrily munched our burgers.

When we'd wiped our mouths on paper towels, and the coffee pot had done the rounds once more, I said, "Let's go and sit on comfy chairs."

As we moved down to the living room, Andy whistled again. "Yeah. I would know this was your space even if I didn't know. A living room suite the color of the lipstick you wear, with splotches the color of Tula's eyes to break the monotony. Interesting." He placed his pinkie on pursed lips, à la Austin Powers.

"You flatter me, Andy. The suite was on sale. It was so funky, no-one else wanted it," I said, as I nestled into the love seat, my knees up, bare feet resting beside me. Tula stood at attention, waiting for the boys to take up their positions on the couch and chair respectively.

Jim snuggled back into the cushion. "Andy and I were saying it's a damn shame we can't call you anything more impressive than 'consultant,' even though you're integral to much of our mystery solving."

"We proposed 'Spiritual Consultant' or 'Psychic Specialist' but there were no takers." Andy said earnestly. "But we figured at least we should work on getting your teammate here certified as a service dog, with a jacket and all."

"He'd like that. Make it light blue to go with his eyes, would you?" I smiled my thanks. Having one of us made official was better than none. "So, chaps, what's going on in Springfield?"

"Hunter Hughes," Andy spat and leaned forward, elbows on his knees. "Twelve years ago, Janice, his wife of 'two glorious years'—his words, not mine—went missing. We suspected the son of a bitch had something to do with it, but there was nothing to incriminate him."

Jim took over. They'd worked together for so long they had an easy, natural-sounding schtick. "Local boys and detectives imported from Boston spent days searching every inch of their home." Jim ran a hand over his closely shaven head in frustration. "We came in and expanded the search with a chopper and cherry-picked uninhabited areas—a bitch of a job with all the marshlands, lakes, woods, nooks, and crannies. And we followed up on hundreds of tips."

Andy chimed in. "No evidence anywhere. No eyewitnesses. We knew from Hunter that he and his lovely wife had gone off to a block party, but he'd left early. Nothing to suggest foul play. Janice's toothbrush remained in the cupholder, her cell phone on the charger near her purse in the kitchen, and her car in the driveway. Hunter reported her missing the next morning." Andy shook his head, his anger clear. "A beautiful, vital young woman just disa-fukin'-ppeared."

I picked up my phone and Googled *Hunter Hughes Springfield* and up popped the kind of image billboards were made for. Literally and figuratively. He was a realtor. In my mind's eye I could see his boyishly handsome, clean-shaven face on a 12ft by 24ft board on stilts, with a 'shining' star inserted above his set of pearly-white teeth.

But I felt nothing.

And I said nothing.

Not yet. Let them get it all out.

Jim continued, "Five pairs of neighbors all hungover from the party the night before were interviewed. Nice people. Nice, safe neighborhood. They recalled Hunter had gone home early, nobody knew why, and Janice, just a social drinker, mixed her drinks—on purpose, it seemed to all at the party, and really got sloshed."

Andy said, "At 1:35 a.m., one of the revelers remembered glancing at his watch, Janice announced it was time for the couch. One asked why not the bed? And she replied, 'Don't want any Hunting going on,' and she'd laughed hysterically. When questioned on how things stood with her husband,

Janice said, 'I have the right to remain silent,' with a giggle, and nobody pushed for more. Several people offered to drive her four doors down, but she refused and said she needed the fresh air before she got home."

"The poor girl was postponing going into her own home." I said, as dread washed over me like dirty dishwater.

Jim followed with, "They asked her if she had her cell phone with her, in case she needed to call them, but of course, she didn't. So, they continued partying and didn't give Janice another thought until the police knocked on their doors twelve hours later."

Andy reached down to give Tula a head scratch. "Janice was a court stenographer, and everyone there loved her."

"Aha, so that's why she said, 'I have the right to remain silent.'" When my mind was going two hundred and fifty-three miles a minute, I had to slow things down. I was impressed Andy sensed my need, and had offered a break in the narrative of the disappearance itself.

Jim nodded and placed his empty coffee mug on the table. "Judges praised her work ethic. All the big, tough bailiffs blushed when they talked about her. Besides the neighbors, she had a handful of good friends. Her father was still alive, but her mom had been killed in a car accident during a fierce snow storm. She hit a tree. Tragic. And only two months before Janice and Hunter's wedding."

"That's beyond awful. Losing someone like that..." I ached for Janice. I knew all too well the wretched devastation and chaos of sudden death. I sniffed my palm... *Ahh, Opium.* It made my world tilt back on its axis. I went to the kitchen and ejected ice and cold water from the fridge door into three glasses, and showed off my old South African Airlines hostie skills. I had all three full glasses in two hands while carrying an open, family-sized packet of mini-Butterfingers in my teeth. Ha! Who was I kidding? There was no tooth-carrying in the airline. The Check hostesses would have your hide!

I heard a Check in my ear, bitching away, but I ignored her and tightened my teeth on the Butterfinger bag as I navigated the one step down to the living room without spilling a drop.

Placing down the Butterfingers and glasses I asked, "So, why is the FBI getting involved?"

Andy said, "It happened here, in Massachusetts, but since it's spitting distance to Connecticut and close to Rhode Island and New York, we led the investigation, looking for leads and similar disappearances."

He took a quick swallow of the iced water and I took a shameless peek at his lips through the bottom of the glass. Even distorted, they were sexy. He put his glass down, and I focused on his eyes; pretty dreamy in and of themselves.

Stop it, Lucky. Don't go there.

I shook my head to clear the untimely dialogue with the universe. The Big U seemed to be interfering a great deal with my little crush.

Don't want me to look? Then find my soulmate will you? I pushed back.

Focus on the job, Lucky!

Andy said, "We couldn't fault the procedures of local detectives or the Boston imports. The leads were all dead ends in the neighboring states. Frankly, we were superfluous. There was nothing more we could add, but we got to know Janice's dad well and it became personal, which is never good."

I bit into a delectable candy bar as Jim took the baton. "This one has burdened us for nearly twelve years. We've been here a week this time; going over everything with a fine-tooth comb again to see if we missed anything. Checked with neighboring states to see if any leads had come in since we were here last, or if anything suspicious was forthcoming after the incident. Nothing. Interviewed park rangers who periodically patrol Hamilton reservoir, Lake Siog and all Springfield's surrounding marshlands. Nothing suspicious there, either. Lots of peculiar things, but none that could help our case."

"So here we are, Tula and me. Your last resort, as usual." I smiled to soften my retort and added, "And happy to help if we can." I patted the space next to me on the loveseat and Tula jumped up. "This has been a cold case for a long time. What new tidbit got you two to drag yourselves to the likely picturesque New England town?"

Jim looked sheepish. "Unfortunately, Janice's dad recently passed away. He went to his grave, refusing to accept his only child was dead. He left her a substantial inheritance in his will."

Andy crossed his forearms over his tight, broad chest and continued, "His lawyer, who knows our station chief, appealed to her to reopen the case in hopes Janice might still be alive to receive her inheritance."

I scratched the top of Tula's head and his eyes closed in sheer bliss. "It's a small town. You'd think somebody would've seen something. But you've revisited all those interviews and heard no alarm bells. The chances of her being alive are indeed slim."

Two heads nodded sagely, and Andy continued, "Her two closest friends said they got the impression Janice regretted marrying her husband—that she wasn't joking at the party. They believe she only went through with the wedding to honor her mom. Janice wanted to hang on to the memories of the big occasion the two women had planned together for a year, far more than she actually wanted to become Mrs. Hunter Hughes."

I pointed to my phone where I'd spotted Hunter's All-American-Boy good looks. "I saw his face, but what's Hunter really like?"

"Smooth and slick as Brylcreem on my comb when I was ten," Jim and Andy said in unison. Clearly a private joke. They smiled at each other like old friends do when they're on the same page.

Envy struck me, and I caught a glimpse of the abyss of my loss. A friend like Alana, who finished your sentences and whose sentences you finished, could never be replaced.

"Fancies himself to be quite the catch." Andy said and rolled his eyes. "Our radar really pinged when we found out Hunter Hughes used to be a park ranger with the Army Corps of Engineers around here. The guy is more than familiar with the area." Andy's brow wore a deep frown. "All the lakes and swamps make perfect dumping grounds for a body. And hungry animals do an excellent job of moving and removing evidence. By that spring, there'd have been nothing left of her but bones. What the hell kind of evidence can we expect to find a decade-plus later?"

"I think the only one who can tell us the story is Janice." I kept my voice flat. They looked at me and nodded.

Silence reigned for a few seconds.

This was a typical pattern with pragmatists. They believed I could use my psychic skills for answers, but they didn't want to have to think too deeply about the source of those otherworldly alternatives. They simply wanted the results to appear magically, so they could continue with their business as if they had generated answers on their own.

"These days, Hunter's a big shot at a prestigious brokerage in Springfield." Jim said, "he drives a flashy car and his wife is similar in age to Janice twelve years ago."

"I'd love to nail him on his smirk alone," said Andy, and Jim comically contorted his mouth to imitate Hunter. I laughed. "Hunter Hughes was our *only* suspect," Andy finished.

"Hunter didn't do it." I said flatly.

Their gaze fixed on me, their confusion palpable, like an uninvited guest at our table.

"Why do you say that?" Jim got out, while Andy's jaw struggled to find its way back up.

"I felt nothing when I looked at his photo," I said.

The two men looked at each other for a minute, and Andy's jaw snapped shut.

"Well, that's that then," Jim clapped his hands.

"Lucky, you've taken our instincts and squeezed the life out of them. That's pretty rude when we're both top-notch FBI agents," Andy chided through a grin.

"I am so sorry, boys, but I tell 'em like I see 'em. Hunter's character isn't strong to kill someone and display his face on a billboard. He's a gatherer at heart, not a hunter at all." I smiled but knew that wasn't enough to restore fragile male egos, so I added, "But he surely sounded like a prime suspect!"

The two looked down. Two naughty boys who'd been chastised.

"Listen, once you get the evidence, if we can spend the

night with her stuff, I bet Tula and I can get a solid handle on Janice's last hours. We'll certainly promise to do our best."

They both nodded and were silent for a bit, then Andy glanced down at Tula. "Your boyfriend doesn't say much."

"That's the way I like them," I quipped. Catching Andy's glint from my double entendre, I busied myself fluffing Tula's hair.

CHAPTER 3

I didn't have to look at him to know those intense eyes of Andy's were still on me and I actually squirmed, suddenly aware of my own body. It had been a long time since a man had made me do that. Well, a real one. Not one from my dreams or my fantasies.

"We're always all-business when we're working on a case. There's seldom time for us to socialize." Andy's voice had an edge of intimacy, like he was telling me something important.

"Yes, Lucky. Truth is we both want to get to know you. The woman Lucky, not just the psychic who helps us get healthy annual increases." Jim smiled, and Andy laughed.

"I'm really not all that interesting," I said.

"Come on," said Jim. "Start at the beginning. Where were you born and when did you first know you had psychic gifts?"

"It's a long story," I warned.

Andy looked at the coffee table, then at me. "May I?"

Fortunately, I'm psychic. I smiled. "Sure. The table's hardly an heirloom. I think I got that at a thrift store."

He put his feet up, grinned, and said, "We've got time 'til

that damn evidence becomes available. It could be days. Take your sweet time."

"Since there are no sleepovers in my house, I'll make it short." I briefly wondered if my insistence was due to the temptation of sleeping under the same roof as Andy.

Jim and Andy both took off their jackets and removed their ties.

"About time you two did that. Now you are officially off duty."

"Don't procrastinate, Lucky. You warned us before it was your flaw. We really want to know about you," Jim said soberly.

"Wow. You think I'm fascinating?" I joshed, glancing at Andy. He was straight-faced and nodding. My heart did another girlish somersault.

Quit your bitching, Big U, the old heart needs some exercise!

"I was born in the depths of Africa, Zambia actually, and it took me eighteen hours to make an appearance, so my mom told me. And when I did, I was silent.

"Almost a decade later, when Neil Armstrong graced the front page of the *Sunday Times*, taking his first step on the moon, my mom exclaimed, 'That's what you looked like when you were born. Just like Louis Armstrong from the shoulders up.'"

The boys smirked as if I'd made a boo-boo. I let them think so for a beat, then set them straight. "My mom always mixed up her Armstrongs." I smiled. "I was thrilled to resemble an astronaut but never had the urge to play the trumpet."

My mom appeared before me, unseen by the Special Agents, bracelets jingling, red hair in disarray. She was pissed. "You always foul up this story. Let me tell it my way. It was me who lived it, after all."

My hand went up, admitting defeat in the face of her fury. Boy, the fellows must have been confused.

"I am so sorry. I know this is super-weird, but my mom made an unexpected appearance from the other side of the veil."

The boys were slack-jawed, but they should have been used to me popping in and out of pasts and presents and channeling those who had passed away. In their defense, they had only seen me as a vessel or a mouth piece for a victim, never my family!

I soldiered on. "My mother just scolded me for claiming this story as my own when it's hers to tell. So, I'm going to give her the floor." I dared glance at Jim and Andy. Both were big-eyed and still as salt cellars as I presented, just like Vanna White, my mother's invisible self to them.

"Okay, Ma. Do it your way," I conceded out loud and literally sat back and watched the show.

Tula squished in beside me and I heard my voice decrease two octaves as my mom began the story I had heard so often. The cadence of her conversation, along with the *Jingle, Jangle* of her bracelets, made me inordinately happy.

"I want you to have the correct version, Andy, and Jim. And by the way, it was Lucky who, in the telling, always fouled up the Armstrongs'. Not me. That little minx...I knew my Louis from my Neils." *Jingle Jangle.*

"So, my child's in the doc's hands and we're still bound by our umbilical cord. There she is, the oddest sight I've ever seen. Arms and legs perfect with this balloon for a head. The veil was thin enough for me to make out her enormous eyes underneath. She was alive, but hidden. Kind of spooky, really.

"I swear," *Jingle, Jangle,* "the doc, the fledgling midwife from Ireland on her first assignment, and I stood frozen. I felt panic rise from my bosom to my throat.

"After doc cut our binding cord, he studied the odd opaque skein. Then he crowed in a most unscientific manner. 'My first caul in twenty years.'

"It hit me like a brick to the nut. This is my child. All shrouded. And I felt my face scrunch in sadness and tears prickled my cheeks as doc went to work, quickly but gently snipping the membrane from my daughter's shoulders. Then she took her first breath and ripped out a scream capable of stopping a freight train at full throttle. Loud when she needed to be. Just like her father. My heart did a little dance. I wished he could see her, but men were not allowed in the delivery room back then.

"Doc plopped the shiny, thin skein on the stainless-steel, kidney-shaped bowl Dawn held out for him. Then he shooed her off to clean up the newest little soul in the room.

"'What's a caul?' I asked, but the question was overshadowed by the soft feel of our creation being gently laid in my arms.

"If I'm honest, she looked a lot like my mother-in-law, which was just a tad disappointing.

"Doc put a hand on my shoulder. 'An en caul birth is a very rare event. Your baby was born intact, but still inside her amniotic sac. The sac balloons out at birth, and she remains inside the unbroken membrane. You went into labor, and the sac didn't burst, causing her to be born completely inside a jelly-like bubble.

"'It's something that happens by chance, and it's not necessarily any better or worse than a standard birth,' he said reassuringly, patting my hand that was curled gently around my baby's back. 'It's very rare but nothing to worry about. You'll never know she wore it in a few weeks, when the skin around her shoulders settles.'

"'Oh, you'll know it,' said Dawn in an ominous tone. Then she quickly glanced away, clearing her throat in hopes her exclamation be mistaken for a noisy sinus issue.

"Doc and I locked eyes on Dawn then looked at each other. I instantly understood the truth in her words, but the doctor, in his scientific guise, refused to hear.

"Dawn looked into my eyes, and said in her Irish lilt: 'She was born psychic. That's what it means. She is a seer.' She enunciated the last four words with reverence.

"Then it hit me and I heard myself declare: 'Well, that confirms it. We were always going to call her 'Lucky' because her dad and I met in line at the racetrack to cash in winning tickets on a rank outsider. He turned to me—a complete stranger—and said, 'If we get married and have a baby, we should call her *Lucky*.' Now here she is!' I gazed down at our daughter in my arms, and an unexpected surge of love infused my soul. Was this the mother's love they talked of? Suddenly I was a believer.

"'Lucky's a fine name for a lass,' said Dawn. 'Mind you, it can be lucky or unlucky to be born with a caul. She has to learn it's not a curse, though it will feel like one 'til she works it out. Will you be keeping it?'

"I was suddenly desperately afraid that this caul thing might mean they would take her away from me. 'Yes!' I cried, holding the little bundle even tighter. I vowed right then she would never be far from me, even if only in spirit.

"'I was expecting you'd keep *her*.' Dawn smiled and continued, pointing to the kidney-shaped bowl. 'I meant this.'

"It was a gooey looking thing. 'What on earth for?'

"Dawn's pixie face lit up. 'It's lucky. But if you don't want it, may *I* have it?'

"'Good heavens, why on earth would you want such a thing?' Doc asked.

"'I need to get home safely to Finn, the boy from whom I fled in favor of an adventure in the sunshine.' She bowed her head and whispered, 'But nothing is bright without him. And the grass *is* greener on the other side. In Ireland.'

"'How on earth can that slimy thing help you get home to him?" I asked, trying not to look at the slippery piece of skin that had stopped my only child's ability to breathe.

"'That caul will keep me from drowning on my ocean crossing,' Dawn said and promptly used forceps to pick up what looked like uncooked tripe. It dangled, waiting for a pot with onions, garlic and boiling water. I realized I would never be cooking tripe again, no matter how much my husband begged for it.

"Then Dawn placed the caul gently into a jar. When she turned the lid she smiled, the kind of smile that made me believe Finn in Galway Bay, way across the vast and treacherous Atlantic Ocean, was a lucky, lucky fellow."

CHAPTER 4

J im glanced this way and that. "I don't hear the bangles, is she gone?"

"You heard bangles?" Andy sounded peeved to have missed out and Jim gave him a look. Poor fellow was nowhere near Jim's level of soul development.

"Yes, mom was never without bracelets. She's gone. Sorry about that impromptu visit. She rarely pops in, but must approve of both of you to appear like that."

"Well, at least that's one big hurdle. I've met your mother." Andy grinned.

I ignored him and Jim saved Andy from being embarrassed by jumping in. "Wow. That's some beginning."

Andy's feet were off the coffee table and he leaned forward, "I'll say. And that your mother herself told us your story...blows my mind. Her voice, the way she uses her words was so different to yours, Lucky, and her accent much harder to understand."

They continued to wear looks of perplexity until, shaking his head Andy stood quickly, causing Tula to jump off the loveseat and block him from getting to me. I was to say, "Tula, let the man do what moves him." But I didn't want to hear the universe's disapproval again. I didn't know what had come over her. She was so possessive all of a sudden.

Alas, he wasn't coming over to embrace me for being born with such great aplomb. Instead, he said, "Lucky, you drive me to drink, and if I can't consume your animal-zonk potion, I'm off to pick up some beers."

"Not me," I chided. "That was my mother driving you to drink."

"Shit, just imagine having a dead but still opinionated mother-in-law permanently in your house." Andy retorted.

"I strongly advise against marrying or moving in with a psychic."

"Are you using that as an excuse?" Andy asked.

I responded with an ask. "Please get a big bottle of 7-Up too?"

"What, you're not drinking?" he asked in mock-shock.

"7-Up and beer makes a great beer shandy." I told him, and he gave me a you-are- distinctly-odd kind of look followed by a half-grin.

"Hold the stories for my return please, Lucky." And Tula saw Andy to the door.

"Jim," I said, "I've always meant to tell you. You have had many, many lives."

He looked shocked. "How do you know that?"

"When I first started seeing dead people, it was their particular smell that made them materialize into forms I recognized. I didn't know of any other ways to see them besides my sense of smell. I spent time with a toy that belonged to a missing girl and found her through her essence. It's how I can see beyond the material items collected in your case boxes. I suppose the more my abilities grew, so did my perception. I realized then my sense of touch was equally strong as my sense of smell. Now just shaking your hand gives me a summary of your life. Well, lives, really."

Jim's eyes were doing things like the cartoon characters and going around and around with this un-scientific information. I was undeterred. "It certainly doesn't happen with everyone, but whenever we shake hands, I see you in different professions over the course of many of your lives. You're a helper. You've been a priest. A prophet. A nurse. A teacher or perhaps that was a professor. Now you're here as a helper for others. Your primary mission is to offer closure and solace, even before solving the crime."

His lovely face lit up like a kid. "Oh, that's great. I always hoped I was an old soul."

His response surprised and delighted me.

"No doubt about it. You've been around for thousands of years born to parents of all kinds, rich and poor on every continent, during different times in history. You've done it all." I smiled.

"Don't you dare let on to that other FBI agent." He jerked his thumb toward the stairs. "He won't be at all impressed that I have such an accomplished soul."

I chuckled. "Your secret's safe with me."

"You know he has a crush on you, right?"

I swear I blushed. "Oh Jim, I think you're imagining things." But my heart had skipped a beat.

"Oh, he is like a love-sick puppy about you. Always has been. It was he who made me call you today. NO reason for us to come up and see you, though I am glad we did."

"You're married with kids, right Jim?"

He smiled a fatherly smile. "I am an FBI anomaly. One wife who I love and two boys and a girl or should I say two men and a young woman now. But don't deflect Lucky. We were talking about you and Andy."

"Honestly, I am not into drama. Potentially great unions filled with lust before real life rears his ugly head is not for me anymore. I avoid disappointments wherever possible these days. I know Andy's been married several times. The last thing I want is someone to disturb my peace with no gain. Sounds mercenary, doesn't it?"

"Not really, but don't cut yourself short or stop having fun. You are alive and fascinating and too vital to deliberately deprive someone else of your wit and wickedness. Someone you trust and care about and who is worthy of you."

"Jim, I have been in love with my soulmate since my twenties, when I dreamed of a life he and I had shared some centuries ago. I've since determined we two have shared many, many lives together." I sighed.

Jim's eyes met mine, and he encouraged me with a brief nod.

"Then I met him again in this life as Roy Moreno-Reyes." The minute I said his name I conjured up his lovely face. Kind eyes. Musky essence. His touch that made me beg for more.

At once I felt bad my body was reacting to Andy.

More than that. I felt unfaithful.

I finally willed my way back from the five-dimensional vision of my true love and saw Jim's face. It was stuck in anticipation-mode. I smiled because he was so sweet, and really interested, so I carried on.

"We spent a few glorious days together and continued our long-lost love in a long-distance relationship, making plans for our future, which we both believed was inevitable. But he mysteriously disappeared. I've held out hope for literally decades that he will walk back into my life."

"Wait! I remember that name. You had asked a few years back for us to check to see if he was anywhere in our databases."

"Your memory is scary-good. Yes. That was him. And you came up empty."

"You realize that's not a good thing, right? We can find anybody," Jim

cautioned.

When I didn't reply, Jim said "That's a long time to wait for someone."

"Don't get me wrong. I enjoy men. I even like non-committal flings now and then. But Andy and I have to work together and I would never jeopardize our casually-professional relationship for a quick roll in the hay."

When Tula flew up the stairs and gave a yip, we stopped our chat and glanced guiltily at the steps coming up into the living area. My hound bounded over and I lowered my face to receive his happy kisses.

Seconds later, Andy roared in with a bag, a dozen Heinekens, and a mammoth grin. His boyishness was a treat.

"What have you kids been talking about in my absence?" he asked. "You didn't carry on with your life story without me, did you Lucky?"

I silently crossed my heart, and he kept his eyes on my small left boob way longer than was professional. Damn. Blushing twice in two and a half hours, a rarity for me.

Stop it!

"Did anyone else from the other side visit while I was gone?" he questioned.

"Don't mock," I said.

"A fair question as far as you're concerned, don't you think?"

I shrugged. He was right.

We resumed our positions in the living room and the fellows marveled at nature showing off all her colors in the looming dusk. They had reason to be impressed. The sunset was enchanting, with her shades of red, orange, yellow, green, blue, indigo, and violet. Every color of the Shakra spilled in through the windows and unadorned glass doors, delivering a kaleidoscope of hues from all 360 degrees.

Andy read my mind. "It's almost as if we are at the center of the prism right here."

Today, he surprised me. No holding back or putting on a macho façade. Andy had to be careful. Sensitivity of spirit was something that lured me like a hungry fish.

We sat in silence watching each of the colors enrich themselves, dim and change. It was a divine light show for my rare visitors. Mother Nature loved showing off her magnificence and this home of mine gave her the perfect stage.

"I will never ask you again why you have to rush off home," Jim promised as he stood and turned slowly, absorbing the colors from north, south, east, and west.

"I swear it feels like we're being energized by all these colors. Lucky, *can* I stay here forever?" Andy's eyes were pleading.

"Nope," I smiled. "And not for too much longer either."

"Why not? Do you think you might enjoy us too much?"

"It's a strong possibility, and we can't tempt fate, right Jim?"

Jim gave me a wry smile and said, "Don't worry, I'm driving, so I'll stop at two beers and move onto coffee. Then I'll drag his horny ass back to Springfield, but not before you tell us your story."

"Pleeeeeeze," Andy begged like a kid, "I want more story."

"Oooookay!" I grinned on my way to the kitchen, grabbed a tall glass and brought it back to the coffee table and poured in a half a glass of 7-Up and half a beer.

"Taste?" Andy put out his hand, and I let him take a sip. I realized later how easily I gave up my glass to Andy. In this post-Covid age one didn't share but with your closest and dearest, but I didn't give it a thought.

"Nice. Refreshing," Andy said, and added, "Just like you." Jim and I both pretended we didn't hear.

I pulled open a packet of Knick Knacks Andy had produced from the bag. I had a moment where I almost felt bad I wasn't rushing around making sandwiches, or frying eggs on toast or something to make them feel welcome. But the inclination passed before I finished the thought.

I looked around. "You okay if I go on with the rest alone, Ma?" I asked the fresh air. The boys shifted a wee bit uncomfortably. When there was no reply, I grinned at them. "Just checking. My mom never liked to be upstaged."

They grinned back although there wasn't much mirth behind their smiles.

"As you chaps know, my last name is van Niekerk. My parents were second generation South Africans. Nobody quite recalled how an English-speaking family came to be bestowed with such a strong Afrikaans name.

"Van Niekerk proved immensely playground-problematic for me. You see, we lived in a society still divided over the Boer War. Totally ridiculous considering that bloody war ended in

1902, when the massive British Empire absorbed the reluctant Boers into their kingdom.

"It is reasonable to assume that these two factions would have compromised on their ideals by the 1960s. Alas, it was not yet so. The English didn't want me on their side of the playground and, as soon as I opened my mouth, nor did the Afrikaans.

"Van Niekerk is a bastardized Dutch moniker that literally means 'from no church.'

"In my first school-going years at the convent, I seemed to rub the nuns' fur the wrong way. The constant reminder that I had to be a heathen because of my name 'from no church' made life dim for this six-year-old.

"It didn't help that I first *smelled*, then *saw* dead people all over the convent. I was delighted to see them, and we'd converse whenever we bumped into each other. They didn't smell in the stinky sense, unless they proved to be stinky in life.

"Everyone has an essence that's different to everyone else's, and my nose identified those soul-smells, if you will, and conjured up a physical form visible only to me."

"You poor kid," Andy sympathized.

"Well, your folks knew you had gifts thanks to Dawn, the midwife, right?" Jim showed he'd been listening.

I smiled at him. "Yes, they were cool with it, and while the nuns had no appreciation for my psychic inclinations, my mom celebrated my uniqueness and I became her party piece. I felt chuffed she'd found a use for my...peculiarity."

Andy chuckled. I really liked that he "got" me.

"She'd schlep me to her friends' houses, stand in the hallway and ask, 'Lucky, do you see anybody else here?' And as if I were a magician's well-trained dove, they'd release my little self into the house to look for chums.

"I often found new folks to talk to—invisible to others—and freaked out some of mom's friends. They usually sold and moved to new homes that had to undergo 'The Lucky Test.' If I was unsuccessful, they signed the transfer papers.

"It was easy to find new friends no one else was able to see. My nose led the way. But soon the *real* kids thought I was weird, so it became difficult to frolic with my invisible friends without ridicule.

"I began to hate my nose. She who so expertly identified things long dead. She who dragged me out of this world and far back into familiar pasts that should have been unfamiliar to a child but, later, history books confirmed my adventures were as real as the (ahem) nose on my face.

"At ten, I taught myself how to block out the gift the caul had given me. It was difficult to learn *not* to smell the world around me and whatever it brought with it, but desperation diminished difficulty. It was something I had to conquer. There was just no other way to fit in.

"My parents moved me to a co-ed public school where, in addition to dealing with my surname, my first name became the target of my peers' jokes. 'Unlucky' they'd call me when chewing gum got stuck in my hair. 'Lucky-she's-not-on-our-team' when a fellow netball player threw me the ball, and I ducked. 'Luckless' was a favorite and when I was older, 'Did-you-feel-lucky? Cruel high school boys laughed loudly because they considered me not cute enough and my boobs not big enough to qualify for a teenage fumble and feel.

"If you'll let me, I will make your sad youth into a vindication celebration with my mammoth appreciation for small boobs."

"Okay, Special Agent Martinez. I am baring my soul here. No taking advantage of the situation!" I chided.

Andy put up his hands. "Okay, Okay. Just trying to be a hands-on-therapist. You feel me?"

"Andrew!" Jim shot him a warning glance. "I will confiscate those beers if you don't quit. You're interrupting a story I've been wanting to hear for years. Now, no more lewd remarks!"

Andy saluted Jim and grinned sheepishly at me. "So sorry, Lucky, do continue. I meant no harm just wanted to..."

"Uppp upppp uppp" Jim put his hand in the stop position and Andy mimed zipping up his mouth then mumbled "Please Lucky, continue."

I smiled shaking my head, but I kept going because I knew they were genuinely interested and I hadn't told my story in years. Nobody really wanted to know. Until now.

"My caul, my name, my uber-sensitive nose and, on occasion, my ability to see things through touch, all shaped me. But it was a trip on an airplane, when I was a mere babe, that gave me a mission."

"An airplane?" Andy asked and took a swig of Heineken, never taking his eyes off me.

"When I was two, my parents flew from Zambia to South Africa. It was the first time my dad, a bomber pilot who'd flown in World War II, had taken a commercial flight. He marveled at the mechanical advancements. The adventure simply delighted my mom.

"But since they were dead broke, they conspired to tell a whopping lie. They assured the ticket master I was eighteen months old to avoid paying for the separate seat required for a two-year-old.

"During the flight, the air hostess mesmerized me. She was smiley, kind, and she smelled gloriously alive.

"Much to my parents' horror and embarrassment, I begged with well-formed, non-infantile words, to help her. She seemed delighted and armed me with a silver bowl and a fancy miniature spoon. My job was to offer tiny sugar cubes to passengers after the air hostess poured them a cup of tea. Down the aisle we went. I was truly thrilled.

"When we disembarked, the air hostess remarked how adorably *advanced* I was for my age. To quell their guilt, my parents headed for the arrival-hall bar, and two gin and tonics later, their consciences eased.

"I was thirteen years old, still at a co-ed public school in standard seven (USA's ninth grade). It was Career Day, and I sat on a hard wooden chair in the massive high school hall. The entire school attended. All the guidance counselors and homeroom teachers were on the stage to dissect the choices of our intended futures.

"After the head had called us to order, he said into the microphone, 'We'll take the first five hands. What do YOU want to be when you finish school?'

"I was excited. My hand reached skyward. I was so clear on my destiny.

"First went the doctor. Then the lawyer and the pharmacist. Blah. Blah. Blah.

"'You.' The headmaster's eyes met mine as he pointed.

"That was me. Lucky number four!

"Unlike the others, my conviction, and pride in my chosen profession propelled me up to a standing position to make my announcement. You'd have thought life would have already taught me swimming against the current had its drawbacks.

"'I want to be an air hostess.' My voice rang crisp and clear as visions of silver bowls and sugar cubes danced in my head.

"Our homeroom teacher, a wet-behind-the-ears frilly little thing, jumped up, grabbed the mike like Mick Jagger, and declared in a voice that made the mic and amps screech, 'Oh, my God.' She glared at me as her face, red as a beetroot, contorted in distaste before she trilled on top of her lungs: 'You want to be a flying mattress!'"

"Fukaloolie." Andy shook his head. His exclamation pulled me out of that dreadful time. But I'd started this saga, now I had to finish it. What in the world had propelled me to spill my guts on my living room floor to two pragmatic FBI agents?

I looked at Jim. His face was a study in horror for that poor thirteen-year-old child. He was indeed a wonderful empath.

Andy's expression ached with sympathy, though I was sure he was just in it for the story.

Suddenly I knew exactly why I was spilling the beans so freely. Despite being strangers in my home, these two have shared numerous lives and deaths with me in this and perhaps other lives.

Tula nudged me with his wet nose.

It's okay. They're okay. They're on our side.

When I glanced at them again, they were fairly hanging on to the edge of their seats to see where the abominable embarrassment had taken me.

I obliged. "A moment of shocking silence ensued before the guffaws, and the hysterical laughter and the pointing began. The headmaster patted our teacher back down on her seat, cleared his throat and said, 'We'll take a last volunteer before we start the program you're here for.'

"The last scholar turned the noise right down with his budding desire to become a florist. My declaration, which seemed too shocking to forget, saved him from being mocked for his delicate choice of career.

"Two girls on my right glared at me, then squished together onto one hard wooden chair—as far away from me as they could get to avoid catching any anticipated cooties.

"I thought my cheeks would explode with heat; I'd bet they were purple. Mortified, I hadn't a clue what had prompted this ridicule. Why was I being shouted at, laughed at? What to do? Where to go? Where to hide?

"And a hand firmly took my arm. I looked to my left. There sat a cute girl with a round face, a bright smile that wrinkled the bridge of a nose dusted with freckles, and a jaunty beret. Everyone else wore school hats, but she'd found a loophole in the rigid uniform code.

"'Why?' I asked the only sympathetic face in my hell.

"'My brothers all read it. It's banned. They wouldn't let me even take a peek. It's called *Coffee, Tea or Me?* A book written by two naughty American air hostesses called 'stews.' They had loads of boyfriends all over the world.' Said the cute freckled girl.

"'Oh, no! Air hostesses are not like that,' I exclaimed, sincerity pouring from every pore. 'They're wonderful. I met one. She was like an angel in heaven.'

"'Well, these stews had loose morals, but they sure had a lot of fun.' She looked at me and smiled. 'I'm Alana. You and I will track down that banned book and find out what all the fuss is about.'

"And we did. '*Coffee, Tea or Me?*' was carefully concealed at my house, behind the Oxford English Dictionary, where my father—an English pundit—later noted dryly, 'I thought that would be a place no one would look in a million years.'

"Having Alana by my side miraculously diminished my mortification. She was petite, cute as a button, and vehemently protective of me, her gangling new best friend.

"Giggling ourselves into a coma, we shared a stolen cigarette and devoured every naughty word behind the bramble bush in our garden, where no one could find us."

Instead of looking through the fellows as I had when I recounted my mortification, I looked at them. I was glad I had shared this very intimate story with them. It was time they knew me better.

They waited.

"I'd made an actual friend for life in every sense. But sometimes, life is too short."

Old grief became brand new and thwacked me hard in the chest as tears sprang to my eyes. Tears that threatened to spill and turn this into a pity party. I swiped viciously at my welling eyes. "Look at you two, making me weep."

"It's not us. It's Alana," Jim said intuitively.

"What happened to her?" Andy stood, came over and took my hand. It was a sweet, unexpected gesture.

I slowly extracted my fingers from his grasp. "That, boys, is for another gathering in the far, far distant future."

CHAPTER 5

High in the navy sky stars winked as I opened the bathroom window.

October's autumn breeze puffed at my hair in passing.

To my left, shafts of brightness shot up from well-angled ground lights, catching the trunk of a lanky paper birch tree in a midnight pose. She swayed gently, rehearsing for winter's wild dance in a month or two. Then, exhausted, she will sleep and awake in April, rejuvenated.

Lucky paper birch.

My eyes settled on the image of curling paper where reams of thin white bark threatened to peel off her trunk.

Paper. Here. There. Everywhere.

How many letters had Roy and I written to each other? Two, sometimes three a day. Being apart after we'd found each other again was torturous. In the eighties, overseas phone calls cost as much as a week's stay at the Sheridan, so we perfected the art of letter writing. It's really a glorious way to get intellectually acquainted, or in our case, reacquainted. There was little time for philosophy and debate during our physical time together. Our bodies did all the communicating.

The essence of Roy filled my senses, and I inhaled him deep into my chest. I held him there until I felt my lungs burn. But I *felt*. Then, with a mammoth exhalation, I released him into the night, so he could go where the wind took him, then materialize and return to me.

It was late.

Those who'd become Very Special Agents had finally left.

Jim was sober as a judge, but not so much his passenger. They were really good guys. I'd known that for a long time but, during their impromptu visit, I realized how good it was to socialize with people I liked. I protected my privacy so carefully, had they not foisted their visit upon me, I would never, ever have invited them. I could not remember the last person—if any at all—who had paid me a visit since my move to America.

As much as I'd enjoyed them, I was glad to have my house back. And my quiet. I in no way wanted to make 'visiting' a regular thing.

I glanced at my watch. I had to be asleep before the witching hour when everything became as distorted as Dali's melting clock. It was my rule.

The Persistence of Memory.

Indeed.

I forced myself to close the window and allowed the air conditioner to do her cool thing as I got ready for bed.

With the pitter patter of determined paws behind me, I climbed onto the high Dream Cloud mattress, then curled up, hoping desperately for a dreamless sleep.

SUPPRESSED MEMORIES, past-life regressions, dreams … What they were called didn't matter. I was locked in their tenacious tentacles, experiencing them as real as the nose on my face.

I was no stranger to being helplessly sucked into—nay, consumed by—one of the many lives I'd lived centuries before.

FLASH!

My heart hammers against my chest, making it difficult to breathe. No matter how hard I try I can't escape the horrifying images surrounding me.

I gag as rosemary, sea spray, garlic, manure, rotten fruit, and acrid sweat invade my senses. Roughly hewn skirts in dull greens and lifeless grays swirl around me, hemming me in.

The fierce hatred of those surrounding me becomes tangible when congealed spittle lands on my cheek like a vicious slap.

I jerk up and swivel my head one way, then another, hoping to find a sympathetic expression in the circle. Alas, there is no empathy. These men and women wear only raging faces contorted with revulsion.

What have I done?

I strain to hear them over the thundering of my heart and the ringing in my ears. Every inch of my body hurts.

"Satan's daughter. You lured my husband!"

"Wicked witch! You told me my son would go blind, and he did. 'Tis the devil's work!"

"Making young girls act like imbeciles! Are you proud of your sins?"

My heart wishes it could thump louder to block out their monstrous accusations.

I stare down at myself, hoping for clues.

I am scantily clothed in blood-red silk scarves, a sharp contrast to the dull yarns encircling me. Splotches of dung, bruises and splatters of tomato pips mar my white, nigh-translucent thighs.

A rough-legged hawk circles and, for the oddest reason, I become infused with loyalty and love. I concentrate on its magnificent wingspan, its beak, its fearlessness. It swoops down and I don't duck. My conscious mind wonders why? Up, up, up he goes and then down again, dive-bombing the circle of haters around me. The dowdy ones cower and cover their eyes lest the hawk should pluck them out, but the rare bird swoops up again as if his aim was for them to witness, up close, the size of his talons.

"Tula?" I reach my arm up to the hawk, "Is that you?" And the bird circles slowly and dips his head in acquiescence. "I thought so. You've been many animals during my lifetimes, haven't you?" The tight circle again. The nod. "And you're always here to do your utmost to protect me. Thank you," I whisper.

He flies down and through the ragged, now screeching circle and settles on my shoulder.

I am no longer facing this dreadful fate alone.

The circle of my condemners widens, giving way for this oddity that is wanton girl joined with a wild bird.

I enjoy the peace and space the shocked silence and distance affords me, but too soon, hysteria resumes a thousand-fold.

"Eeeee." "She's indeed a witch." "No mere mortal would

attract such a bird!" "And a vicious hawk we've never seen in these parts at that..."

"Take her!" A course voice instructs, and brawny arms grab my arms from behind. The hawk lunges at my captor, but the women band together to shoo away my protector.

Three men lift me up like I am but a tree branch.

"Nooooooooooo," I cry. "Tula, stay with me, please."

Between violent kicks aimed at my pallbearers I see Tula above me, still circling, letting me know he is always with me. I am still for a second, allowing gratitude for the agape love from the Tula the hawk, to infuse my soul.

The men push and prod me into their desired position until I feel a hard beam against my back and my buttocks. I look up at the looming wooden post to which I am now tied, hand and foot. I look down and see the women piling kindling around my ankles.

Above me, as close as he can, Tula circles.

Everyone steps far away from me and my head lolls back in relief, allowing me to admire Tula's circles, but not ten seconds pass before a skinny man hurls a long, flaming torch into the firewood surrounding me.

"Go now, Tula, save yourself. I will see you in my next life and the life thereafter. Go. Live! Be safe." And I watch as the hawk rises and disappears beyond the smoke.

I hear the pyre spitting and surging as the flames crawl demonically toward me.

Ferocious fire leaps and fans quickly. I cannot hear my scream through the roaring flames as my feet melt.

The torment is so intense I feel myself slipping into...

...Roy, as I know him in this twenty-first century life, blocks the excruciating agony, the sounds of crackling fire, and smell of my own burning flesh.

All I see is unconditional love in his expression.

"Save me," I cry, but his face disintegrates, becoming part of the smoke, and all that's left are hungry flames.

My tears bubble and boil against my soft cheeks, as billowing smoke sears my lungs. I cough, and unbearable pain shrieks from my chest. I wonder briefly if the pain is because of loss of Roy in this life, or loss of air in the ancient one I'm enduring.

I must find breaths so I may force out words to beg forgiveness for that which I cannot remember, so I need not come back to this earth and do it again. But my tongue is on fire, and my throat has sealed itself off from the fumes and I can't breathe.

Come back to me, Roy. If you won't save me, then at least let me see your beloved face, let me hear your deep, comforting voice, let me taste your lips, let me feel your passion before I perish...

And then my face becomes wet and warm in slow, almost languid bursts. It's not Roy, but it is a great comfort, one into which I wish to disappear—but not too far, lest my soulmate cannot find me.

The pain of missing Roy is ever-present. And it is that ache for my soul to touch his again that makes me struggle for a last living breath until...

BACK!

And as I inhaled, my eyes opened to a blue-eyed stare.

My hand wiped away his doggy kisses. "I'm okay now, Tula. I'm okay." I smoothed my dog's worried brow with my thumb and tugged gently at his fluffy ears. "And I am so happy you're a dog this time. Though you surely were a handsome hawk."

He kept looking at me until he saw me inhale and exhale

enough to make my racing pulse slow. Only then did he lie down. I shrugged and said, "I suppose this means I can add 'witch' to my list of past identities."

Figuring any danger to me had passed, Tula lay with eyes closed. A not-so-subtle hint for me to keep schtum so he could finally sleep, but the need to share exceeded my consideration.

"Whether I was a true sorcerer in the seventeenth century or a Cambodian Buddhist monk in the fifth century, you and Roy were there to share my joys and sorrows, lives, and deaths. Sucks that our souls grow mostly from hardships. What say you, Tula?"

My faithful but exhausted companion yawned. He was there to console, protect and advise, but not to listen to idle chatter when sleep called.

While attempting to find Roy in my past lives—an excuse to regress at will so I could experience all the emotions of being with him—I had to face my own baggage that was dredged up from each of those ancient lives. Sure, I'd been able to acknowledge the dark leftovers, thank them for their lessons, exorcize them and move on, but my dalliances—as cleansing as they were —brought me no closer to Roy in *this* life.

I patted Tula's fluffy head then nuzzled his neck. "But no matter where I go next, Tula, you better believe you're coming with me."

He looked at me as if I'd just wasted my breath. *Of course I'll be there. Just like always.*

I still smelled hints of garlic and rosemary from my imminent-death-of-a-witch turn. The aromas reminded me I was not responsible for what I did in a past life. But the tactile immersion into the horror was hard to brush off. It would remain an open wound until I intentionally sewed it up.

Rising from the bed I opened the window, took a deep breath of sea air, and then said, "Thank you for reminding me of that life, those feelings and that fate. I acknowledge those experiences served my higher purpose, but now I let that guilt, that fear and that shame go. That life and those lessons no longer serve me and they *must* leave me. *Now!*"

I exhaled every ounce of air. Then I perceived those destructive emotions I'd carried with me for centuries being sucked out of the room by a passing breeze.

Relief was instant as I watched them tumble away from me, twisting and turning in a gust of wind. Those past life lessons swirled from me, overpowered at last by nature's substantial force. They sailed further and further away, lessening my load with every knot, until a vicious gale-force wind swept them up and out toward the vast, forgiving ocean.

I closed the window and, feeling a life lighter, I lay down to resume a more peaceful slumber.

I melded my body around Tula's powerful, seventy-pound one.

"What a good boy," I whispered and considered that my witch 'extermination' was a little close to home. Here we lay on my comfy king bed on a quaint peninsula across the bay from Boston, not too far from Salem. Nearly a full circle.

The smell of rosemary was suddenly overbearing, and my heart sank.

Had I left one of the witch wounds open?

Tensely I lifted my head up and spied a little brown bottle of the concentrated herb on my nightstand. "That's the culprit!" I blurted.

Tula's head shot up, eyes darting, head cocked.

"That blooming lash serum with rosemary I slathered on

my eyelashes last night. It's meant to make them grow up a storm. That pong caused the hullabaloo from three and a half centuries ago to come back and haunt me."

I, of all people, should know better than to mess with smells before bed.

Tula gave me a dirty look for creating such a big fuss about such a little bottle.

"Ha! In spite of that horrid dream, if my lashes grow in a couple of days, I'll try it again, just not at night. Then I will flutter them at Andy and divert his eyes from my wrinkles when we delve into Janice's disappearance. But alas, I think it might be too little, too late. I should have started with self-improvement the moment I saw Andy had potential."

I laid my head back down on the pillow but guilt pelted my mind like a vicious summer hail. *What the hell am I doing thinking about Andy?*

Since Roy and my other losses, I'd deliberately lived my life without depth. Without vulnerability. I kept everyone on the surface, except those involved in my job. And then I only let the dead ones in.

Until now.

Spending a delightful afternoon and evening with two people I've known for years was an eye opener. Not only had I shared my very private home with them, I'd shared parts of myself I hadn't shared with anyone for decades. My mild flirtation with Andy, pointless but oh-so-pleasant, made me see what I was missing while I waited and waited and waited for Roy.

Suddenly, molten passionate anger began in my gut and moved north until my head throbbed, promising to erupt in fury.

Where the bloody hell are you, Roy?

You're always with me in spirit, but now I need to feel your physical presence. It's no longer possible to be satisfied with you showing up in my head then disappearing. I need your actual presence to whisk me away from the horrors that this life sometimes pulls me into. I need your soothing hand, the one whose every single line and crevice I can trace by heart. I need you to touch my face after past-life adventures regurgitate and scare the living daylights out of me.

And you didn't save me from the fire I just endured. You could have tossed all those tiny May Flower-ites aside with one hand and ripped the ties that bound my hands and feet with another. But no. You just became smoke and wafted away, becoming part of my demise. And you're not preventing me from giving in to the temptation of a fling with Andy, even though it's a really bad idea. Do you even care anymore, Roy?

I damn well can't go on loving your memory, your ghost. I just can't. But how the hell do I get over you? How? What must I do to NOT ache for you every day of my life? That bloody universe has made me so many promises. I've believed her. I've always "known" she would deliver you. But enough's enough! You hear me Miss Freakin' Universe? ENOUGH!

CHAPTER 6

In late 1986, as a South African air hostess, I found Roy in a dream on a 747 in the crew rest. It was so much more than a dream. It was an awakening. A first in so many things: the first past-life regression I'd experienced; my first *only* all-consuming love affair; my first visual encounter with Roy, though, even in the dream, I knew we were already intimately familiar thanks to our relationships in many other lives. It was the first time I'd felt the depth of being in love. When wakefulness ripped him from me, it was as if a bear had eaten a body part, such was the magnitude of my loss.

A year later, fate played its hand—we were forced to make an emergency landing on a small island, on the very same day and ironically, on the same 747. 316 Passengers and crew had to have a layover in tents, sleep on cots and eat in a mess hall. US Marines entirely occupied the island.

Imagine the chaos of 316 passengers being herded, cajoled, and forcibly encouraged to take a step onto a bobbing inflatable slide attached to the open doorway of a 747. One look at the two-and-a-half story thrill ride on a giant chute slung from cabin to tarmac produced an adrenaline rush that beat any modern-day roller coaster.

There was no logical reason the instrument panel failed at 30,233 feet, but there were two reasons for the passengers to take the plunge.

First, the cockpit crew were unaware of what was wrong with our bird and had no warning of what might happen, even once the engines were off.

Second, for most of the women passengers, my gay friends, and all the hosties, there was an added incentive to reach the ground. Buff men in t-shirts, camo trousers, and army boots stood at the bottom of the slide, with big smiles and muscular arms to catch us safely.

We crew were last to jump. Since I worked business class on that flight, I was two bodies before the cockpit crew. Our captain, like all others abandoning severely wounded vessels, would be the last to jump.

I took off my shoes and nylon pantyhose to prevent my legs from burning because of friction, and I quickly stuffed them into my cabin bag. Then, I launched my cabin bag, along with my first aid kit, down the bouncy slide before taking the plunge.

You can train till you're blue in the face for such an eventuality but, in real life, emergency procedures are chaotic, reactionary, and scary as hell.

Whoooooooa!

My bum hit the slide. In a seated position, the tarmac was a death-drop away.

There was no turning back. Someone ripped control from me, and my body flailed as I flew down, down, down and into the strongest arms that had ever held me.

It was his essence that embraced me before his hunky arms caught and steadied me.

I knew his feel.

I knew his smell like I knew my own.

And I knew his deep voice.

"Are you okay?" he asked softly, in that divinely familiar baritone. It was a voice I'd heard in a hundred languages from a hundred past lives. This time, an American accent tinged its deep timbre.

My body went limp in the safety of his being.

I looked at him, and he looked at me.

We knew.

Our eyes locked and nothing around us existed.

A divine reunion after too much time apart.

Even the shout from above—the first-class hostie needing me to clear the path—didn't deter us. My soulmate simply maneuvered me off to one side and one of his men took his place.

Real life was but a distant hum.

When he looked into my eyes and into my soul, there was nothing but us. No air. No hours in a day. Nothing but my soulmate, me, and lost time.

Two missing parts joined together to become whole once more.

Stronger we became with the love we'd re-found. Stronger we needed to be, to learn the lessons ahead.

I knew Roy from the inside out in milliseconds, and I loved him deeper than I had in all our past lives together. I knew beyond any shadow of a doubt that Roy felt it as richly as I.

Our stolen moments were more precious than a suitcase full of diamonds. Our need for each other exceeded logic, safety and even conversation. Our bodies yearned to express what words couldn't describe.

Reality rudely intruded. Decorum dictated we two people in uniform should pull away from each other in spite of our needs. Before we did so, his lips grazed the tip of my ear. That touch zinged through my body like an electric current from head to heart to pelvis and it melted there, thick and wanting.

I'd read once that when we got to the next astral plane between lives, there was infinite understanding and compassion and clarity. But no sex. Thank God for this life because that's what I needed more than oxygen.

I'd never felt such raw lust. Such desperate desire. Such determination to consummate a union—a homecoming—a celebration of our bodies since our minds had been so long in sync.

Roy was a lieutenant, twenty-nine, with dark curly hair, golden-hazel eyes and the sexiest mouth I'd ever seen. He possessed a key to the base's armory, one of the few in existence.

During the tour of the island, given by the top marine brass, each 747-passenger group learned the island was used to quickly reach troubled spots in South America as a launching pad. The current mission was to keep a sharp eye on Panama. The base served as a perfect training ground for air, sea, and land combat, and had a runway big enough for our 747. Since it was a peaceful time in that part of the world, the armory remained empty most of the time.

As the cabin crew, we took care of the passengers assigned to us onboard. Although anticipation replaced my blood cells, I did my duty. I made sure all my allotted passengers had the chance to clean up in the rows and rows of ablution blocks, feast on fabulously prepared hot food, and get to bed on cots in the officer's mess hall for first and business class passengers. The airline assigned bunks in the mess hall to economy class passengers who were traveling alone.

Any groups or parties of two or more from all 747 class cabins slept in efficiently erected tents (thank you for your service, Marines) close to the shore. Rumors spread that those beach bums had the unexpected vacation of their lives.

I, along with three stewards and the first-class hostie and steward, had a semi- private area in the officer's mess hall behind a partition.

We took turns watching over the passengers, most of whom couldn't sleep but stayed on their cots. On duty, we hovered with water for the thirsty, delicious American cookies for the peckish, and a firm arm for those who needed help to the closest bathroom. Words of comfort and first aid kits to treat or patch up any minor or imagined ailments were frequently called for.

Each crew member had two hours off and six hours on.

On my first break I walked out of the officer's mess, stretched my arms upwards and threw back my head to take in a billion stars roaring above me. A balmy sea breeze caressed my face.

I felt him before I smelled him. That confirmation endorsed the fact that this was not our first, second, third or fourth rendezvous.

I turned.

"I'm Roy," he whispered, moving toward my mouth.

"I'm Lucky," I managed through the pounding of my heart.

We stayed a half-an-inch apart, inhaling each other's familiar essence. His breath was mine. Mine his. Not daring to touch for fear of getting carried away to places from which we'd never return in this public area. But Roy threw caution to the wind and grazed my parted lips with his own.

That *zing* again. It whizzed through me, waking up—nay, *igniting*—every nerve in my body, speeding up the blood supplying oxygen so my heart and my body quivered like I'd had a giant shot of adrenaline. I was teetering on the very edge of a precipice.

He simply scooped me up into his strong arms, his stare penetrating my soul. How many times had we done this before as bride and groom across the centuries? How many lives had we shared through the ages?

In silence he carried me, though I swear our hearts were chatting up a storm.

Our mouths were far too slow for all we had to share.

He gently put me on my feet, and it was a miracle I could stand with my body in such a frenzy. He unlocked the first metal door and opened it as quietly as he could. Then he did the same with another steel door. He took my hand. Once inside he closed one door behind us, then another. In that moment, locked in the pitch dark, what could have been the most suffocating, fearful, claustrophobic horror, was indeed the most illuminating. All distractions were blocked out. It was only Roy and me. It was as if our inner lights illuminated all we needed to see. I saw the joy on his face as he saw mine.

When he switched on the light, we saw the details.

Later, when I recalled our first tryst during my loneliest nights, I couldn't remember how our clothes came off. It didn't matter. They were simply in the way of us getting as close as possible. Perhaps our desire burned through them.

No audible word had been spoken since I'd given him my name.

Stepping forward, I lightly caressed his chest with my nipples, and I could sense his manhood poking at my pelvis. Ready. Willing. Oh, so able.

"Roy," I whispered against his mouth. His hot tongue seared my lips, and I didn't care if my mouth burned to a crisp, as long as our tongues were dancing through time. We tasted tenderness and passion and tenderness again in waves of lust and cerebral union, then he lifted me up as if I was feather-light...

...And just enough of him entered me.

I was flying, tethered only by powerful hands holding my posterior and his hot and pulsing lifeline.

But just enough of him was enough no more.

My body ached to feel every millimeter of him inside me, and I wrapped my arms around his strong back and pulled him in desperately. I was a drowning sailor, hoping for relief for my trembling body when it hit the sturdy vessel.

At last, he slipped in all the way. I felt my core tighten to welcome him home in a burst of pleasure. He maneuvered us and the motion made our roots that fit so perfectly into each other, cling all the more tightly, to stop gravity getting in our way.

He lay me down gently on top of our uniforms—a muddle of sky blue and camouflage.

My pelvis contracted, but he was gone. And I was empty.

The flash of my crew rest dream replayed in my mind and I realized it was a recollection of a past life Roy and I had shared. A dream in which he'd starred as my beloved. But when I lost him in that life, the crew rest dream had ended.

Suddenly it was clear. I had loved him in many lives, yes!

But I had lost him in more lives than I could consciously remember.

I couldn't lose him again. I wouldn't lose him again.

My body arched, aching to be filled. And then, with a hot rush of pleasure, I felt his succulent mouth where his root used to be. Soon my hips were thrusting, unbidden, as his expertly probing tongue had its cunning way with me.

As I shuddered and quivered, quivered and shuddered, I cried out for him to give me his all.

And he did.

We came in unison. An earth-shattering climax that went on for many eternities during which we held each other, as close as two people could be in mind, body, and spirit.

We didn't move, we dared not be without the touch of each other's flesh for fear of the raw yearning we'd feel. His hot tears were on my cheeks as mine were on his. His thoughts were mine, and mine were his. It was a place of spiritual wonder and supreme physical satisfaction that quickly turned to acute yearning for more. More. MORE!

I was an hour late returning to my post, but I had a wonderful excuse. I'd been lost. What the Flight Service Officer didn't know was what I hadn't known either: I'd been lost without my soulmate.

But with Roy, I was found.

Chapter 7

We stayed on the island for three days, waiting for experts that had been flown in, along with the military pundits to unravel the mystery of a haywire instrument panel, and then fix it.

Roy and I spent every spare moment together. I had never laughed so hard, spoken so many truths, nor felt such a need to really listen and remember every detail of another's life. I had never loved a body nor had my body loved so thoroughly; not before or since.

Naked in the harsh overhead light, we were oblivious to the weapons of immense destruction surrounding us as we'd planned our new life. Together.

After too-few days of stolen moments and intense connection with my Roy, I floated a foot above the aisle of the restored 747 as we flew home to Johannesburg.

Together we were divine. And divinely intoxicated with each other.

I still couldn't believe that the cause of our emergency

landing was an eclipse of moths that had somehow infiltrated the instrument panel of our jumbo jet. The powder-like residue on their wings—scales actually—made the instrument panel go haywire. Even with her unmatched powers, the universe *really* had to stretch her imagination to make that coincidence happen.

As we flew back to base, I was beyond amazed that this girl who never wanted to marry or have kids, intent on a stimulating career and many dogs, was floating on dreams buoyed by Roy's and my mutual commitment, and the delirious hope for our future together.

We planned and penned, over the next ten months, another glorious life we were destined to share. Dreams made solid in blue ink between his continent and mine. Hundreds of love letters.

Occasional exorbitantly expensive phone calls kept us physically linked. The sounds of each other's voices were so rare, and so exhilarating, mere words brought us quickly to climax.

Then followed an odd turn of events, and as suddenly as the weirdest happenstance had so brilliantly pulled us together, another ripped us apart.

But what had actually happened, I had yet to discover.

We'd dared to make plans when both of us knew the universe loved to upend them.

It's one thing to lose someone you love when they die, it's quite another when they simply disappear.

I had endured both.

Strangely, despite having a penchant for blaming myself for everything, I knew I had nothing to do with Roy's vanishing. I never suspected he'd deliberately done so to remove himself from my life. I never doubted his intentions.

Still, he was gone.

I mourned him, wailing like a middle-eastern woman over the body of her loved one charred by vicious war.

Eventually, the emptiness he'd left in me was equal only to the gratitude of knowing that great love was indeed possible for me in this life.

And I would find him if it was with my last dying breath.

Back in the late 1980s there was no Google, no Facebook, no way of finding someone in a different zip code, let alone a different continent.

I'd lost my father and my best friend within six years. Each had its own kind of pain, its own life-shattering effects on my soul, and all changed the way I looked at the world. I'd never see my father again in this life, it was highly doubtful I'd ever see my best friend again either, but I *never* believed that Roy was gone forever.

I consoled myself that the universe would make it right—that Roy would eventually appear, and we would at last, live our lives together. Happily, and ever after.

But as time passed, I had no option but to teach my heart to harden. I couldn't risk being vulnerable without my loved ones by my side.

The only way I could make it through this life was to make bloody sure I never cared deeply for anyone else.

I succeeded.

When I found my calling decades later, it was only dead people who mattered to me—the dead, and those who'd caused their earthly demise. Some would imagine my life was full of people who mattered, but when I'd tied a bow on each case, the only one I had to protect and love and lavish and share with, was my dog.

I'd had many fleeting lovers, but much more importantly, a number of fine canine companions over the years—all of them exactly what I needed. Now, mercifully, I had Tula. He was my protector and more than enough company for me.

Keeping things on the surface served me well. Insulation against disappointment was essential for my survival.

I waited and waited as the universe continued infusing me with hope, but she hadn't produced the man I loved—*yet*—but I believed with all my heart she would.

Fifteen years ago, circumstances forced me to rediscover my gift in order to find a missing celebrity in South Africa. The media sensation it caused led to an offer for me to move across the Atlantic and put my psychic powers to good use in the USA. I saw it as a double chance. I was doing what I was destined to do: consulting with law enforcement around the country and earning more than I had ever dreamed. And I was on my soulmate's continent. Surely that would make things easier for her esteemed self to deliver him to me?

Still nothing happened.

No Roy.

Sure, by then I could Google him and search on Facebook.

But he was nowhere to be found.

I was relieved in a way, because I didn't want to find him married or, God forbid, dead, though the latter was unlikely. Such was our connection—had he left this life, he would have come to me in spirit.

Guilt burned in my chest as I realized how close I'd come to revealing my heart in its entirety to Jim last night. And much of it to Andy too. I'd just left out the Roy part with Andy because my vanity enjoyed his flirting. If he found out that I was in love with someone else, I would lose that too.

But the chances of me truly going below the surface, even if it served me, were slim to none. In fact, I'd come too close to doing that last night and I vowed not to let it happen again. I felt vulnerable and afraid that having anyone *really* know me would expose a chink in my protective armor.

CHAPTER 8

Thanks to immersing myself into our delicious time together, my face was feverish and wet with lonely tears. The tenderness of my feelings and the poignancy of my love for Roy Moreno-Reyes were so intense that it caused me physical pain. My body literally ached for him.

If ever I had a doubt about letting him go, recalling precious moments pulled me back to my promise to wait for him and never just settle for anyone else. Once I learned to conjure up, through my soul's immense memory bank, our times together from the age when the earth was new, I had fresh memories to experience and ponder.

But memories were all I'd lived on for decades. Was that fair to me? There were, after all, just so many withdrawals you could make from a memory bank before you went broke.

I was nearly broke. So, what kind of fool was I?

I was getting long in the tooth. In all the years he hadn't been physically in my life my yearning for Roy had never waned.

But there was little point in being too old to enjoy him.

It was 4:01 a.m. when I made the biggest decision of my life.

I would give Ms. Universe one more shot to bring Roy back to me. Only because ours was a love worth living for. A love worth dying for. So, trying one last time to find him didn't seem too preposterous.

Shit, I could find dead people I didn't know. Why the hell couldn't I find the man who belonged to my heart?

The universe enjoyed doing things her way—organically—but enough is enough. It was time to grab her by the wings and have a good heart-to-heart.

I sat up, ready for combat. "What can I do to enable our worlds to collide once again?" I asked her with all the passion Roy mustered in me. "I just need opportunity. I can do the rest."

Nothing. No response.

I was mad as hell.

"I've just about had it," I warned her.

Eventually, I got over my anger but spent another hour wallowing in perplexity.

Then I did what every confused girl should do.

I acknowledged defeat, snuggled down with my faithful pup, closed my eyes and prayed to whoever was up there at this ungodly hour.

"Okay, Miss Universe, in case you're not hearing me, I call forth all my guides, ancestors, angels, God, and everyone else who might be listening and feeling a mite sorry for me. I need your help. I need an answer to my question when I wake up." Inhaling deeply, I prepared myself. "Please show me how to find my soulmate. If you don't show me, I will have to move on. I can't go on like this. What sort of life are you making me live? A lonely one! I found that out tonight with the impromptu visit from colleagues who became friends."

First, I had to remove Roy—who'd earned a permanent spot in my head—then I visualized a divine white light passing through a triangular prism and separating into its component colors: red, orange, yellow, green, blue, indigo and violet.

I concentrated as red emblazoned the window of my mind, locking out other thoughts and intrusions. Then orange, and so on. When I reached violet, I let myself drift into a purple-blue haze of deep sleep.

I awoke with great expectations.

But all I got was a whisper: *Help others to help yourself.*

"That's it?" I sat bolt upright and looked menacingly at the ceiling. "That's all you've got? 'Help others to help yourself?'"

The silence from above was absolute, but the essence of my Roy was back—musky, soapy, ambrosial and tasty as he filled my head, my soul, my heart. And, as always, it went south from there.

No, Lucky, focus!

I'd come to know the universe well. This was her way of promising me that, if I did as I was told, my soulmate would be at the end of the rainbow. But, *help others to help yourself*? What the hell did she mean?

How? Who?

A million questions.

"I *am* helping others to help myself. I get handsomely paid to find dead people, which helps those left behind. And it helps me live in this lovely house and feed my dog. That fits the bill, right?"

Nothing.

"You want me to volunteer? I could go to a dog shelter once a week. Would that do?"

Nah.

"What is it you want me to do? Start a dating service?"

Silence.

"Will I find him in my work environment?"

Silly.

She was right. I would have found him by now if it were as simple as that.

Think, Lucky. Think. Go back to the beginning to find the end.

Had she had too much ambrosia?

Where did you first find your soulmate in this life?

"At 36,000 feet!" I gasped, and Tula jumped at my exclamation. "You want me to help others to find their soulmates? But who?"

The scent of oranges enveloped me.

"Oranges?" I asked, truly perplexed.

Not a smell. Color.

"Orange. Orange..." This was more difficult than Jeopardy Masters. "Orange... Ha!" My shout made Tula so pissed he went to lie on the floor, but I was in the groove—or was it *grove?*

Then it hit me. "South African Airways!" I began jumping on the bed like a three-year-old. "What is the tail color of the fleet of aircraft that took me to exotic places as I crisscrossed continents in my youth?" Damn Jeopardy Masters.

Consider others.

"I have to help others in my situation before help will come to me?"

Someone slapped their forehead in a quick vision. It was enough to propel me out of bed and soon the computer's light illuminated the guest bedroom.

Countless dead ends and then there was a rogue Facebook

group for South African Airways crew members called "Crazy '80s South African Airways Crew."

As I sat there peering at the screen, Roy's essence embraced me. I breathed in deeply, capturing his intoxicating bliss while these words slipped from my fingers and onto the laptop's keys: *If you had a weird dream in the crew rest of a 747 that changed your life, or still haunts you, email me.* The sentence shone on the screen, lighting up my face and my heart. I added my email address, clicked to post and felt instant relief.

A mountain just climbed. A deed well done. A boulder off the shoulders.

"Where do I go from here?" I asked the universe.

She was silent.

I was just about to push back my chair and give sleep another try when a message popped into my email. And another. What? Another? And even one more.

Holy shit. How did you know I needed to talk to someone else about this? Brie.

ME! ME! I do. How? When? Where? Moxie.

Wow. I would be very interested. Chantelle.

I-n-t-e-r-e-s-t-i-n-g. MORE! BJ.

I had no answers for them. Had Miss Universe the grace to tell me how to execute the plan that would have been helpful. But, alas, she was nowhere to be found. Jaunting off with other more 'important' people or souls, I would imagine.

Why these four? Still no reply.

We five went back and forth via email.

As the one who initiated the gathering, it was assumed that I would provide the venue. Tula was an integral part of the process so a mid-Atlantic rendezvous would never do. I looked at Tula and he gave me one of his *suck-it-up* looks I knew only too well. I tried to delay the plans to avoid thinking about my impulsive decision, but these women were having none of it.

It seemed I'd opened four of Pandora's boxes. They wanted to jump on the next flight. All of them reeked of a similar desperation as I, and were eager to explore our dreams *now*. I managed to delay them for a week. It was the best I could do. I shivered.

When at last I rose from my computer chair, I had a WTF moment that made my stomach lurch. A huddle of hosties on my doorstep in a week? Four desperate women coming to me for answers after thirty-plus years. I couldn't help but wonder why specifically those four out of thousands during the eighties.

Fate.

There was no other answer.

CHAPTER 9

One thing was clear. Miss Universe wanted me to explore Roy before I explored Andy.

Okay then. I'd give her two and a half weeks. One before the hosties arrived and six days while they were here and three days of final contemplation. If Roy failed to appear in my quest to 'Help others to help myself' then I would not only seek Andy out, I would bed him immediately. If that turned out titillating enough, hell he could move in and we would let life take us where she liked. If it interfered with our professions, well I knew there were many other law enforcement divisions that needed my particular help.

I had it all worked out.

But first, a bevy of former South African Airways air hostesses, coming from all over the world, would stay *in my very private fortress* for nearly a week, interrupting my blissfully hermitic existence. Oh, boy!

The pressure was on. They were coming for one reason: to decipher their crew rest dreams starring lovers they thought were their soulmates.

These old hosties were all clearly in a state of flux if, decades later, those dreams were still affecting their lives. "A state of flux" pretty much defined *my* position.

I still hadn't determined the ideal words to convey to four women that they shouldn't disregard deep, heart-tugging emotions for a "familiar" man in a dream as just a dream.

I had to make it crystal clear that the specific dream was our subconscious mind emerging, providing evidence that we could endure the darkest adversities if our soulmate was by our side.

When we'd woken from *that* crew rest dream and felt all-consuming love, it was a gift and a promise that *this* was how our hearts would sing when we found our person. Before and after the dream, every lover became inconsequential until we found our soulmate again. Soulmates could make even the worst life worth living.

All we had to do was find them.

This was a first. I'd never had to put into words that which was part of my DNA and something I took for granted. I'd never had to explain myself.

"Wait!" I shouted, and Tulu jumped to attention. I patted him quiet, and he lay back down with a *humph*. "I never proposed a retreat where I had all the answers; rather a think tank with all hands-on-deck."

That thought calmed me down some. Still. *Better get your act together, Lucky.*

I didn't know their beliefs or their religious inclinations. I'd start with what I sensed, what I'd always believed: we needed to experience the entire spectrum of this thing called "life" many, many times. Some said we were reincarnated one-hundred-and-twenty times, others said more, before we qualified to go to work on the next plane with bigger responsibilities. I surmised being born over and over and living various lives was to practice becoming a decent human and polishing our moral codes, irrespective of who we were born to.

Then, armed with thousands of years of knowhow, we would become excellent guides from on high to help people we loved on earth.

Time flies. Before I knew it, they'd be on my doorstep.

I specifically refrained from Googling or Facebook stalking these women who contacted me. I did not want to prejudge them by knowing who they'd become.

I thought equal ground and in-person impressions were better for my intentions.

All email responders were familiar, albeit vaguely. One had been instrumental in my joining the airline though she likely didn't know it. I'd had a trip with another. The third I'd seen around, and the fourth was an airline legend.

The latter was the one who made me more nervous than anybody else. The masses of cabin crew that surged through SAA feared her for a decade and a half.

Besides buying booze and rushing orders of South African treats from shops in Canada to bring a taste of home to the shindig, after the first couple of days I'd done a whole lot of what I did best. Procrastinating.

What specifically would I do with them for six long days?

I breathed in for a count of eight, held for eight, out for eight. Of course, we'd examine their 747 crew rest dreams and get all the ins and outs—ahem—of their soulmates from centuries past. They might have to let me hypnotize them to delve deeper into past life experiences. That way we could unearth what happened after the dream ended. There we'd dredge up well-hidden memories, likely unpleasant ones, that particular life had etched into our souls.

Consider the magnitude of horrible things we have bottled-up simply to survive. The deep-seated damage within our subconscious molds our perception of the world in every subsequent life.

That angst-power of many lifetimes of unopened baggage must be cleared out. Like an old storage bin with crap in it we no longer need. Unwanted goods must go, so we can use the bin for the latest of our most joyful memories. Then we can live a better life.

In my late thirties, when I was first honing this power, I had mistakenly thought I was all caught up. After a hundred or so past life regressions, surely all my baggage was neatly unpacked, leaving nothing that needed ironing out. Alas! 'Twas those lives I had *not* seen that were the hardest to unearth. My subconscious went to extraordinary measures to hide those nasty experiences, so as not to dull this time on earth.

That was a revelation. I was nowhere near as evolved as I thought myself to be. There was more I had to learn.

Help others to help yourself.

Whoa! I've struck a deal with the universe.

This revelation did not come without a hefty dose of neurosis.

I had some acquaintances. I was the self-proclaimed queen of light banter. I socialized superbly for two hours—three, tops —before turning into a grumpy pumpkin and dashing off to my waiting bed. My dog. My home. My solitude. My smells.

Help others to help yourself.

I panicked. "Ha! Easy for you to say. How can I possibly tolerate the idiosyncrasies of others for more than three hours?

How will they tolerate mine? Two work buddies who I could talk shop with for hours was one thing, their smells are familiar. But this lot will bring in their essences all in one fell swoop. How will I cope with all those smells? It's been years since I've had to face the masses and then only after I'd switched off my smell-button. And I dare not switch it off, lest I can't switch it on again...and there goes my job, my life. Shit."

You are overreacting. It's only four new smells. Get over yourself.

Sheesh, she could be rude sometimes.

I shivered and addressed her in a very ballsy fashion: "You do know I am only doing this so I can get Roy at the end of this ordeal, right? If you don't deliver after all you are about to put me through...well, I can never trust you again."

I was trying to hit a nerve. Trust in her book is paramount.

When there was no reply, I sniffed my palm, breathing in my elixir, and my heartbeat slowed.

I hugged my handsome fellow, which also did the trick. "But now it's just you and me, kid. Blissfully quiet and in control of our aromatic surroundings."

I snuggled into Tula, breathing in oatmeal, dog shampoo, and unthreatening sea air wafting in through my open bedroom window.

Then he passed wind.

"Phew," I complained, and pulled away to breathe. He looked hurt.

When at last sea air diffused the rotten odor, I said, "I bet now that the foul stuff you've been hoarding deep inside is all gone, you'll feel much better."

Tula gave me a look and I heard him say, "Well that's what *you* need to tell your visitors!"

CHAPTER 10

"Lucky, we've got the evidence box."

The call came four days into my countdown. Damn. "Lucky" my ass. That left me with just three days to prepare for the Feared Four. Of course, I'd done sweet nothing in preparation. That's my jam. Some would call it a giant flaw. *To-may-toe. Tah-maaah-toe.*

Could I say "Can it wait, Jim? She's dead and not going anywhere and I have to…"

What came out instead was "Tell me exactly where to meet you," and he gave me the name of a pub in Springfield.

I tossed an outfit or two into my overnight bag, along with all the toiletries my fly girl days taught me were essential, Opium, and MAC's Ruby Woo. Sadly, vivid red lipstick was the only thing Taylor Swift and I had in common.

Tula traveled light. I got his collapsible bowl, scooped grain-free food into a baggie and checked his insulin. After his diabetes diagnosis some six months ago, I'd fashioned a clever little bird's-egg-blue insulated pouch that he wore on a thick leather cord around his fluffy neck. It helped to have his lifesaving drug readily available and it gave him the vibe of a hip sixties dude with it dangling on his hairy chest.

Three and a half hours after hitting the road, we walked into Barnie's Bar.

I stopped, Tula next to me, to allow our eyes to adjust to the darkness. Jim and Andy, dressed in their usual suits and ties, looked out of place at a bruised wooden table in the rough-n-tumble pub. They leaned toward each other, deep in conversation. I felt my eyes drawn to Andy, and they lingered long enough for him to look up. Those bedroom eyes looked directly into mine and his face lit up. That did wonders for a girl's ego.

Jim turned, grinning, and they both stood. I appreciated their old-school manners.

As Tula and I made our way to them, I mentally blocked one nostril to the years of spilled liquor, biting and sweet, embedded in the thick carpet. Nostril number two I closed off quickly to prevent the deeply entrenched aroma of decades of disappointment and desperation making their way into my psyche.

By the time I got to them, I was breathing through my mouth.

Andy stepped forward, shook my hand a little too long and grinned down at Tula. "A woman with red lips and a good-looking partner walked into a bar." He winked.

Always the flirt. That was fine by me. Even if I was giving Roy a very last chance to appear. I smiled and waited a beat. "What? No snarky follow-up zinger?"

He lifted up palms and shoulders. His dark, smoldering eyes were the kind that captured yours, whether you were friend or suspect. "Keeping a psychic like you guessing makes me more intriguing, Lucky," Andy chuckled.

I peered up at him. "I'm not dying with curiosity, but when you come up with a dazzling punchline to your bar joke, let me know, would you?" He nodded and gave a slow wink. Boy! This one had *it* and knew how to flaunt it. "But I won't wait up for it," I threw over my shoulder as I tried to dim my flirty grin.

"Nice to see you, Jim." We shook hands, smiling.

I wiggled into the hard wooden bar chair, my posterior searching for the most fitting bum-print of the thousand before me, as Andy moved off saying, "I know what you need, Lucky."

He returned to the table carrying three big mugs in one hand like an Oktoberfest hostess, along with a bowl of water in the other. Tula lay down close to the wooden legs of my chair so he could anticipate my every move, and gave Andy a quick lick of thanks as the agent placed the bowl down for him.

I took a sip of the beer shandy, reveling in the bitter sweetness.

"Hey, lady," a very drunk patron shouted from across the room. "You can't have a dog in this pub!" He ended with a hiccup.

I ignored him, but the agents opposite me both jumped up as they saw the man weaving toward me and Tula, slinging his thumb toward the door. "Get outta here, mutt!"

Tula positioned himself between me and the man, his lip raised without a sound.

"Hey buddy," Jim stood and held up his hand. "This here's a service dog and our friend can have him anywhere she likes."

"Bullshit. No dogs allowed." The man bent to lunge at Tula and Andy leapt putting himself between the lunger and my dog. Miscalculating his steadiness, the lunger hit the floor. Andy stood over him and pulled his jacket away from his hip, while Jim extended his hand to hoist the man back up.

Lunger was upright again but his eyes were still glued to the spot where he'd been given a close-up of Andy's full holster and shiny badge. He bowed and gave a sloppy salute, "Thank you for your service, man."

"Wrong uniform, sir, but appreciate it all the same." Andy's tone was sarcastic as Jim body-guided Lunger back to his bar stool.

I was amused and inordinately chuffed they considered themselves mine and Tula's guardians.

We settled around the scarred three-legged wooden table once more, and Jim asked, "How've you been, Lucky?"

"Waiting for your call, boys, how about you two?" I smiled and glanced at Andy to include him.

"We've been mulling over your early story," Andy began.

"And we're moved. You sure had a rough start." Jim finished.

"Oh, don't fret. I turned out okay." I flapped a hand in dismissal.

"You sure did." That was Andy.

"What doesn't kill you makes you stronger, that was a song, wasn't it?" Jim asked.

"One of my faves," I said, "Kelly Clarkson." And quickly changed the subject to deflect any more self-talk from one-loose-lipped psychic. "Let's get down to business, shall we? Since I saw you, I've developed a pressing time frame. A batch of hosties arrive on my doorstep in," I checked my phone, "two-and-a-bit days, and I need every moment to prepare."

Andy put up his hand. "Wait! What's a 'batch of hosties?' And what the heck are you going to do with all those cupcakes?"

"I'm still figuring that out, Andy."

"Seriously, I want to know."

Hmmm. Andy was a little possessive. That was unnerving. Perhaps it was just his passion showing through.

"Seems you boys and your fine company inspired me. I invited four South African girls—well women—to my house for six days."

"Did our fun night together completely transform your reclusive life?" Andy was fishing.

"Yes, something like that," I said, avoiding Andy's intent gaze. "And time's a-wastin.'"

"So that means you realized your childhood dream?" Jim's face was hopeful.

Andy was a beat behind: "And what the heck was that...a-wastin'? Don't tell me you're losing your South African accent?"

I laughed, all about keeping it light. "I was trying out my New England hick on you two. My new thing is to use it for the employees at the Cumberland Farms near my house. They struggle with my accent. As I left the store a few days ago, I heard one clerk whisper to another, 'She doesn't have an accent. It's a wicked speech impediment!'"

Jim chuckled but Andy nudged his way in: "Did you become an air hostess?"

"That my dear fellows, is a story for another time. Another place. But I will tell you, I was never a flying mattress!"

"Now you ruined a fantasy." Andy exaggerated his look of disillusionment and Jim cleared his throat.

"Hand over the box, Jim," I said. "Let's begin the beguine."

As Jim lifted the box up to the table, Andy asked "What's a beguine?"

So much for Andy being a hair slower than his partner. "It's a West Indian dance similar to the fox trot."

"How do you come up with these strange words?" Andy again.

"I have many past lives to draw from." I smiled Jim's way and reached for the big cardboard box marked: HUGHES.

I touched the lid and felt the churning inside it. The fellows were glancing at each other and, by the look on their faces, I knew they were hiding something from me. *Should we tell her? Shouldn't we tell her?*

I waited a few beats to see if they would spill the beans.

Nada. I was disappointed but I moved on, taking a deep breath and bracing myself for the unexpected. "Let's see what we've got."

Then I lifted the lid.

Apart from some files and miscellaneous paperwork, everything was sealed in either paper bags or zip-type transparent plastic bags.

I rifled through the stash and found a pair of earrings. I didn't know a woman who washed her earrings, so there was a strong possibility residue of her essence was left behind, no matter how long ago she'd worn them.

"Where did you find these?" I asked, holding them up.

"On the bathroom vanity. Recently worn, we assumed," said Jim.

Andy flipped open his pocketknife and handed it to me. "Go ahead and cut the seal now if you want."

Though this dingy pub was hardly the ideal forum for a psychic experience, over the years I'd learned to block out my surroundings to do my job. I carefully slid the blade across the evidence seal and returned the knife to him. I took a few seconds to center myself, then opened the bag.

Powerful odors only I could detect—thanks to my gift—emanated from the dangly, oblong turquoise, and silver earrings within.

Sure enough, Janice's soul-bouquet was embedded in the stones and that would allow me to feel her; *be* her.

I lifted one earring from the bag and placed it in my palm and slowly closed my hand, enveloping her soul.

What came to me nearly knocked me sideways from my chair.

My thoughts swirled. Beyond the stench of stagnant water came visions of a girl in her mid-twenties with jet-black hair, green eyes and a fair complexion...

FLASH!

...Sulfur in the air singes the tiny hairs in my nose. I hear the crackling of the sparkler she's holding in her left hand. She twirls and twirls like an ice skater with a glittering wand. Her head is thrown back as she laughs, exposing a long, slender neck before she loses her balance. Giggles.

Tightness around my throat cuts off my air supply. I try... I try in vain to draw a breath, clawing at hands I can't touch, but the pressure is intense. My attempts are useless, not one teeny bit of air filters through. I can't breathe... I can't...

I open my mouth to scream, but no sound comes out...

BACK!

My eyes flew open, forcing me into the present. Tula had jumped up, his front legs in my lap. I stroked his neck until my heartbeat eased and he got down.

I placed the earrings back in the bag and swallowed, then

gently massaged my neck from chin to chest as I took several deep breaths with my eyes closed.

When I opened them, Tula was still close, watching me. "Okay, boy. I'm okay." I smiled at him.

I looked first at Jim, then Andy. They looked stunned.

But I remained silent and, finally, Jim gestured at Tula and asked, "Did you train him?" How well they knew me. *Take her away from her vision, so it's easier for her to talk about it when it's not so fresh.*

"No. I found his skinny self in a pound up north. Saw him on a news channel showing off as the shelter's Pet of the Week. They thought Tula had fallen off a boat and washed up near Great Boars Head in New Hampshire, because no-one in a twenty-mile radius had seen the dog before. And he wore the remains of a tattered life jacket. Must have been hard to find food in the woods with hints of luminous orange still around him. The potential forest-food would see him coming a mile away."

Andy snorted, and I took a long sip of my shandy. The fellows waited courteously for me to continue.

"He was a mess when he landed on a good Samaritan's doorstep and she took Tula to the pound. When I got him two years ago, they estimated his age at two years, and I just hope he has longevity in his genes. There are two strange things about him. He becomes desperately mournful when we're on the beach. He puts up his head and howls like a heartbroken wolf. It's almost like he's calling somebody. Or something. And, even stranger, he has a tattoo of a pair of wings on his tummy. You can't see it unless he's been shaved, but I thought that was an odd thing. I feel sad for his owner because he was clearly loved and cared for, before his dire and lonesome adventure.

"He's been my angel since he arrived. When he witnessed my first regression, he jumped on my chest, bringing me mercifully back to the present."

I'd babbled on so, I stopped to gauge their interest and was surprised to see them leaning in, fascinated, so I continued. "It's seldom fun back there," I jerked a thumb behind me, "and he's rescued me every time since. We're a dream team." I smiled at them.

I realized how peculiar I must have seemed, having a vision in front of everyone in the pub. "I hope my minor episode didn't upset the locals."

"Nah." Andy glanced at me. "A couple of cutie-patootie twentysomethings came into the pub, and nobody gave us another glance."

"Story of my life," I said flatly.

"I wouldn't say that," Andy said with an enigmatic grin.

"Fine dog you got there. Knows your job and his own," said Jim, rubbing his chin, clearly moved by Tula's story and his and my connection.

I'd seen the same emotional reaction often before from other seasoned law enforcement officers with whom we'd worked. One would think those who encountered plenty of tear-jerking situations every day would be immune, but they always seemed particularly touched when witnessing our bond.

"He's my best boy. Australian Shepherds are surely the smartest of them all." I leaned down and ruffled Tula's ears again before I said flatly, "I saw Janice with dark...no, black hair, green eyes, a fair complexion. She had a sparkler in her hand, and she was twirling, happy. She was left-handed."

In the silence that followed, Jim and Andy's eyes became

much like Mutt and Jeff's, round and loopy and popping out of comic books in 2D.

"I'll be damned!!" exclaimed Andy. "Yes. Yes. And hell yes! That's exactly what she looked like, right down to the left hand. You haven't lost your touch, Lucky."

"We deliberately didn't tell you the date or the occasion, and you nailed it with the sparkler. It was the Fourth of July, 2012 that she went missing." Jim focused on me in a bit of a daze.

"Does Janice live on the edge of a pond or close to water?" I asked, remembering the dank smell of trapped water.

"No, but marshes are all over the place down here, even between houses," Andy replied.

Hmmm, it wasn't that. "I think she was strangled. I felt her air being cut off, her inability to speak, to breathe."

"Strangled?" Jim sat forward.

"By whom?" Andy demanded.

"Don't know yet, and there's a chance I never will. Let me look for the where, then you chaps can work on the why and who." I looped my bag over my shoulder. "Did you book us a hotel room?"

They nodded in unison.

"I hope it's decent this time. Tula and I have standards, you know!"

"We know," they said together.

Grinning, I stood and Tula followed, Andy behind him. Jim threw some bills on the table, picked up the evidence box, and joined us as we walked to the door.

"Hey, what happens to her inheritance if you determine Janice is dead?" I asked over my shoulder.

"It all goes to a cat shelter in Watkins Glen, where Janice's old man lived for years," said Andy.

"That's lovely. A good cause, though my fellow here would prefer a no-kill, free-roam dog haven to be the recipient."

Tula wagged his tail.

CHAPTER 11

I begged off dinner with the chaps because my time was tight, and my brief foray into Janice's world earlier had left me woozy. I was all about a little self-nurturing before I put my nose to work in someone else's deadly business.

I'd be famished when this was all over, but there was always twenty-four-hour room service, courtesy of the FBI. Tula had his food and his insulin injection, and that was all that mattered, for now.

On the way to the Marriott, Andy had explained, "Jim wanted to book you into the Paws A While Inn down the road. They tout it as the place where pets bring their owners to rest. Then I heard it was an older building that had been revamped, and I reminded him about the time before last. Remember? We thought we were doing you a favor in Savannah and booked you into the most expensive hotel, but it turned out to be the oldest one in the city."

"Oh, yes, you chaps plum forgot I was psychic. You left me with not just the victim's ghost, but the entire city's long-dead lost who popped in for a visit." I laughed, remembering at the time it had been disastrous to my psyche and worse yet for my poor Tula, who worked like a Trojan to keep me sane.

"How do you get rid of them? The ghosts, I mean?" Jim asked soberly.

"You thank them for coming, then nicely tell them to go. If they don't, get firm and tell them they're not wanted and they *must* leave." I turned around to look at Jim and wondered how many other-worldly visitors he'd attracted, given his empathetic soul.

TULA and I lay on one of the queen-size beds in the elegantly sterile room of the Marriott and watched the sun set through the sheer inner curtains. I ran my fingers over the pristine white comforter, appreciating the chain's corporate commitment to divine cleanliness and tight 500-thread-count sheets. The neatness and angular corners of the beds would have pleased the prickliest army major general.

I needed to clear my head before I got to the business at hand, and a brief procrastination would recalibrate my world. I had forgotten to bring the latest book by William Kent Krueger. He quickly whisked me away to entrancing, brilliantly constructed worlds. I dare not get involved in a TV show I enjoyed because it would be hard to drag myself away. I just needed a little time to help me put off the inevitable, so I opened my computer and checked my inbox.

What the hell? There were nearly forty fresh emails. The string had been started after the hosties and I had confirmed our plans. Seemed I had four Chatty Cathies coming to play at my house. *Shiver.*

Moxie: *How did you guys get into South African Airways?*

Brie: *A pilot recruited me.*

BJ: *Aha! 'Recruited' a new spin on sleeping your way into the airline.*

Chantelle: *BJ! Don't be so mean. Brie is as pure as the driven snow. I know her.*

BJ: *And I've known snow. There is nothing pure about it. It's white, but it covers a shit load of shit lying underneath.*

Moxie: *Now. Now. Be nice.*

Chantelle: *If you're going to be as bitchy as your reputation, BJ, I will cancel my flight.*

Moxie: *I will have to cancel mine too. No bitchiness allowed at Lucky's house, or else.*

Brie: *It's okay girls, thank you for sticking up for me. But too many sticks and stones have tried to break my bones, words no longer hurt me.*

Chantelle: *Oh, that's so sad, Brie. Have you had a hard life?*

Brie: *No! My life is bliss. I am so lucky.*

BJ: *If your life is so bliss, why the hell are you going to Lucky's to delve into your crew rest dream?*

Moxie: *Why the hell are you going, BJ? You were too good to talk to us in the airline. So full of yourself you were. Only when you were forced to, did you lower your nose and look down on us from first class. We were just serving the plebeians in economy or business class, not up to your standard, apparently. What's changed to make you as vulnerable as the rest of us?*

Her fight surprised me. Then I remembered Moxie was called "Little General" in the airline.

A day later:

BJ: *You don't know me, missy. Don't judge what you don't know.*

Brie: *Come ON, girls. This is an adventure for all of us. Let's not let old assumptions and stereotypes impede having fun while we solve mysteries in our own lives.*

Chantelle: *Wisely said, Brie. Moxie and BJ, you two behave!*

Moxie: *Why me? I was just sticking up for Brie, now I'm in trouble.*

BJ: *We are not in first grade. Nobody's 'in trouble'.*

Chantelle: *Stop it right now, BJ or cancel your flight!*

Brie: *Whoa. Nobody's doing any such thing. We four will all make sure we have the time of our lives. Which part of the world are you girls coming from?*

Moxie: *I quote Lucky: "You are not allowed to discuss where you're coming from, who you're married to, or what's ailing you before all five of us are in the same room."*

Brie: *You're quite right, Moxie. Sorry, I forgot. How did you get into the airline BJ?*

BJ: *With ease.*

Moxie: *Well! That's not exactly being open and forthright! Isn't that the goal of our reunion?*

Chantelle: *Enough. Let's focus on a merry time together. I joined because I flunked out of university.*

Moxie: *Why?*

Chantelle: *I forgot about my hatred for chemistry. I was just happy to have a varsity that thought I was good enough to be accepted. A year later, I listened to my heart.*

Brie: *Sounds like a good move to me.*

Chantelle: *Is Lucky in this conversation too?*

A day later:

Chantelle: *I guess not. Bet she's preparing her castle. Can't wait!*

Brie: *So much to do. Must away!*

Moxie: *Nobody waited for my answer. I joined the airline because I was too short to be a Sun City Showgirl. Damn. I was dying to wear a G-string and nipple caps on stage.*

BJ: *Please God don't let's have an 'Act Out Your Fantasy Day' on this trip. I couldn't stand to see any of you old ducks naked.*

Moxie: *Speak for yourself, you old duck. I am fabulous naked.*

BJ: *Even at YOUR age?*

Moxie: *Stuff you, BJ. Stay at home if you're going to be an old cow.*

Brie: *Girls. We are old enough to be and let be. Now I'm really logging off. Bye for now.*

Chantelle: *Agreed. Be nice and see you all in your best frames of mind.*

It seemed these four former air hostesses were already at odds. Oh lordy, what had I done? I detested conflict. It scared the shit out of me. These women were at odds on *email.* Imagine when they were all in one house with three beds!

Still in my clothes, I snuggled under the lovely white linens and, to avoid the coming days, I covered my head with the comforter and thought about my own airline beginnings.

CHAPTER 12

Benoni, South Africa: 1980

I was fighting jealousy and self-pity by pointlessly looking at the latest fashions, which I could never afford, in a boutique in our town center. I dipped to check the price tag on a stunning jumpsuit and groaned. *That slice of couture divinity will never slide over this body.*

Between the racks of trendy creations, I saw the sign. Kitty's Cafe. A beacon to my aimless soul.

Our school friend Kitty had inherited the place from her deceased parents. Just thinking about her made me smile. Kitty's parents were Hollanders, and she spoke only Dutch at home. She'd struggled with English and always screwed up her words, much to Alana's and my great delight. In standard eight (known as tenth grade in my new country), she'd told us she spent the evening pushing back her testicles.

It took two whole minutes with Kitty's ten fingers waving in front of us to realize she meant she'd pushed back her *cuticles.*

We sheltered innocents didn't talk about testicles at school.

Kitty didn't mind at all that she was the butt of our jokes and laughed joyfully at herself along with us. Goodness knows Alana and I sported enough quirks for Kitty to get her own back. Ours was an unusually wonderful threesome.

Kitty saw me come in and waved, as I made my way to a table.

Four years after that epic testicular conversation, and what had changed? Well, I'd lost my virginity with no marching bands passing or glitter falling from the sky. Grave disappointment was an understatement! I'd met him in my matric year on holiday with Alana and my parents. He was the assistant manager of the hotel in which we stayed. He wooed me by mail and phone calls for two years. Then he arrived on my doorstep and whisked me off to his hotel room.

Two years of anticipation and all I got was a wham-bam-not-even-a-thank-you-ma'am, and I never heard from him again. A meaningless notch in a belt. That was me.

I slumped over. My bank account was teetering on the lip of the toilet bowl. The chain had been pulled and my confidence was already careening its way down the porcelain. My life, such as it was, had long been floating in the sewage system. Up to shit even before it had really begun. Oh, pauvre de moi! I was studying French during my boring Girl Friday job. I had vague thoughts of working for Club Med. Ambition lurked dimly but sans any conviction.

That morning, Kitty's place was filled to the brim. Everyone was trying to stay one step ahead of the next downpour.

A year older than me, Alana was cute and sexy and flying around the country as a South African Airways air hostess. I was thrilled for her, jealous as hell but still thrilled. I felt dull and one-dimensional next to her, especially when she was wearing the fabulously tailored uniform of my once-dream job.

I watched patrons lift steaming coffee cups off Delft blue saucers. I could smell the air, rich with chicory, and, as I closed my eyes, I had an epiphany.

It wasn't that I was afraid people would think of me as a flying mattress. I was afraid they would wonder how in the world I could *ever* have qualified as one.

Truth was, if I didn't apply to the airline, I couldn't be rejected.

I just had to face it. I was too plain to be a glamorous air hostess, even though Alana promised I would love it and she thought me perfect for the job. But she was my best friend. She saw my heart and not my instantly forgettable Average Josephine face.

One didn't forget an air hostess.

Kitty delivered a titillating platter before me, but after a quick hug, someone pulled her away. Even our lovely Kitty had a mission. And here I sat, nineteen and dull, dull, dull.

The steaming croquette on the plate threatened to bring back a miserable life in Amsterdam in 1232, not a good year for me. I fought it with all my might and focused on the aromatic beef shin, flour, parsley, garlic, peri-peri and breadcrumbs fried in deep oil.

Hunger and a watering mouth soon quieted my threatening hyperosmia, and subdued my self-pity.

The bell above the door tinkled, and I automatically looked up. It was Brie, the pretty girl who worked at the bank. I'd wondered why she kept herself hidden from the world behind bars. Her beauty was captivating. Shivering, she shook herself like a cat emerging from a cold bath. Rain flew in all directions as she searched for a place to settle, but Kitty's was abuzz. Catching sight of me, she smiled. I felt bad I was hogging a whole banquette and motioned for her to join me. She nodded with relief.

On her way to the table, she tripped over...well, nothing I could see. I was sure it wasn't on purpose to attract attention. Brie did not need to do that, with her heart-shaped face, cascading thick dirty-blond hair, bronzed, flawless skin, and broad, genuine smile. She was in the one percent of the world's naturally beautiful people. The rest of us worshiped at her shrine of loveliness. Yet she was in equal parts unassuming and kind.

She collected herself and slid into my vinyl-covered banquette with a relieved sigh. Fragrant geranium shampoo wafted towards me, and I waited patiently while she discarded her rain jacket and hung her bag onto the back of the booth.

"Thanks, Lucky! I was dying for Kitty's special coffee. How've you been?"

"Okay, thanks, Brie. You?" I asked. Though she looked the same, a layer beyond her shampoo didn't smell like the same Brie at all.

"You won't believe what's happened! It's like a fairy tale. A client at the bank is a pilot for South African Airways. He thought I'd make a good air hostess for SAA, but I was too young. I had to wait a whole year, but I did it! No more boring bank!"

"I wondered what happened to you," I said. So that's why *her essence is different.* She was free of her bars and flying high. I felt a stab of despicable envy.

I studied Brie's face as she shared her fantastic tales of life as an air hostess. She underwent training for over three months and learned fifteen subjects. She was flying internal routes all over South Africa, having a wondrously social time.

Though I'd tried to live vicariously through Alana's wonderful life as a "hostie," I suspected jealousy blocked my complete immersion. It was Brie's new life and her interesting scents that struck a match and reignited my imagination.

If only.

"I'm doing my conversion course and learning a new language to go on the overseas roster. I can't wait," Brie said with no hint of bragging in her soft voice.

My heart sped up with excitement. "Which overseas places will you fly to?"

"Every continent except the north and south poles." She smiled. "North and South America, all over Europe, Asia, Australia and, of course, Africa." Her beaming smile was so bright, I almost ducked.

Then it struck me. There was no such thing as coincidence in my world. Brie had surely come to sit at this table to give my life direction. But how could I fool SAA decision-makers into hiring such an unexceptional candidate?

I fluctuated between holding my breath and breathing in deeply to discover for myself all of Brie's adventures.

I told her my best friend was also flying, and she said it was such a marvelous opportunity because we lived so close to the international airport. The world had changed, she said. The fleet of 747 jumbos was growing and growing. Passengers were hungry for world travel and companies had an urgent need to spread their corporate wings internationally. South African

Airways, our nation's only airline, desperately needed cabin crew.

It was the word "desperately" that drew me in.

Out of the blue, Brie interrupted my reverie with the very words I'd longed to hear. Not from my best friend who loved me, but from a virtual stranger: "You should apply," she said, straight-faced.

A glimmer of hope lifted the corners of my mouth. "You think?"

"Of course. Do it, Lucky."

But I looked like the ugly stepsister to Brie's Cinderella, and I could never be called cute and petite like Alana.

"Not yet. Lots going on. I mean, I plan to. I'm just not sure I'm, well, *pretty* enough to be—" By the way she watched me, I figured my expressions told her more about my insecurities than my words. My face was an open book. Not something I was proud of.

I took a breath and came clean. "Brie, I have but one hand of virtues. I cook a fabulous chicken à la king and I am faithful, presentable, polite and ridiculously loyal. But that's it. That's all I've got."

I smiled and swallowed down my remaining assets: *My powerful schnoz can whisk me off on other people's adventures and occasionally draws me back to my long-ago past. Oh, and I taught myself how to block out dead people but they've come back. I think it's because my best friends are so busy living, they have no time for me.* My fate as a lunatic would have been sealed by those confessions, and the people at the next table would have committed me if Brie hadn't.

Brie reached over and laid her hand over mine and, by the

look on her face, I knew I'd managed to keep my oddities a secret. "Oh, heavens no. You're lovely. You *must* apply."

Her face was a study of kindness, which I may have mistaken for sincerity. But her encouragement was really all I needed. Beautiful Brie, my dad who worshiped me, Alana who loved me, my loyal friend Kitty, all thought I could do anything...

So, what was the harm in trying?

I hung on to Brie's kindness like a nursing puppy attached to her mother and secretly applied to South African Airways.

IQ tests were first up. Then weeks later I was called back for the medical. Perfect eyesight was necessary—any need to wear glasses immediately nixed a girl from her dream job. And hearing? It had to be at a hundred percent.

The woman inside the dark booth with the machines emerged and said, "Sorry, your hearing is impaired. Sign here."

The paperwork coldly stated: *I acknowledge that I have impaired hearing and that I am unable to progress in the position for which I applied to South African Airways.*

I don't know where I found the balls. My parents were dead against balking at authority, but one wrong flick of a button, and my dream was dead as Elvis. I wouldn't—*couldn't* let that happen.

Words tumbled from me, "I do not have any hearing loss. Please, please test me again." I pleaded, "One mistake and my life's dream will be taken away from me." My passion must have made an impression, because the lady complied.

When she signed off, I was in. I breathed a sigh of relief so great, a few of the lights in her booth flickered.

I didn't tell a soul. I still had the hardest part in front of me. But if I failed, it would be a private affair. I ached to tell my folks, Alana, Kitty, and Brie, though I never saw Brie again. She was too busy getting on with her extraordinary life.

But then came the most terrifying of all the quests. The interview.

Facing the strict, somber, snooty panel of four top tier South African Airways brass was more intimidating than an ordeal I'd endured in the school change room.

The time when—pre-Alana—I attempted to don a T-shirt in front of a gaggle of mean girls when only one boob had blossomed. My mother thought it a waste of money to buy a bra for just one "nin." In my haste to cover my perceived deformity, the stretchy fabric got stuck between my arm and opposite shoulder. My one and only boob-bulge with distended nipple was suddenly on display for all to see. And fumble as I might, the odd little thing was exposed for what felt like two days while the left side of my chest lay flat as a pancake.

The entire menagerie of mean girls glared unflinchingly, but left the building before their giggles exploded. I felt the same scrutiny as eight eyes graded me in that interview and I feared afterward they'd laugh up a storm at my impossible dream.

In their presence I felt underdressed, overexposed, and sporting only half of what it took for such a glam job.

How I refrained from running for the hills and throwing myself over the fence and into the Kruger National Game Park to be eaten by lions before the second question they threw at me, I'll never know.

The unsmiling, disinterested four interviewed me in English and Afrikaans to ensure I satisfied the "fully bilingual" necessity.

They fired political and religious questions at me as fast as speeding bullets to check if I managed to dodge them with the diplomacy required.

I was instructed to approach their long table, where a giant world map was cut in half, elongated, then trapped under thick glass. Unsmiling and officious, they asked me to point out Christchurch, then Anchorage. All this so the panel might assess my posture from one end of the table to the other.

How the hell *did* I save myself from not falling off my new, deeply discounted, slightly scuffed high heels?

The exercise was more than a geography test; it allowed the panel to examine me closely. Did I have dandruff? Was I a nail-biter? Did I have skin as flawless as Snow White's? The latter, not so much, and I prayed either my Max Factor was working its cover-up magic or I'd have the chance to tell them about my masterful one-dish show-stopper as a compromise.

Long days became long weeks while I waited for a letter from SAA.

I rehashed the interview a thousand times.

Cloistered in my dread, too ashamed to share my angst lest I had failed the mammoth quest, I threatened to explode within. I checked the post box five times a day for that bloody letter.

I worked my dull job while channeling Norman Vincent Peale. *Yes! I am worthy. Miracles happen.* But my secret grew larger and more ominous as long days passed. I began praying to the Air Hostess Goddess.

The day finally came. I swear, when I pulled the letter from the narrow steel box, I felt it red-hot and throbbing with news.

But what kind? Bills cradled the letter, blocking disappointment or possibly cradling good news. So much for the usefulness of my psychic instincts!

I stood breathless at our front gate as I ripped open the

envelope with such gusto, I tore off the South African Airways emblem.

My eyes flew over the content.

And then again.

Pain exploded through my stomach, into my heart, then my head.

That bloody rejection letter crashed my now-airless ride to the unyielding earth, leaving my body parts and bits of brain distributed all over the path from the postbox to our home's front door.

What the hell made you think you could?

My only salvation was nobody knew how terribly I'd failed. Nobody but me, my worst enemy. I slithered down the brick wall of our family home, feeling far, far from anywhere familiar. And I cried. And cried.

I really had no Plan B.

There were no reasons why I was "unsuitable" listed in the automated notification, but a bazillion reasons reared their ugly heads, unearthing my inadequacies.

I was positive I'd answered every question correctly, pointed to all the right places, and had no gangrenous appendages.

But this Dear John letter was confirmation.

I was ordinary. Unremarkable. Plain as plaster. The airline was 'desperate' my arse!

To lessen devastation, I tried a condensed milk diet. I added two Cadbury flakes to each sitting for motivation to rise from my bed. But SAA's refusal rendered even the power of sugar and chocolate tasteless.

Once my self-esteem had been marginally restored, I finally shared my devastating disappointment with Alana, my parents and Kitty. The friends I cherished were sympathetic and supremely kind. My dad raged, "Those dumb bastards have no clue what they're missing by not snapping you up." And my pragmatic mother reminded me that *aanhouer wen*. She who persists, wins.

We lost my dad soon after that, in a mere six weeks. He went from healthy to dead without warning just after my twentieth birthday.

Once I'd emerged from the thick fog that shock lavishes on the survivor to keep them sane, I begged my dad to show me he was still around, still within earshot, still within reach.

But he didn't come to me. I couldn't touch him. I couldn't smell him. Me, his darling. Me, who could once see any dead person who was visiting or struggling to cross over. Me, who'd closed off my gift because I wanted—no, I *needed* to fit in. To be normal. I wanted him back; in any form he could muster.

But still he didn't come.

When I recovered enough to function, I changed my job to a career in public relations. I felt stimulated and successful, but I still held onto my juvenile goal. *I damn well will become an air hostess,* I said. But only to myself.

Once, when I saw Brie rounding the corner, I crossed the road and ducked into Woolworths, too embarrassed to face her.

One night, the beloved, and familiar fragrance of my dad's rugged skin with a hint of Dunhill and a heady scotch infused my senses. Warmed by his presence, I heard the strange little noise he made in the far reaches of his sinuses when he was deep in thought.

Love surged so forcefully through my body my heart ached. Then his protective touch grazed my cheek. I saw his smile, and my heart smiled back. The curtain in my bedroom to which I'd pinned his WWII wings fluttered, even though the window was tightly closed.

He was showing me his wings because he understood my heart.

There was no doubt. His message was simple.

And if my daddy believed I could, I could. And I damn well would.

CHAPTER 13

I sniffed my Opium-splashed wrists to haul me from my past and rolled out of the white-as-a-lily Marriott bed.

Tula and I went for a walk. We explored the hotel grounds for his evening constitutional. As we rounded a corner, a familiar figure, now in jeans and a tight black t-shirt, ambled towards us, hands in pockets.

"Special Agent." I smiled, trying to avoid looking at that broad chest.

"Tie's off, it's just Andy," he said with mild sarcasm, and followed with, "Kinda missed you at dinner." Concern etched his face, although he had not yet met my eyes. After a moment, he busied himself scratching Tula under the chin. "Did you two eat?"

"We're all good." I brushed his arm to make him look at me. "You're telling me you only came to check on my sustenance?"

"We seldom have time, just you and me. I thought we might get to know each other a bit more, without Jim around."

It was a shock to see Andy so unsure of himself. So UN-cocky. *Stop it, Lucky!*

I didn't need him to tempt me away from my deal with Miss U. Who was I kidding. I was a girl of my word and the entire argument with Miss U was that she wasn't living up to hers.

Here was a kind man, open and vulnerable. He'd been perfectly lovely when I was in that same state a few short days ago, so I owed it to him, not as a prospect, but as a human being. *Be kind and listen, Lucky.*

I sat down on a wrought-iron bench and unhooked Tula's leash. Andy sat down on the opposite end then scooched over till we were two feet apart. I watched Tula, a perfect excuse not to look into those dancing dark eyes next to me. They were all kinds of trouble.

Last chance Roy.

"That sounds nice." It also sounded a little bland. I was out of practice. I glanced at him.

"Well, what do you do when you're not finding dead people?" Andy's eyes were reluctant to hold mine. When the chips were down, he turned out to be just as unpracticed as I.

"Wish I could tell you I danced on tables or practiced for marathons but, in truth, what you saw on your visit is who I am. I enjoy my own and Tula's company. I can brandish about some idle chatter if really necessary though I'm forced to rush off before my shine wears off, so those I've left behind don't suspect I'm really as dull as a toilet brush. How about you?"

"Hey, Jim and I must be pretty damn special. You managed *not* to kick us out for seven whole hours."

I laughed. "You're right. You are two Very Special Agents. But don't avoid the question, what do *you* do when you're not special-agenting?"

"Well, as I think you know, I am unmarried after three

tries, but between us, my life is rather lonely. Not surprising. Who the hell wants to be with a man who's never home? And when he is, he's worrying about a case, and can't chill long enough to sample the real world. Or so they tell me. The wives. The live-ins. The girlfriends. I've been doing this since my late twenties. I don't know a world more real than this one. I try to escape into their worlds but it just doesn't work."

"That's sad. Though I understand. Your perspective and theirs. I reckon we choose our destinies before we take this earth assignment. We know what we're signing up for; we know the lessons we're meant to learn; the challenges, the heartache, all of it. It's what we have to endure to strengthen us, make us more empathetic, so we can eventually earn our wings."

Andy smiled. "Speaking of wings, was being a flight attendant a fun job?"

"Trying to trick me into telling you the end of my story without Jim?"

"Yeah. I reckon it will make me feel pretty special if I'm the only one who knows the outcome of your passionate mission."

I mulled over that for a minute. He was right, I'd given Jim a private taste of my life, didn't I owe it to Andy to give him the same?

Probably not. I didn't owe anybody anything. But somehow, I thought Andy should know.

"When I was flying for South African Airways, we were called air hostesses. Cleaning toilets for passengers during thirteen-to-sixteen-hour flights was a lousy job. Twenty-eight-hour work days most of it in a pressurized cabin fouled up your metabolism. It was a demanding career that sucked you empty as a plastic beach ball in winter by the time you landed. But you helped people. I didn't know then how much I needed to do that. Helping people was my calling.

"And it was a job that held the key to faraway places; to ten-day night stops in exotic destinations, staying in five-star hotels; loads of sustenance and a travel allowance you could spend on shows and live concerts from Bob Dylan to Dire Straits, The Moulin Rouge, Broadway, The West End. Mini trips to countries not yet explored, castles and impromptu island getaways. It was perfect for free, young spirits. Now it feels like someone else's life." I heard my wistfulness.

"And now here you are. Dealing in death and ugliness."

"Quite the contrary, though sometimes it gets me down. In truth, I'm so lucky to do what I do now. To help people find closure. I miss out on seeing the families' reactions when they hear the news that their loved ones have been found. But I imagine them transitioning from not-knowing to knowing. Then putting their loved ones to rest and at last finding some peace. My mission feels accomplished and I am sublimely grateful I was able to be a part of all that."

I felt a pang of guilt as I saw Alana's face—so dear—then an icy shiver worked its way from the bottom of my spine up to my head, which shook like a Jell-O mold taken too early from the fridge.

Thankfully Andy didn't notice because he commented calmly, "That's very noble."

"Not that lofty. Satisfying but not noble. Don't you think what *you* do is noble?"

Andy contemplated that for a minute or two and then, for the first time, he looked into my eyes. "I do, now that you've made me think about it." Then he looked away and said, "But there's no time for reflection before the next case demands attention."

We were companionably silent as we watched Tula pee on every second blade of grass. After marking his territory on each unsuspecting tree, Tula came back to make sure I was doing okay.

Damn, I love this dog.

Andy leaned close enough for me feel the pressure of his shoulder against mine. My cheeks burned and my once-automatic response to pull away was nowhere to be found.

But Roy's face was suddenly in front of mine. Wistful, Warm. Wonderful.

And suddenly there was no doubt what I had to do.

"So, these 'girlish' women who are coming. Are they hostesses too?"

"Were. Hostesses had a ridiculously short career with South African Airways in my day. The moment you turned thirty, the brass had a mission to get you out before you were called an "old bag.""

Andy laughed. "That's pretty mercenary."

"You have no idea."

He put his hand on mine and squeezed.

After Roy's image reminded me of my priorities, my first reflex was to rip my hand away. But that would have been rude. Instead, I extracted it gently and said, without looking at him, "Since we work together, we shouldn't change our dynamic. Might make things awkward."

His eyes were on me; they burned into the side of my head, so I smiled to ease the tension. And then glanced at him.

He was blushing too, but hastily turned his face away "I thought it would be fun."

"Oh, it would be!" I tried not to have a visual. Temptation was a bitch.

I continued pretending I was watching Tula sniff and cavort. "Andy, you're a hunk. If I wasn't in love with someone else, I'd say, 'To hell with the future, let's make hay in the hay while the sun shines.'" I smiled my best smile, hiding my almost-regret at losing an exciting, albeit brief interlude.

I had a girl to find. Guests to prepare for. A final deal with the universe.

A distraction—which was all it would be—was not in the cards. And no matter how spectacular the rendezvous, regret would inevitably follow.

But more important than all the important rest, was Roy and my love for him. I had given the universe a last chance. She knew I'd reached the end of my tether.

"Who's the lucky guy?" Andy asked, shifting a stone between his feet.

"My soulmate." I said simply and immediately regretted doing so. How fanciful it must sound to a pragmatist. I felt compelled to explain a little more. "Someone I've loved for many years..."

Even that little felt like too much.

I looked at Andy. He was looking at me, his dark eyes were no longer flirty. Just intense.

I continued quickly lest I lose my nerve and my chance. "I mysteriously lost him. He simply disappeared. He was a lieutenant in the Marines."

"How long ago?" Andy asked. He bent and picked up the rock he'd been kicking and started tossing it from hand to hand.

I chickened out and tried to change the subject, forcing a laugh. "Tula's fascinated by you playing with that rock. Look at him! His head's swinging from left to right, right to left, like he's watching a Wimbledon tennis match."

I felt the sharpness of his stare but dared not meet his gaze.

"Tell me how long," he repeated. Such was his tone; my Tula nudged his knee and gave a sharp bark as if to caution him.

I owed him a better explanation. "Since 1988."

Andy threw back his head and laughed. "Nineteen-eighty-fuking-eight. You're kidding me, right?"

It sounded so asinine out loud. I shook my head.

"You've been waiting for this 'soulmate' for thirty-five years? Good God, Lucky. I pegged you as the smartest woman I knew."

He shamed me further by using past tense.

All my insecurities, which I'd fought so hard to quash, threatened to come back wearing party hats. This wasn't my first brush with doing something for which I might be mocked. But the shame of trying and trying and not succeeding, well that never got old.

As soon as I got to the States and became involved with law enforcement as a psychic, I had asked my co-workers to check their data bases and those of Interpol for Roy Moreno-Reyes.

I did this with every new law enforcement team I hooked up with on a case. I was not required to state my reason, so none was given. They believed I was searching for a person of interest, if not in their case, then another. Two or so years ago I'd asked Jim to do the same. No luck. It occurred to me that I had waited to catch Jim alone to ask him. Perhaps my crush on Andy went back that far.

Jim and Andy were the only ones in America and in the last week, who now knew I was looking for my soulmate. And here

I was, eliciting ridicule instead of understanding. *Dammit it, Lucky, you should know better. You do know better.*

I stood up. "Well, that was fun. Let's do this again soon," I said sarcastically, as I hooked Tula up to his leash.

Andy grabbed my arm. I turned slowly.

"I am so sorry, Lucky. That was uncalled for. Who am I to judge? Shit. Are my failed marriages and relationships smarter than you searching for your soulmate for over three decades? At least you're faithful."

I waited.

"Sit for a while. Please." His eyes were imploring.

I didn't.

I blew the air out of my cheeks. "No, I haven't been faithful to him. My heart and soul, yes, but not my body. That's why I couldn't get involved with you, Andy. Because I really like you. You wouldn't just be a passing fancy for me. And your track record is lousy. Even so, if I thought for a minute that the man I love is dead or spoken for, I would give up and optimistically see where this" I waggled my finger between us, "would go." I smiled, sadly perhaps. "But I don't feel he is lost to me. That's why I'm holding on with all my heart."

He looked up at me and smiled a beautiful smile. "Lucky bastard."

I bent down and touched his cheek with the back of my index finger.

The little *zing* was gone. As I left to go and find Janice, all I felt was sorry for him.

CHAPTER 14

I soaked in the tub laden with blissful lavender salts. Tula lay next to me on the clean, tiled floor. Purple essence quelled the bathroom disinfectant, and I luxuriated in the calming perfume until...

FLASH!

Lazily, I looked up at the enormous kosso tree and thanked it for its shade, then glanced down to the chaise lounge on which I lay.

Dark-skinned young men with bare chests and yellow turbans took turns fanning me with huge palm fronds. Ethiopia in the fourteenth century—was I the Queen of Sheba?

BACK!

Was every life I slipped back into my own? Or someone else's?

It certainly felt like I was inhabiting the bodies of the people in my centuries-old dramas, because each of my five senses exploded with awareness. Never an observer. Always a participant. Though my time-slips usually have a beginning, middle and end, occasionally, like this time, it's just a preview for a longer adventure for me to revisit.

With my hasty return to the Marriott room in the twenty-first century, water splashed out of the bath. Seems there was too much going on in my mind to let myself linger in the body of the languishing queen. Pity. It could have been fun for a change.

I slipped on the Downy-scented, cotton dressing gown I found in the closet, dabbed on more Opium, picked up the evidence box and plopped down on the bed I wouldn't be sleeping in, placing the box gently beside me.

I removed each piece of evidence slowly. When I used my nail scissors to cut open the bags, my fingers tingled as if my digits warned my nose about what was coming.

Inhaling the Opium on my palms kept me from being dragged back half-cocked. I had to surround myself with *all* Janice's smells *and* find her true essence before I let myself go.

Tula stood at the foot of the bed on high alert. His nose twitched, and his head moved as he caught the myriad of unfamiliar scents. Though his nose was ten thousand times stronger than mine, he was thankfully spared the experience of being yanked back in time...or was he? I thought of the hawk he'd been during my witchy demise.

Janice needs you. Grasshopper brain!

I laid out Janice's possessions reverently, respectfully.

Her cell phone, toothbrush, hairbrush with a tangle of pitch-black hairs, a discarded cotton nightie found in the spare room or so said the evidence tag, a favored pair of jeans and a sweatshirt retrieved from the laundry basket the day they searched the house. All these items were laid out on the king-size bed. I added a pair of her favorite shoes from the evidence bag and emptied her handbag. Lip gloss, a red pen, a locket without a chain, Tampax camouflaged in a pretty little plastic box and two Excedrin fell gently onto the stark white comforter.

I opened the locket. A color photo of Janice, as I had imagined her, was on one side, while the opposite oval held a picture of an older Janice. Her mom. I laid down the open locket to bring them in to help me.

I placed the handbag down, and Tula's nose hovered over the bag, sniffing long and deep. "What?" I challenged him. His eyes never left the camel-colored Nine West purse. With one hand, I lifted it upside down and showed him the trinkets on the bed. "Tula, that's everything."

But he wasn't convinced. I needed to take heed. I massaged the pliable, glossy leather this way and that until my fingers touched something hard, flat and rectangular. I turned the handbag inside out. There was a hidden slit in the pocket with a business card slipped between the lining and the bag. No wonder the police missed it. Janice had created a masterful hiding place.

I pulled out the business card of a lawyer in Springfield: *Mr. Jeb Winston Esq., Attorney at Law*. In smaller print, it read: *A firm practicing in family law, expert at resolving legal family disputes*.

As I was about to place the bag with the rest of Janice's things, Tula whimpered. "What's with you? I found the card."

His intense eyes moved from the handbag to me and back again. I put my hand in the secret slit of the pocket deeper than before, through another tiny slit and into the bag's hard base. My finger touched glossy paper. Inventive, secretive Janice.

I gently worked it through the slit and out. As I smoothed it with tingling fingers, I recognized it as a sonogram. That it was hidden alluded to this baby being a secret. And then there was the divorce attorney's card.

The tampon and Excedrin were possibly wishful thinking before the confirmation this little piece of paper provided. I checked the date on the bottom right corner. One day before she disappeared. Janice had been with child when she went missing.

The dual loss became a physical blow to my gut and I hunched over as Tula hovered. When it eased, I whispered, "At least they're together now, Tula, and next time they're born, they'll be close in one form or another." I found great peace in that.

I leaned over, held Tula's fluffy head, looked into his arresting eyes and said, "You are the cleverest detective in the whole of Massachusetts."

I could've sworn he grinned.

I left all the lights on in the room and lay down carefully between Janice's possessions. Tula still stood on the floor, his eyes on me, watching raptly. He wouldn't move a muscle for as long as it took.

I closed my eyes and allowed my nose to follow its destiny.

And my immersion into Janice's world began.

CHAPTER 15

Were it not for my suddenly busy social schedule, Tula and I would have slept in after our hectic night. We'd only snatched a couple of hours of sleep after following Janice's deadly path.

Time was not our friend, and Hull called. I tried not to think about all I *wasn't* getting done before the huddle of hosties landed.

Jim and Andy waited downstairs, and we all checked in for the hotel breakfast.

"You look like hell," said Andy.

"Just the look I was going for," I replied, munching on a piece of bacon and slipping Tula his own sliver under the table. "That's what you chaps do to me. You lay the life of another on me, then wonder why I look like hell the morning after."

"So sorry," said Jim, looking mournful.

"You'd still turn a head," Andy muttered without looking at me.

I smiled on the inside.

They didn't push me for information. Starvation must have

been painted on my face. There'd been no time to order room service.

Once I'd eaten everything laid on the table before me, I checked that Tula had finished the last of the sausages Jim had slipped him, and he'd had his fill from a bowl of water under the table. I sat back, holding my coffee cup in both hands and inhaling the Marriott blend of java.

"Why didn't you tell me Janice was pregnant? Did you want me to prove myself to you?"

They both hung their heads sheepishly. Neither would look at me.

"After all this time," I knew I sounded like a nagging wife but I wasn't done yet. "Look, as of a few days ago I trusted you with *my* most intimate secrets, but you don't trust me enough to share what you know about the victim?" I was more pissed than I should have been professionally, but I had shown my vulnerability to them, my most private past and yet they couldn't share this vital information?

Andy's eyes were so apologetic I didn't want to linger there. I needed them to know this was unacceptable.

"We found out when we followed the trail Janice's computer and calendar led us on. The Gyn confirmed the pregnancy when we were first working the case." Jim hung his head.

"I am so sorry Lucky," Andy said. "Old habits die hard. We're trained not to trust anyone but our partners. We can't afford to be too open."

"I guess that's why you've been married so often." Boy that was a low blow but I couldn't help myself.

"I'm truly sorry, Lucky. It will never happen again." Andy said, misery seeping from his tone.

"We trust you almost as much as we trust each other," Jim said.

I retorted, "Take out the 'almost' and we can move forward. When we're on a case together, we *three* are partners and don't you forget it." Now I sounded childish and I knew it. Tula sensed the rise in my blood pressure and nudged me with his wet nose. I breathed in slowly and felt calmer.

"I can speak for both of us when I tell you, we marvel how *much* we trust you, Lucky. We can't say the same of anyone else we work with. Please don't take offense." Jim's face was so contrite it took away my anger.

"Okay, but from now on, we discuss the case in its entirety. You don't leave out parts so I can prove myself."

"Promise," they said in unison.

"Okay, spill, chaps. I need to know it all."

Jim nodded, and Andy said, "Janice was maybe six weeks pregnant."

"Oh, how dreadful." Sadness overshadowed my professional or was it personal slight.

Jim's face was as sad as I felt. "She told her dad, and only her dad, on the last day anyone saw her."

Andy took over. "Her dad said he didn't know why such good news should make her so sad. She'd spent an hour crying. He remembered his late wife—Janice's mother—blaming tears on hormones when she was pregnant with their only child, so he put Janice's emotions down to that. He didn't know about her disenchantment with her husband."

"Such a shame. Maybe she was crying because she didn't want to bring a baby into a broken marriage."

Andy nodded. "But of course, we weren't going to disillusion him. The poor old man had already lost not only a precious child but a grandchild, too."

"I see why this one grabbed you in the gut," I said, as my stomach took an invisible punch.

We sipped the last of our drinks in mournful silence. Tula gave the tiniest whine, one likely only I heard. It was enough to pull me out of my sadness and into the present. I had a job to do.

"I hope you chaps are ready for a long drive," I warned.

"Whatever you need," they chimed together.

"We need to get moving. Thanks for breakfast." I got up, disappeared to the loo, mostly to replenish my Ruby Woo red lips, and then claimed shotgun in their luxurious, tinted SUV.

Jim and Tula sat in the back, Tula behind my passenger seat. "Our tax dollars are well spent," I said, wiggling into the ultra-comfy seat and enjoying the distinctive aroma of new leather, which always made me feel spoiled.

I pulled my hair off my face and slipped an elastic band around the loose ponytail on top of my head. Ready for business.

"Which way, Lucky?" Andy asked, turning to me.

I opened my third eye, then my heart, and I allowed my super-nose to lead the way.

"Right at the next light," I heard myself say from a place far away. "Go ten point two miles straight ahead."

It had taken me too long to realize that when I let instinct rule, amazing things happened.

As we drove and I barked out directions through my logical brain, I experienced a myriad of sensations that were not mine, but they became so...

FLASH!

...I am light-headed. I can take on the world. I am no longer Mrs. Hughes, nice girl, obedient wife, disappointed partner. I am a Woman of Substance, Woman of the World. Woman of Intrigue. Unfettered by my wifely status, I am Sultry Janice.

A rush of heat to my pelvis, and my body sways in surprising undulation. Ahh, tequila. I giggle. It *is* all it's cracked up to be!

Sultry Janice can move!

"Did you bring your phone?" somebody asks.

"Who'm I gonna call? You're all here!" I laugh and make an exultant exit in my new and forbidden skin.

Balmy July air cocoons me. I am hotter, sexier than I ever imagined. And proud of it. I must flaunt my new sexuality. And I can in my empty suburban street, with the streetlamps trying to upstage the stars. Traces of extinguished fireworks hang in the air, as if they're holding on with all their might to their very last impression, hoping to remind me of their earlier brilliance.

I sing Matchbox Twenty's "Unwell" and spin and fall but not all the way to the asphalt. I laugh at my uninhibited body and unabashed confidence.

I love me.

Not Hunter.

No! I giggle. Hunter is a dullard, not wild enough for Sultry Janice.

Lights.

Aha! At last, the spotlight I deserve. My body becomes boneless as it sways and turns and my head rolls like the MTV dancers of my youth. "I'm not crazy..."

Loose pebbles spit out from slow-rolling wheels. A car. Aha! My limousine to whisk me away to greener pastures? My spotlight turns off, but the pebbles keep popping. And then the car is next to me.

A Prince Charming for Sultry Janice? Should I show him how I can dance? I shake my head. Who is he? My head spins and I see white-white skin, dark eyes, black eyebrows. The contrast is intriguing. And a sensuous mouth. Fat lips. I like fat lips.

I lick my own. Ahhh, tequila. I smile.

My new love is powerful and commanding. His name is Tequila.

The big man in the compact car is vaguely familiar—but not.

Unthreatening, his smile is wide, teeth ever so slightly crooked. "Can I take you safely home?" he asks, his alluring smile the best invitation in two not-so-glorious years.

I laugh and laugh. "It won't take you long." I point to my solid, prim home, two houses down.

"Janice, you need to sober up before you get home." He sounds like my conservative friend, my father, my conscience. I am disappointed. Sultry Janice has no room for a conscience.

"Away with you!" I point at his nose. "I am free. I want to stay free." I twirl, feeling free and safe and confident.

And then I trip and I land hard on my butt. Ouch.

I open my eyes to see him unwinding out of the small car, a slow jack-in-the-box, making me wonder briefly how he fit in at all. He has on blue jeans and a loose T-shirt. He is lean. And tall. Oh, so tall. Hunter is too short.

He extends his hand. I shouldn't accept a hand up from a stranger. I should refuse and get up on my own, that's what I should do. And then I should walk home. But instead, Abba spews from my lips, asking him to take a chance on me, as I take his hand.

He pulls me up and I stand like that for a few seconds before I remove my hand. Embarrassed laughter bubbles up. "It's not an invitation," I promise, blinking hard, "just a song."

He smiles. No judgement. No threat.

I like the look of those lips. Puffy, even as they spread across those slightly uneven teeth.

Sultry Janice smiles back, and she looks up at him, her most charming smile. I must remember how I did that. Puffy Lips is clearly impressed with this new smile.

He takes my hand and leads me around the back of the car and opens the passenger door, ushering me inside. A gentleman. "Why, thank you, kind sir," I remark, amusing myself as he softly closes the door.

He starts the car, does a U-turn, and we cruise with the lights still off, away from my cul-de-sac.

"Where are you taking me?" I ask conversationally.

"To heaven," he says, and his voice is thick with lust. I am amazed I recognize the sound of lust. I am fascinated by it. Fascinated and a bit turned on.

I turn abruptly to face him. "Do I know you?" I ask. Then, through tequila's haze, I remember he called me by my name. "You know me."

"I've seen you. You looked at me once." His voice is flat.

"Only once?" I tease. It's an old car. I see the window winder and consider how Hunter wouldn't be seen dead in this car. 'It's so yesterday' he'd say. Then I turn to the driver whose head is a hair away from scraping the roof of the car, and banish my dull, thin-lipped husband from my thoughts.

Puffy Lips puts a huge hand on my knee. I examine it like a

bone uncovered at a zoo dinosaur dig. Nails well-clipped. Fingers long, like a piano player's. A tumble of black hairs dust thick white knuckles.

But his physical touch interferes with the freedom of my imagination.

My mind may do anything, go anywhere. But a stranger's hand touching me? I'm suddenly uncomfortable, and a niggle of doubt neutralizes some of the tequila.

I move my jean-encased leg out of his long arm's reach. I no longer feel so comfortable.

"Seriously." My voice has an edge. "Where are you taking me?"

"I am taking you to where you're longing to go. I am taking you to your zenith. To your utopia."

Sultry Janice jumps out of the window, but I am still in the passenger seat. My buzz is gone. I am Conservative Janice. Devoted Daughter. Loyal Friend. Exceptional Employee. Wife.

And fear attacks like a swarm of hungry mosquitoes. Not deadly yet, but most uncomfortable.

I think Frightened Janice should leave the way Sultry Janice did. I am small. Perhaps I can get out of the window.

But I notice for the first time that the window to my right is broken. Shards of glass poke upward and downward, and when the car turns and hits the open road, wind rushes in a big hole where someone has plucked out glass. A hole just big enough to get an arm in from the outside, so fingers might flip up the door lock.

Did he steal this car?

Terror bites my toes, real and threatening, and works its way up.

Oh, God, NO! I must get away.

I put my mouth close to the jagged hole, careful not to get too close, and I scream bloody murder.

He laughs. "No one will hear you. You wanted me just now. I saw it in your body. In the lust of your eyes, in your tongue, on your lips. You're going to get me, Janice. Every. Inch. Of. Me."

The last four words are said slowly, each laden with a promise of evil so violent, it sends tremors of terror down my spine.

I look back through the rear window. There are no lights. No cars. No houses. The car's beams reflect colors and shapes. Woods. Marshlands. Dark asphalt. Rippling shallow water.

CHAPTER 16

FLASH!

My head throbs, and I touch something wet and sticky on my neck. I remember the thud and pain when my skull hit a rock as he hauled me out of the car by my feet.

I kick with all my might. To no avail.

Twigs and leaves and stones scratch my face as he drags me through the woods, weaving in and out of the trees randomly.

I have no breadcrumbs to help me return.

Concentrate on the stars.

The once-interesting face turns, and wild eyes bore into mine. His mask of humanity is long gone. Features are wicked. Twisted. I scream, but there is no sound. He has taken off my blouse and bound my mouth with the sleeves, so tightly I can't move my tongue. The sound from my larynx resembles a trapped animal far away.

Brambles, sticks, and uneven stones tear at the skin of my back with only a lacy bra to protect it. I refuse to contemplate the inevitable. I will fight him for all I am worth.

"I may be little, but I am fierce," I tell my daddy. He smiles and ruffles my hair like I'm a boy. I love it. Think of Daddy. He's alive. Like me. I am alive.

My jarred body produces unbearable pain, but then it's replaced by acute sadness and loss. Mommy I miss you so. I beg for the physical pain instead.

But suddenly she is before me. Shimmering and loving.

I love you, Mommy.

I have found a coping mechanism. My mother gives me loving solace as we share beautiful memories. I accept my long, agonizing journey. The metallic odor of blood invades my nostrils. It's my own. My back is battered. Bruised and torn by sharp spears and rocks and unyielding obstacles tearing at my skin, but my mommy makes all of that just a vague discomfort.

It is when we stop that my desperate fear returns.

Mommy, where are you?

I sob.

But she lays long fingers on my forehead as if I have a temperature.

Her concern pacifies me.

Then *his* arms are around me, and I shiver in fear and disgust. Screams in my ears from my bound mouth are those of a confused, raging, rabid animal, then he hoists me over his shoulder like I was a two-year-old.

Look, Mommy! I'm a sack of potatoes!

I can no longer see the stars.

The bump-bump-bump of his shoulder bones box my internal organs with each gigantic stride.

Let's make up a song about a sack of potatoes.

I am so happy my mom has come up with such a fun idea. We work on words and tunes to go with the rhythm of the bumps, and the pounding of my liver, my spleen, my innards, subside.

And then he throws down the sack of potatoes and I hear the air in my lungs being expelled by the sheer force of my body ramming the earth. I am stunned. My eyes dart around to catch something memorable. A giant tree leans toward me, offering sympathy and solace.

Oh, God. Please, not that. Not that. Sultry Janice was just visiting. I wouldn't have let her stay. This is me. Janice the prude. Janice the good girl. Please, please, not that. I'm sorry. Sultry Janice will never be back. Never. I promise. And I never break a promise.

Knowing what's about to happen, a familiar sense of helplessness threatens to choke me as tightly as my assailant's hands.

I gag on the bile rising in my throat...

BACK!

...Breathing deeply, I pull a well-worn invisible, shield up to protect myself. This way I can safely allow the images to continue when I am ready. I feel the extreme comfort of Tulu's breath on the back of my neck. I am not alone in this frightening place. Tula is close, watching over me. Remember, I am observer, not participant. The shield is powerful and will protect me from any negative forces wishing to attach to me, but to doubly indemnify myself I repeat: *This is Janice's past, not mine.* A mantra.

Safe, I choose to be completely connected to Janice once again.

FLASH!

I see myself as a little girl curled in the safety of my mother's lap. We huddle on the window seat, which is covered in pink flowered cushions. When the seat lifts up, I'll find my

Monopoly and Chinese checkers. My mother's lilting voice reads 'Brer Rabbit.' I watch her mouth as it moves. Her lips curl up in a little smile now and then, and her eyes, when they look at me, burst with love so tender. I am safe. No matter what. I am safe.

He's back. So is the fear, but not so much because my mommy is close by. She urges me to grab at something around his neck. He doesn't see me coming because I'm left-handed. An unexpected southpaw. I think of my dad's animated face watching boxing on TV, and I almost smile before revulsion pulls me to the present and fuels me to pull with all my might.

I do.

How does he not feel the tug at the back of his neck?

You did that, right Mommy?

She nods.

Thank you.

His evil eyes are on me. I drop my head back, depriving him of taking my eyes hostage.

Gigantic hands move towards me and heat sears my neck as they encircle me. I shut my eyes. Tight.

I think of something important.

I too could be a mother. I try in vain to touch my belly but he is in the way. I have toyed with severing those ties deep within me. No number of visits to confession have succeeded in making me unselfish enough to choose my child's life over my own. I am so sorry, my child. I feared you would tie me to Hunter forever. That is a fate worse than the guilt my actions towards you might prove to be.

Mommy?

I feel her fingers thread through mine.

Mommy, is this punishment for my selfishness?

No, my child. There is no punishment in this world or the next. This is where your contract on this earth ends. You have served your time, just as I served mine.

I accept mommy's infinite wisdom.

"Look at me!" he commands in a thick voice.

At last, *I* can decide. I can choose to look at him or not. I close my eyes, shutting him out, tight. I choose to insult him. Refusing his angry demands. He tries to pry my eyes open with his fingers, but the hurt is lessened by my victorious refusal to comply.

He swears, grunts, and probing thumbs leave my eyes.

They push down on my windpipe instead. I give it a last, sterling try and, releasing mommy's hand, I put both arms out to the side, not in acquiescence, or the beginnings of a snow angel, but to find a rock. First, I push that which I've pulled from his neck under the dead leaves.

My fingers move either side of my body like two crazed tarantulas as I search for anything large enough to kill the enemy. All at once I am spurred by a maternal instinct to protect my offspring.

I must smite this enemy, not for my sake but for the sake of my child.

But there is nothing within my grasp but twigs, leaves, and little stones. Not enough... Not enough.

I have failed you, my child. I cannot...

I try... and try...I just can't take a breath.

My tarantulas are giving up. They're dying.

I am so sorry my child. You did not have to wait until you were born for me to disappoint you. I am so desperately sorry.

Mommy, help me. Help us.

And she is there.

But Mommy, what of my child's life contract? Will her commitment to this life be left unfulfilled because of me?

No, Janice. Your child's contract only begins when she is born. Not before.

Then I am not hurting her by letting go of my own life?

Mommy shakes her head and smiles. Then she opens her arms.

Wide enough for both of us.

CHAPTER 17

B*ACK!*

"STOP!"

I jumped at the sound of my own loud shout.

Tula's back legs were on the floor at my feet, his front paws on either side of my butt, nose inches from mine as Andy hit the brake.

"God, it's been an hour of watching you agonize," Andy said in a shaky voice. "No wonder your poor partner here is worried sick."

"I'm okay, boy, I'm okay. Thank you." I placed my cheek next to Tula's and held him there for a minute until we both relaxed. Then he jumped back to join Jim.

"Shit. Excuse my language, but what you do scares the life out of me, Lucky," Jim said from the back.

"Me, too, Jim." I suspect it's harder for others to watch me than for me to experience things. It was as if I was saved from full immersion by a thin skin—or perhaps a magical birth skein that separated me from whomever I became.

That's the caul protecting me from being consumed by

someone else's plight. This was not a new thought but an old revelation. *And the caul becomes the shield because it's easier to visualize.*

"Now what?" Andy asked, pulling me back from my self-enlightenment.

"Park just short of the bridge, and we'll head through the woods and the brush the same way he pulled Janice."

Her fear was tangible. It came in great waves. I was grateful when it ebbed because that meant she was oblivious. Her pain on her back and shoulders, the sticky feel of wet blood on the back of her neck, was mine too.

Tula's cold nose touched my hand now and then, assuring me he was right there. Keeping me in the present.

Tula and I led the way, zigzagging through the busy floor of the woods, over rocks and stones and sticks and branches I could have avoided. But that was the way Janice sent me.

I recoiled at the essence of the tall man as he pulled Janice like a butcher with a meaty carcass. He had the dark, vile odors of a teenage boy's untended bedroom filled with old and recent secretions, stinky sneakers, and immaturity, mixed with something oddly sweet. It didn't make sense. The man was every bit full grown, a giant of a man, long past the teenage stage.

And the sweet, cloying, vaguely familiar scent was one I could not, for the life of me, for the life of Janice, identify.

Nearly half a mile north along Garnet Lake, the branch of a gigantic tree blocked my path. Literally and figuratively. The latter because it felt like the tree leaned over to stop me, lest I wasn't paying attention.

It marked the crook of a small elbow of the lake that petered out into the marsh. Nobody would take such a dead place too seriously. Not hikers or anglers. Slime shimmered on the strip of shallow, stagnant water the size of a skinny lap pool. Where slime wasn't, lily pads were, and the whole pond was bordered by thick, tall reeds. A typical landscape for untended marsh-lands in Massachusetts.

"This is where he raped her," I said flatly as I stood under the tree. Fear and resignation, disgust, and lust permeated the air around me.

His putrid smell, the sight of...

My stomach roiled in revulsion and I turned, Tula at my heels, and retched behind the enormous tree.

I hated when that happened, but better out with the ugliness.

I inched back in front of the tree, where the two agents stood statue-still waiting for me.

"He strangled her right here." I pointed.

I felt a stillness.

My legs move as I float above, distancing myself from death. I watch the evil bully become a four-year-old having a tantrum because he deliberately broke his own toy. Heaving with great big sobs and hysterical cries. He lifts Janice reverently and carries her like a groom crossing a threshold, a bride in his arms, to where the reeds grow thickest.

He lays her down like Moses in the bulrushes.

"What did you just say?" Andy's voice jolted me back to the present.

I had to think. "Like Moses in the bulrushes. I have no idea why." Then I shivered.

My feet moved unbidden towards an exact spot on the bank. I felt as if roots grew from my Wellingtons down, down, down. I couldn't have moved if I tried.

"He lays her down between the reeds, in shallow water." I

gestured. "Then he finds rocks and packs them into her jean pockets and inside her bra. Unties her blouse from her mouth and fills the front pockets with stones, then ties it around her waist. Janice slips under the water. He searches and searches. Finds a giant boulder. Lays it gently on the submerged Janice's chest and her head disappears, lifeless legs still floating on the surface.

"He lumbers off in search of another, returns to the bank and lays the second boulder down while he assesses his work. Then he hauls up the huge stone with both hands and lays it down gently, so as not to hurt her, over her lower abdomen and pelvis. He weeps loudly as she disappears in the moonlight."

I watched him for a bit as he worked, busy as a basket weaver.

"He pulls the reeds from one side of her and knots them with those on her other side, creating a tight, natural-reed coffin, sealing her in. When he's finished weaving, he steps back on the bank and examines his handiwork from this angle and that in the moonlight. But all he sees is a clump of reeds within other clumps of reeds. Nothing to find.

"Janice is long gone. Janice is at peace. With her mommy and baby," I said, and wiped away my tears, holding on to Tula's collar with all my might.

Andy's arms were around me, holding me tight. But once I'd calmed, he dropped them and quickly walked towards the elbow of mucky water.

Jim called in a potential crime scene and demanded a forensics team.

When he clicked off the phone, he called out to Andy, who was already gently wading in to search for himself. "Can you take it from here?"

"Yes. Take Lucky and Tula back to the Marriott, and I'll see you back here. Lucky, I'll call as soon as we find anything. Thank you. Thank you." His face was a study of gratitude.

"You haven't found her yet," I said, "but you will."

As we turned away from Janice's resting place, the stench of rotting reeds and slime was replaced by the smell of blood. No. Like blood, but metal. Yes! Something metallic and silver was once smelted into a coin...but not a coin.

Tula's wet nose brought me back. I stopped, turned to Andy, and raised my voice. "Look for something round and silver close by. Maybe near the tree. It's important."

Andy stopped what he was doing, nodded vigorously and stared into my eyes for longer than he should have. I broke our electric eye contact first but, in spite of our grim surroundings, a tiny buzz of delight coursed through me. Perhaps just to remind me I was alive.

CHAPTER 18

After the ordeal, there was no way I could navigate us safely home. Besides, by the time we got back to the hotel it was already dusk. So Tula and I spent another night in the soothingly clean Marriott with the lights on. I'd returned all Janice's possessions to Jim when we got back. Then I'd checked myself into a new room on a different floor with a view of the pool. The change in orientation made it easier.

My senses reeled as, out of the blue, I smelled his musky scent.

The joy of feeling Roy again triggered my body before my mind could find its logic. Fueled by longing, my arms reached for him. Spawned by decades of hunger and deprivation, my soul guided my movements.

But all too quickly, the smell that had so piqued my senses dwindled. *Panic.* With every fiber of my being, I wanted to hold onto him... But the last remnants of the only man I'd ever loved vanished into thin air.

My face tickled. I reached to scratch it and found my cheeks wet with tears. The terror of never finding him again made the empty feeling bottomless.

I really wept then. Great big tears of self-pity.

Tula standing over me, licking my cheek, nudging me with his wet nose, had no effect. I wanted to feel sorry for myself and almost told him to leave me alone. But God forbid I should scold him on this one occasion versus scores of others when I needed his rapt attention and loving care.

When my sobs subsided, I hugged his neck whispering: "So sorry, my Tula. I am just so very sad."

Where are you, my Roy? You wouldn't have left me on purpose. You couldn't. Our souls were destined to be together again in this life.

Reaching for my phone, I typed into the URL: *World disasters, conflict, and mayhem between late 1987 and early1989.*

It wasn't the first time I'd tried to work out where he'd gone, but it had been a while.

"The Piper Alpha oil platform disaster of 1988 in the North Sea was one of the worst offshore oil disasters in the history of the petroleum industry and claimed the lives of 167 workers... The 'Great Storm of '88,' an extratropical ("southeaster") storm that struck the Pacific Coast from Baja California to San Francisco and produced the largest waves ever measured in the Southern California Bight... Iran Air Flight 655 is shot down by a missile launched from the USS *Vincennes*, killing a total of 290 people on board..."

Geez, there had been enough disasters to keep Roy otherwise engaged for a lifetime. I could be here all day going down the rabbit hole of excuses for my soulmate to disappear.

"Hurricane Gilbert devastates Jamaica and turns towards

Mexico's Yucatán Peninsula causing an estimated $5 billion in damage... Pan Am Flight 103 is downed over the town of Lockerbie, Scotland, by a terrorist bomb, killing 270 people... In Alaska's Prince William Sound, the Exxon Valdez spills 240,000 barrels (11 million gallons) of oil after running aground..."

Too many reasons he could have been lost to me. I would just have to ask him myself when the universe delivered him on my doorstep. I smiled, buoying my spirits, and ordered room service: a slice of death-by-chocolate cake, lentil soup, and a marrow bone for Tula. Then I slept a mercifully dreamless sleep with my trusty side-kick curled up behind my knees for what remained of the night.

I grabbed a Marriot coffee to go, left Andy and Jim a note thanking them for their fine hospitality and loaded my bags into the jeep after Tula hopped in. Home at last, to my fortress. My brick-and-mortar security blanket.

As we left Springfield I glanced at Tula—riding shotgun, of course, who looked decidedly pleased with himself. I was pleased, too. We'd come to do and we did. I pushed the Janice situation as far out of my mind as possible. I had one sleep and whatever was left of this day, to prepare my domicile.

During that long, traffic-jammed trip home, I thought of the four former air hostesses who were on their way from who-knew-where to my sanctuary.

BJ.

I didn't know her, nor had I ever flown with her, but she was known as The Queen of the airline. A legend. One you'd rather hear about than actually experience. BJ had a penchant for Shakespearian slurs long before they became popular. She threw around The Bard's insults like a shot-put athlete. With contemplation, precision and all her weight behind them. Nobody was exempt. Not cabin crew, cockpit crew, and not even first-class passengers. If they were less classy than she expected them to be, they were targets but they never reported her. Strange. She must have something, I conceded.

Dread crept in. How in the world would I handle such a woman in my home for six long days? Holy cow! Sanctimonious and ready to whip me into shape with her insults? Not my idea of fun. Kinda sucked that she was one of the four who'd had The Dream. BJ caused the heaviness in my chest.

I shivered. How would my less-than-perfect housecleaning and catering standards upset her? To heck with her. It was my house, my rules after all. I smacked my chest, sort of resetting my heart to rid it of any angst that had crept in because of the most dreaded guest.

Fiddling with the radio, I found a seventies and eighties rock station.

Also on my "Imminent Arrivals" roster was Chantelle, who I couldn't remember from those days, and Moxie who I'd witnessed being chastised by her instructor for bossing around the girls in her *ab initio* group. She was in a different class, along with forty others, at the same time as ours.

I thought of Brie. Beautiful and kind. In what ways had the past few decades altered her? I hoped she'd not become jaded; she'd sounded compassionate and kind in the emails I'd found in my inbox. I'd know soon enough. If indeed she was the Brie I remembered, she might balance the mean BJ.

CHAPTER 19

My cell phone rang, and I sprang back from my reverie and moved to the slow lane. Wh was I kidding? All lanes were slow and I was still miles from Hull, hours away from cleaning my house to impress the imminent barrage of bodies.

Such good intentions.

"Hello?" I heard a flurry of voices in the background.

It was Andy. "Lucky, we found her!"

An icy shiver traveled from my coccyx to my brain. "Poor Janice," was all I could muster.

"Yes," said Andy, his voice breaking up not because of a poor signal, but for a lost girl found. "It was just as you described down to her lacy bra and the patterns on her blouse. Fragments of both were caught under a rock, and a small piece of denim under another. I know it's her—we all do. But a fast-track on forensics and dental records will confirm. She hadn't moved from her 'coffin of reeds,' as you called it. Moses in the bulrushes. It's exactly what you said, Lucky."

There was an awe in his voice I dared not consider. Pride had no place in the underbelly of my world.

I nodded, though he couldn't see. "Now find the silver coin or medallion. It's close. Don't leave 'til you find it, Andy. It will lead you to answers, to her dad's and Janice's ultimate peace." I was overcome by emotions, and tears poured down so hard, I had to pull over, pissing off all the cars behind me. So be it.

Andy hung on through my weep, and I would have bet he was having his own. Then he said simply, "Thank you, Lucky," but the three words were loaded.

After I hung up, the metallic taste was so strong only a drive-through's mocha java could quell it. Tula guzzled up his kid's size grilled chicken nuggets.

On the road again, traffic-tedium pulled me back to where I left off, and I was whisked back to the early 1980s with a little help from Cat Stevens who was looking for a hard-headed woman.

In the two years I waited for my dad to come to me, I'd created ice walls around my heart and garnered my courage. I walked with confidence on the outside and faked it on the inside. I vowed the world would never see the vulnerable me again.

I'd discovered bright red lipstick was a marvelous antidote to unremarkable features. And I smiled more, demanding attention to my well-tended teeth, and, by people's response, I seemed fractionally more interesting.

The question was: did my strong façade and my red lips make me interesting *enough?*

I took the proverbial plunge, slipped on a pair of cast-iron panties, retook the IQ and medical tests, and presented my very best and smiling face to the new—and even more intimidating

—Panel of Four. My desperate hope was they would see in me something worthy the last panel had missed.

Since I got my scoop from the most reliable SAA source, Alana, I knew the demand for cabin crew was greater than ever, and I figured at some point they'd run out of really good-looking girls. Perchance high demand had decreased expectations. A girl could always hope.

This time I was prepared for the interminable wait for that blasted letter. I steeled myself for rejection while working relentlessly on the career I was carving out in PR—my more viable Plan B.

My mom had sold our family home, and she and I moved to a block of flats close by. I taught myself to walk slowly down four flights of steps to the postbox, like it didn't matter if there was no letter. But ten days later, there it was, naked as a jaybird, no bills insulating its news. There was no heat, but I banished all potential signs. Good or bad.

But I knew better than to open the envelope in the lobby. I refused to be seen as a melted pile of mush on the dirty linoleum floor. I slowly took the four flights of stairs up to our flat, but they might as well have been Mount Kilimanjaro. A zenith you hoped you'd reach, but if you rushed and forfeited the anticipation of the climb, the summit might prove to be a disappointment.

The letter burned a hole in my palm. I concentrated on breathing and counting just to keep from considering its importance. I held in my hand what could be the end of my lifelong dream.

It had taken all of my gumption to try a second time. There was no such thing as third-time-lucky.

I considered having a tête-à-tête with the Air Hostess

Goddess, but her divine self was pathetically ineffective last time. Then I scolded myself for thinking negative thoughts. *I am worthy.* My dad said so.

Unlocking the front door, I slipped inside and called for my mom. I groaned when I remembered she'd left for her tennis match. Hmmm, probably best I was alone.

I slid down the door to the floor, unable to walk any farther on rubbery legs. I ran my finger under the lip of the envelope and along the edge.

"Ouch!"

The hiss slipped out when the sharp paper cut reminded me that this was real—the letter had *really* arrived. I sucked the droplet of blood from my finger before ripping the envelope open the rest of the way.

Pulling out the functional white paper with the distinct orange and blue SAA logo, I glanced at the neat black electric typewriter print. My eyes flew over the neat paragraphs, once—looking for negative words I'd seen before; twice—when they blurred and ran together, and a third time, when the words were easy to read. A hiccupping sob caught in my throat and released a mewing sound worthy of a midnight tomcat.

I inhaled a deep, shaking breath and forced myself to read the letter slowly, as if I were in first grade reading a story out loud to my teacher for the first time.

Yes.

HELL, YES!

By some otherworldly intervention, I had passed the Panel of Four's wickedly intense scrutiny, and finally, mercifully, this time I was accepted into South African Airways as an air hostess.

I hugged the letter of success to my (thank the Lord) fully

developed, albeit meager chest. A slightly hysterical laugh slipped from between my lips, followed by another, and another, until I was lying on the floor, breathless from mirth.

I lifted my injured finger and thumbed my nose at my past adversaries: the mean nuns; cruel school girls; the young teacher who'd publicly made me think less of my longed-for profession, and less of myself for wanting it so badly; the bastard who deflowered me then disappeared; the first Panel of Four; and a whole lot in between.

"Take that, world! I did it. Dad, you said I could. I did. Thank you!"

I cried, missing him as if he'd left me just yesterday.

But glee overtook any sadness, and I lifted both feet into the air and kicked wildly, laughing at myself, my self-doubts, and all my insecurities until my sides ached.

As I stared up at the ceiling, a sense of calm descended over me. But it was short-lived. Unadulterated panic sucked at my angst like a tsunami pulling back billions of gallons of water. Then when the giant wave built to its zenith, it came back to my conscious with a vengeance, changing the landscape of my life.

How will I cope with the plethora of smells that surround hundreds of people at a time?

Dammit. I would find a way. I would live in the moment and relish the excitement of traveling to places about which I'd only dreamed. My sights were never set on local travel I could drive to. SAA was my ticket to the world. And to get there, I had to reel myself in.

If I could stop dead people from showing themselves unbidden when I was just ten years old, I could find ways to cope with my hyperosmia at twenty-two.

This deserved a celebration!

I lifted the big black phone off the heavy base and dialed.

Alana said hello. I screamed. A massive scream that likely had the neighbors calling the cops, but I didn't care. Her scream matched mine. No need for words.

"Kitty's?" I asked.

And I knew we'd both rush off to meet with Kitty and share my victory. That's how we rolled. I marveled how we, who never ran out of things to talk about, reverted to minimal communication when anything important happened because there was no need for words. Many lifetimes together will do that for you.

On my way to the car, euphoric with the success I'd been so long denied, I held tighter to the written proof that *aanhouer wen.*

I lifted my head up to the skies and shouted at the top of my lungs: "UN-Lucky? Not on your life!"

And ... a drop of bird poop landed in my eye.

A group of young boys snickered as they passed me.

I dug in my jacket pocket for a tissue, cleaned the gross excrement from my eye, and glanced up—a little more warily this time—at the endless skies I would soon fly in.

As I found a bin, then headed to my car, a smudge of poo still blurring my vision, I ruefully conceded: *The gods sure know how to keep a girl humble.*

_____

CHAPTER 20

Two months later, I was well into my first action-packed week of the three months of *ab initio* training at cabin services. I was blissfully happy.

Our classes were tough, exhausting, and filled with enough information that I thought my brain would explode. It was clear the glamorous life came with a lot of do's and don'ts. But I was in!

We went from learning how to tame a firehose loaded with gallons of pulsing water and writhing like a mamba ready to strike; to becoming ofay with what wines were paired with what entrées; to the deportment and makeup class and a host of new things in between. A veritable finishing school on steroids. It didn't get any more fun than this.

I was as high as a 737.

It was my turn to learn how to accentuate my best features, and I settled into the instructor, Ms. Venter's, hot seat.

As I waited, in the mirror I could see the other *ab initio* class from our intake of new hosties. They were taking turns walking in high heels with books on their heads to improve their deportment. A petite blond girl was shouting out instructions to her fellow would-be models "Straighter, Getruida!", "Not like that, Victoria," until their instructress said "That's enough from you, Little General. Place 'Gone with the Wind' on your head and see how *you* manage."

I was eager to see the book fall off the Little General's head. It didn't. I was quite disappointed.

Our instructress, Ms. Venter was a sexy, buxom woman in her late forties.

She stared at my reflection in the mirror. "Why are *you* here?"

Taken aback, I turned away from the mirror and looked her in the eye. Her face was impassive so I thought this was a lesson in grace and I should humbly declare what my actual worth to the airline might be.

Turning back to the mirror I began: "I love people. And I'm a good listener. I will strive to understand passengers' needs and will always do my utmost to..."

She held up a stop-hand, tipped in pink polish. "No. How did *you* get in here?"

I glanced around in confusion. Perhaps I was in the wrong classroom? But no. My new friends were walking in high heels with books on their heads.

Thank heavens Ms. Venter spoke, because I was at a loss for words. It wouldn't be until I looked at the scene in retrospect that I wished she hadn't spoken at all.

She leaned in and whispered in my ear, "I vetoed you the first time you applied to SAA."

Shocked, I pulled my head back and looked at her. Damn, I *knew* she looked familiar. Ms. Venter was on the first Panel of

Four who had sent me the bloody "You're not Good Enough" letter two years ago!

"Why?" I croaked.

She leaned down, and her hot breath tickled my ear again. This time, my nose picked up a mixture of Estee Lauder's Youth Dew and mints covering the stench of garlic. Images fought to form in my mind, but I squashed them down. I didn't want to know about her—or her life, which must surely have been miserable if she could pass on such wretchedness.

Her whisper was buttered in the bitter batter of a sweet smile I witnessed in the mirror before me. "I'll never understand why the stringent enrollment board overlooked your ugly nose the *second* time you applied."

I stared at Ms. Venter in horror. And as if she'd never spoken such cruel words, she gently turned my head back to the mirror and called, "Girls. Come along. Let me show you how you can maximize almond-shaped eyes, how to minimize your lesser features, and how to wear this length hair to its best advantage."

No one would have guessed how, with so few words, she'd regressed my confidence back to sewage pipe status. Not only that, she'd just ruined my life by pointing out my schnoz was the reason I was not good enough for the airline.

I was right. They had decreased their standard. It was the only reason I was there.

My nose? I'd always considered it a burden but not a physical one. She'd given me something else about which to be ashamed.

The rest of the day passed in a blur of misery covered by a thin veneer of pretending to have fun. Anything to save face, so to speak. It wasn't until the drive home that I pulled over to the side of the road and cried like a baby.

Howling, I looked in the mirror and saw, between the twin rivers of black mascara in full flood, the biggest nose ever to be slapped onto a mortal's face in the world's history. Every one of my self-doubts not only resurfaced. They amplified.

The rest of the way I mulled over how my very ordinariness had indeed paled in the shadow of the ugly nasal appendage that I'd missed in the mirror for all these years.

I sat in my designated parking spot on the asphalt in front of our flats and slapped the steering wheel so hard, I felt the need to apologize to it.

Then I smelled my Dad.

It was as if he sat in the passenger seat. His kind eyes buoyed my spirits and his lazy smile slathered Superglue on my heart to repair the massive tear.

I stared at him as he spoke, his words etching themselves into my soul. "You *are* worthy of this profession. You've earned your place with hard work and consistently high marks in all subjects. Deep down, this is the only career you've ever yearned for. Why let someone on her own miserable journey in this life, bring you down? Remember what you heard recently? *What others think of me is none of my business.* Nobody has ever made a fuss of your nose. You will never see this mean-spirited woman again. Why do you even care?"

I consciously steeled myself against her ugly, wretched words that had so easily sliced away my newly learned self-esteem. How dare she use her own bitterness to dash my young-girl dreams?

He said "She will hurt you, but only if you let her. So, don't! Just don't!"

He laughed that laugh I missed like a ballerina misses an amputated leg. He smiled and said, "That old bitch's just jealous, Lucky. Jealous and bitter. Make sure neither of those real flaws makes it into your arsenal."

A determined smile curved my lips. I pulled a paper serviette out of the cubbyhole and blew my now red nose.

She can't hurt me now.

I'm IN!

I must get an even brighter shade of red lipstick for subterfuge.

And I flipped the bird in the direction of the cabin services training center to show him that from now on, she wouldn't matter.

But when I turned toward the passenger seat, my daddy was gone.

CHAPTER 21

I jumped this time when the phone rang, springing thirty-something years forward to the present. Tula, sitting beside me, was watching the highway as any good copilot should.

I answered.

"Lucky, you won't believe it... Stupid me, of course you will! We found a thick, masculine silver chain ... under that tree." My heart matched the pace of Jim's unusually quick words. "Because of you, we commissioned the metal detector, and there it was, hidden deep, under a million compacted leaves."

"That's great," I managed. "I wonder why it wasn't found when it was more visible twelve years ago?"

"The initial search didn't reach Garnet Lake. Even the mammoth workforce of volunteers we had combing the area limited us to a search radius of twenty miles from Springfield. The lake is sixty-odd miles from ground zero," Jim said flatly.

"But a jogger, a walker, a hiker?" I asked. A shiny object was always worth picking up. And then I remembered how Janice had deliberately pushed the necklace she'd ripped off his neck under an existing pile of leaves, so he wouldn't find it.

Jim was still talking, "...years of leaves upon leaves upon leaves created a layered carpet two feet thick. Besides, this spot is way off the beaten track. No walking trails, no traffic encouraged at that end of the lake at all. You've facilitated a miracle. We would never have found her without you. And as for this recent clue? Not in a million years. I wish Janice's dad was alive to see this happening." Jim sounded choked up.

"Don't worry, Jim. Janice and her mom and dad are watching you work, cheering you on. I'm sure of it. But keep searching. There was something on that chain. Something round and heavier. Look for it close to where you found the chain, but deeper. It will help us. Give us a clue to that bastard's identity. I'm sure of it. Don't give up till you find it." We hung up.

Peter Frampton was singing "Baby I Love Your Way" to me, so I let my mind meander to those airline days so I would have something in common with the four former hosties. I needed some cohesion, and that was all I had. Well, that and our soulmates.

Peter and his guitar guided me back to my bedroom in 1982, where I slipped easily into my twenty-two-year-old skin and stood in front of the mirror. I permitted myself to feel fabulous for thirty seconds. It was all I was allowed. I knew all too well that pride came before a fall, so my goal was to avoid a gargantuan landslide.

This wasn't just *my* adventure. I was doing this for my parents as well: my mom, who'd been smitten with airmen since she'd come of age during World War II, and the RAF fighter pilot she snagged with her winning ticket at the races.

My only chance to see the world, and I was gripping it with six hands.

Dad's embroidered WWII wings suddenly lifted high by what had to be a gust of wind (or was it energy?) into a short, clean salute. The window was still closed tightly. I smiled. It was so good to have him close. Glancing down at my new, shiny, gold-plated single wing, I saluted back to him.

We were flyers, my daddy and I.

Less than six months before, Mr. Oosthuizen, head of cabin services of South African Airways, had pinned this treasure to the lapel of my SAA sky-blue jacket in an elaborate ceremony.

After *ab initio* training, I'd spent four months on internal flights, six weeks on the 747-conversion course, and finally, today I moved to the big leagues—International Air Hostess with emergency proceedures and conversational German under my belt.

What other chance would I ever get to see the world? I'd be too old to get off the plane by the time I'd saved enough rands to cover exorbitant ticket prices.

I was not graced with my mom's hourglass voluptuousness, but the jacket miraculously created a waist for my straight up and down form, likely aided by the stylishly-nicked Vs which exaggerated my hips. Wow. I had a figure!

A pang of sadness marred my elation. Oh, if only Dad could witness this day! But had not the salute of the curtain proved he didn't have to be flesh to be here?

I smiled into the mirror but not at my image. I felt him like I felt the soft fabric of my new uniform's collar. Close, soft, and colorful.

"Mom," I called, just needing her softness, her breath, her warmth, her pulse.

The sudden death of one of your parents will do that to you.

In seconds, she was there.

As I hugged her, both my parents hugged me back. A distinct benefit of being a psychic.

My mom held me at arm's length, a tear glistening in her eye as she said, "You're in the *Air Force* and going overseas. I am so darn proud!"

I laughed and shook my head. "Don't be telling your friends that, Ma. They'll wonder why you're so excited I made it into the typing pool. A woman could *never* be a pilot in the South African Air Force." I hugged her. "And the Air Force certainly don't need air hostesses. I'm not in the *Air Force*, dear mother. I'm in the *airline.*"

"*Airlin*e. Air Force. You'll be flying for a living," Mom chided with no embarrassment at all.

Oh, would that I had my mom's ability to let a soft chastisement roll off me so easily. With a dismissive wave, a tinkle of bracelets, and a waft of rooibos tea, my beloved mother left my room.

Left again to my mirrored image, I smoothed down the collar of the off-white blouse with its wisps of dark orange leaves.

In my suitcase, I'd neatly packed the other five of the six bodysuits in various colors and designs, all issued by the airline. These shirts pulled down and snapped together in the nether region below. The look skillfully eliminated unflattering lines, perfect for the illusion.

The just-wider-than-pencil, knee-length blue skirt had a back slit, high enough to allow gallant strides in leather pumps with four-inch heels. Pantyhose turned freckled legs to smooth, tanned skin.

I deftly shaded my now obvious nose and tried not to look at it again once I applied fire-engine-red lipstick.

Sticks and stones may break my bones, but don't let them lie to you, kids, words can also hurt you. Sing with me now...

That ballsy bright lipstick was initially applied as a means to be noticed. Thanks to Ms. Venter, vivid red lips were now an essential subterfuge.

Listen to your father! You are the only one who can damn well UN-hear that bitter old witch's words, Lucky van Niekerk!

"HERE WE GO AGAIN," Whitesnake warned. The memory made me smile. *I've come a long way since then,* I mused, checking my red lips in the rearview mirror. *But old habits die hard.* Those years when lipstick application was as important as brushing your teeth, had made a lasting impression.

I thought again of beautiful Brie, wondering if she'd found the life I thought she deserved. Unlike the rest of us mortals who had dozens of flaws, Brie only had one. She tripped on fresh air. It was like the universe was balancing things out a smidgeon by making her a wee bit clumsy. I smiled. I was looking forward to seeing her. She was the saving grace to my dreaded shindig.

I glanced at Tula. He'd crashed on the seat, bored with our journey. I focused back on the road and lost myself in my first overseas trip and the discovery of the elixir that would be my salvation.

And then I let myself drift back to studying my reflection in my handsome blue uniform. There I was, grinning broadly.

London, here I come!

I picked up the precious pear-shaped bottle with rich gold liquid and a cap the color of a queen's cape and thought back to when I'd first pointed the nozzle of the sample bottle of *Opium* at my wrist. The spritz had not yet landed when I recognized its power. The store suddenly became bright and sharply in focus, as if a veil had been lifted.

I realized I was, at that moment, completely in the present. And Opium had an amazing effect. It cut off the hundreds of past lives that always hovered on the periphery of my soul, my psyche, to take over my NOW.

I couldn't afford the perfume, but I knew I couldn't afford to live without it.

Opium. My elixir. My shield.

Now I sprayed a tiny dab on each wrist, my temples, between my breasts, behind my ears and on the suprasternal notch at the base of my neck. The aromas of black coffee, white flowers, and sweet vanilla enveloped me like a cloak.

I pirouetted, capturing every drop of fragrance before I reached down, chose a cyan scarf from the ample selection, and skillfully knotted the silk at my throat. Then I stood still, rooted in the moment, enhanced by divine anticipation and confidence.

London!

Finally.

Opium would shield me from three hundred fifty-six passengers and fifteen crew members who'd be sharing a closed vestibule with me for a dozen or more hours. No longer could they, would they, be able to pull me unwillingly into their worlds, past or present.

London was 12,840.4 kilometers away. My tummy did a double somersault. I'd be walking all the way to London tonight on a 747!

I buttoned up the jacket and checked my long, red-painted nails before I slipped on white cotton gloves, smoothed down my handsome blue skirt and took a last glance in the mirror at my wavy auburn hair. Once it'd grown a half an inch and touched my shoulders, protocol required it be swept up. No wild hairs would be tolerated in SAA.

We didn't wear a uniform.

We wore an image.

CHAPTER 22

A fter a flight briefing and a crew bus to the terminal, the check hostess's office was our first stop. I lined up with the rest of the women for final inspection while the stewards strolled off to buy magazines or cigarettes.

"Why don't they have to be scrutinized?" I whispered to a seasoned hostie behind me.

"You're a girl, doll. Did you forget that if we hostesses put on weight, it will throw off the aircraft trim? Besides, think of how the world would end if we had unpainted nails! We'd start a global rebellion."

When it was my turn, I stepped on the huge industrial scale and, like I was a lab specimen, the check hostess scrutinized my makeup, hair, nails and uniform. Without comment or expression, she signed off next to my name on a sheet of paper with three holes, ready for filing, and waved me away wordlessly. Intense scrutiny was the ticket to being allowed to strut in the concourse and board your flight.

A collage of scents swirled around with the cool air of the

ventilation system in the International Hall, but one whiff of my wrist, and I regained my equilibrium. *Thank you, Opium!*

The march through the airport was a trip—not in time, but in headiness. People stared. Women and men in uniform, I was to discover, made an impression. I was thrilled to be part of all this fuss. I'd never noticed anyone turn to look at me before I wore this uniform.

They never lost an opportunity to drill into our young heads: "You are not just air hostesses. You are ambassadors for South Africa. You are always watched. So, behave!"

Across the tarmac we strode *en masse* toward our beacon: the ginormous orange-tailed jet. As we got close, the registration number ZS 216 came into focus.

I slowed as we reached the steep metal steps and looked up toward the open cabin door, nearly three stories above us.

Getting up there was no easy exercise in four-inch heels while carrying my cabin bag and heavy first aid kit. I was hot, sweaty and breathing heavily by the time I finally ducked through the doorway. But, oh, it was so worth it. The jolt of excitement hit me again as I took my first step inside the cool cabin as an international hostie. I literally pinched myself.

The fragrance was clean and interesting on the surface, then thousands of comings and goings for millions of reasons almost sent me tumbling backwards down the stairs.

The crew member behind me put a steadying hand on my shoulder. "Are you alright?"

"Yes, thank you," I replied with a shaky smile as I pulled my wrist past my nose.

I snapped to attention when the senior hostess barked, "No time for dilly-dallying. To your station and prepare for boarding." And she bustled me along to do what I'd been well-schooled to execute.

We hung up our uniform jackets, donned polyester pinafores and changed sexy heels for boring, institutional-looking, one-inch-high cabin shoes. London was a long walk from Johannesburg.

The large half-moon-shaped aft galley required a "galley slave"—usually a senior hostie or steward who'd sworn off mixing with passengers—plus two junior hosties, one senior and one junior steward.

When the laden, well-dressed passengers tumbled in, I fluctuated between holding my breath and sniffing my wrists, just in case. I paused to wonder how many thought I might have a strange affliction.

On her tour of the cabin, I saw the senior hostie lean over a male passenger sitting in an aisle seat. She shook her head and walked off. *Wow, she was rather rude.*

Once the safety announcements were made, I fumbled through my first live German welcome and safety instructions, while the crew in my section did the silly-looking, lifesaving actions. Since I was facing the sea of passengers in our section, it was a good time to take them all in.

My eyes—or was it my nose? —were drawn to a girl, probably my age, sitting next to the window. My heart swelled as I wondered if I was still a girl, since I'd thought of her that way. Her head was resting on the Perspex window as she gazed vacantly ahead. Her eyes were red and swollen, and she kept wiping her nose. Whatever was upsetting her was unusually disturbing.

On my way to check on her before takeoff, the man on the

aisle—the one who the senior hostie had walked away from earlier—was still struggling with his seat belt.

"Can I help you, sir?" I asked.

"I just can't seem to get this thing right," he said, looking morose.

I leaned over and pulled on the sturdy nylon of his seat belt.

"A little tighter, please," he begged, and I obliged. "Tighter." His voice became demanding. When I looked at him, his face was a study of strained bliss, and I realized this was dead wrong. I fled, red-faced, to my galley.

The steward asked, "What happened?"

"The guy in 41C asked me to help him with his seat belt," I said, flustered.

"Oh, that old trick." He chuckled. "It gives them a thrill. It's probably the closest he's had to a hand job for months."

"Oh, that's disgusting!" I erupted with nervous laughter. "What a pig. No wonder the senior disappeared from view, shaking her head."

"Well, it won't happen to you a second time. We've all had our firsts in dealing with seat belt masturbation."

I had never heard the "M" word said in company, let alone in uniform. A new and strange world just opened up to me.

The memory shivered me into the present.

That feeling of defenselessness and naivete was just too close to experiencing the horrors Janice had endured.

Reaching over to the passenger seat, I absently played with Tula's ear. Sensing my slight distress, he lifted his muzzle high enough to give me a lick across the back of my hand. The quick thudding of my heart subsided.

"No matter where you are in the world, there'll always be a jerk who can mar a memory," I murmured to myself with a shake of my head. "See, Tula? I don't need any male nonsense in my life. I am only equipped to handle yours." I might have said that with too much emphasis, because Tula gave me a one-eyed dirty look that said, *I'm trying to catch forty winks here. Let's not have a long discussion!*

I WAS BACK in the eighties and in my aft right single jump seat for my first flight. We were finally ready for takeoff and I glanced at my watch. It was 9 p.m. I'd started preparing for this flight fourteen hours before, and my work day had barely begun.

But I forgot all that the minute that giant 747 bird of steel lifted its nose up to heaven.

Milliseconds later, my stomach lurched, and an excitement I'd never felt before embraced me as we soared ever skyward. Nothing will ever come close to the euphoria of a jumbo's takeoff for me.

Once in the air, when the seat belt signs were turned off, the two-and-a-half-hour dinner service began. I could not get the weeping girl out of my head. I was serving on the opposite side to where she sat and kept checking on her. She looked like she was comatose.

The end of dinner didn't mean peace and quiet for the crew. It was as if passengers, paying a small fortune for their seats, thought up new requests just to "get their money's worth." But the longing to see London Bridge from the air kept my eyes on the prize.

I'd been worrying about the sad girl all night. My frequent checks confirmed her head had barely lifted from its resting place on the window in the nearly four hours since she boarded.

Her tray table remained bare. She'd rejected food and drink. Her face was morose, and every time I looked at her, my stomach contracted.

The aisle was free of working trolleys, and there was no one between her and the masturbation-guy on the aisle. When I saw him leave to use the loo, I nipped in between the tray table and his seat, then leaned over and touched her arm. "Are you okay? Anything I can get you?"

She was surprised out of her trance and looked at me in shock for a minute, as if wondering where she was.

I waited. Nothing. "You seem so terribly sad. Can I do anything at all to help you?" I asked, my heart even heavier seeing her up close.

"No, nothing." Her voice caught in a sob, "Thank you."

But something made me push a little harder. "It's a long flight. Gives you way too much time to ponder something alone. Do you want to share? Sometimes it helps. Eases the pain. I am not here to judge. Just to listen."

She looked me in the eyes as if assessing my sincerity and as she did so, I had a profound thought.

Sister.

"Is it your sister?" I asked oh-so-tentatively.

Her eyes grew twice their size. "How did you know?" she asked.

"Sometimes I see things," I said and flinched. I'd already said too much.

But the floodgates opened.

"My sister is missing. She left to seek fame and fortune in London. Just up and left with no game plan and little money. She's a dancer. Studied jazz, modern, and contemporary dance all her life. There is such a tiny pool of commercial dancing jobs in South Africa. In London she could be a star. She's fabulous." She almost laughed, but a hiccup of sadness diffused it before it could leave even a smile.

"I haven't heard from her for ten days. Every second day she would call me from a West End callbox. We spoke for a mere sixty seconds—but I heard her voice. Phoning home is so expensive, but she'd found a friend who'd schooled her on how to trick the ticky-box. It sounded like she was having a blast. She was happy. But there's been no sound from her for ten long days."

"What was the last thing she said to you on the phone?" I asked.

"She said she loved me."

"And what preceded that lovely confession? Try to remember her exact words," I encouraged.

The man came back to his seat. I tried not to think of how he'd humiliated me as I moved closer to Janice and turned my back to him so Janice and my conversation could continue privately.

"Her last words to you?" I prompted, looking straight at her to assure her of my genuine interest.

"She said, 'I have an audition tomorrow. If I get the part, I'll ring you. If I don't, I'm going to do something for the family. I'll call you in a couple of days.' I asked her what she meant. Our remaining family is merely our mom and me, but she said, 'Trust me. I love you.' And that was that. Not another word."

And with that, the girl burst into fresh tears. I leaned over and took her hand. Her fear of loss and the heavy dread of the terrifying mission before her transferred to me. Where did she start looking in a strange and unfamiliar metropolis?

"I'm going to bring you a concoction my mom makes. A

warm brandy, milk, and honey. It soothes and heals the human spirit. You'll see." I smiled at her, wishing the drink had more magical powers than I knew.

When I came back with her hot toddy in a steaming cup, I excused myself, glided by the man and resumed my position close to Janice. She took the cup from me, and I saw a ghost of a smile.

"I'm Lucky. What's your name?"

"Stephanie Smith." She smiled a lovely smile. "My sister is Susan Smith. I wonder how many Susan Smiths there are in London?" A rhetorical question.

I swear, I did not intend to get any further involved. It was not my place. But my voice had a mind of its own that night. It must have been the high altitude. "Do you have anything on you that belongs to your sister?"

She looked at me oddly, and it was the mental slap I needed.

What on earth was I doing? I had safely closed off my psychic tendencies—well, for the most part, through immense will and fortitude, and here I was on my virgin overseas flight poking at oddities. What the hell was I thinking?

"I am so sorry," I apologized. "Forgive me. Drink that. I promise it will help you face tomorrow." And I whooshed myself away and into the galley, where the breakfast prep kept me busy, though Stephanie's pain jabbed at me like a hot poker.

I was selfishly relieved to avoid opening a vault of trouble by meddling with long locked-up things for good reason.

_____

CHAPTER 23

Our drive home to Hull continued at a dismally slow pace. Tula was unsociable. The FBI boys were doing their thing. I felt myself slip back to that first trip to London.

I found out pax—as we called passengers—would pass the night's long and boring hours galley-hopping: a cup of coffee here, a tot of brandy there, and engaging in small talk with cabin crew from forward to aft.

Crew had little desire to have tête-à-têtes with bored strangers at 2 a.m., especially those who hoped to pick up the scoop on how mile-high club members earned their wings. I quickly learned to smile and change the subject when the question reared its suggestive head.

Smoking was allowed onboard. There were ashtrays built into every armrest and in strategic places in the galleys.

My steward and I sat on heavy dry stall bins we'd hefted from their secured place in the galley. We smoked and chatted, and cabin crew from the other galleys popped in. It was wonderfully social as we got to know one another. We'd be spending a week together. What better time for making friends than en route?

Our roster was designed for us to be in the air no more than twenty hours a week. The flights were inordinately long because politics forced us to fly around the bulge of Africa.

Happily, we earned a ton of downtime in each exotic place. We were free to spend glorious days in vibrant cities we'd only previously seen on a map.

With over two thousand cabin crew members in our fleet, we seldom flew with the same people twice in our careers. We could request to fly with friends, but the privilege had to be earned by airline longevity, such as it was.

The Flight Service Officer or FSO ran the cabin. In the eighties, and only in the theater and in the airline, could a sturdy, bearded, well-groomed man, reeking of Shalimar, proudly sport a badge reading "Callas" though his name was Gert Joubert.

When Gert came to work, he was "Madame Callas," who sang impressive operatic bites while working in the first-class cabin. Not even butch pilots turned a hair and passengers loved the free flight entertainment.

Madame Callas came bustling into our galley and announced it was time for the second shift to go to the crew rest. I hoped he would burst into song, but alas, he reserved his performances for first class and, I later found out, fabulously fun nights in London.

On that first flight, I checked that all the back toilets were clean and polished as was my mission. Then I hurried to the crew rest as soon as I could. I was dead tired.

Just before I pushed back the thick curtain that hid our sleep-hole from prying passenger eyes, a hand touched my arm.

I turned. Stephanie Smith.

I smiled. "Hi."

She handed me a Glook. It was a kids' toy made in the UK in the late sixties. A weird, fuzzy little creature stuffed with sponge rubber on the inside and covered with long hair you could brush in any direction. This one was electric pink with a few bald spots, likely from too much combing and cuddling. I was warmed by the thought. This well-loved little dude was twenty-something years old now. He stood seven inches high with big eyes, a red nose and big, black felt feet.

"I brought Susan's favorite toy with me. For my comfort as much as hers...when I find her. If I find her." And she burst into a violent set of tears.

I put my arms around her. When she stopped sobbing, I said, "I've not tried this before, but may I keep the Glook and see if I can get a clue on where Susan might be?"

Eyes bright with hope, she nodded like a small child at Christmas.

"Stephanie, I can't promise you anything, but..."

"I don't have anything. That I have your empathy is more than I had before I boarded. Just keep her Glook for as long as you need. I think she'd like you to have it for a while." She smiled wanly and returned to her seat.

I stood with a lead lump in my gut, fear of overstepping my ability in my heart, and a gnawing guilt in my craw for giving this grieving, helpless girl a glimmer of hope. Not to mention a bright pink Glook under my arm.

The small, inconspicuous crew rest near the aft toilets was hidden by a heavy wool curtain. Passengers rarely noticed it, as was the intention. Inside were three narrow bunks on each side, from floor to near the ceiling. The seventh—you couldn't exactly call it a bunk—was a thin mattress squashed between the two lower bunks.

Being the first, I settled on the top bunk with the electric pink Glook in my arm. I was careful to cover us with the sparse square that was the royal blue airline blanket. I had a quick look around the compact space and marveled how exhaustion made the crew rest feel like the Sheridan's presidential family suite.

Still alone, I pulled out the Glook and gave it a long look. "Now, I don't want to go back to that seat without anything to report to the poor girl, you hear? So, show me Susan, Mr. Glook." I felt the fuzzy pink thing was a boy in spite of his girly color. I dare not piss him off when so much was riding on him being the conduit of Susan Smith's essence while we slept.

CHAPTER 24

Exhaustion had her way with me before any dreams or immersions into Susan's life could begin.

But snickering dragged me from oblivion. The privacy curtain in the doorway had been replaced with a tableau of gaping cabin crew members.

I jumped, realizing my bum was in the air, courtesy of the flimsy, synthetic blanket that had lost its fight with my nylon stockings and polyester body shirt.

"What?" I asked, sitting up abruptly and knocking my head on the all-too-close fiberglass bulkhead. The Glook! I'd never be able to live down clutching a comfort toy in the crew rest. Thank heavens it was dark. I didn't want to be a sissy in my airline legend. Hell, I'd prefer not to be a legend at all. I ripped away the tiny blanket barely covering my crotch to frantically cover my wild-haired bunkmate and hoped, quite desperately, that darkness toned down electric pink.

I wiped the deep-sleep drool from my chin with the back of my hand and pried the second eye open using my thumb and index finger. *Damn. Sleep juice and mascara should be marketed as uber-super glue.*

"What did I do wrong?" Other than my nigh-nakedness and the Glook, what airline sin could I possibly have committed?

"Your first flight and you think you've earned top bunk?" Madame Callas's authoritative bark bit through the hum of the air-conditioning. "Top bunks are for FSOs. At your level, you're on the ground, doll. Floor, center mattress. So, get used to being walked over."

"So sorry," I said, meaning it, and started down from the high bunk which, without a ladder, proved to be as hard to nail as a double back pike gymnastic dismount with the Glook and blanket under my armpit.

The snotty, most-senior senior hostess's voice shrilled, "Where is your decorum? Don't you dare sleep without your pinafore on. We can all see your bum. This is not the dressing room for the Rockettes. Get out, get properly dressed for the crew rest, and get lying down where you belong. Bottom middle mattress. The rest of the off-duty crew is on their way."

A distant *ping* of a needy passenger yanked the dark shadows away from the doorway, and the soft darkness of a 747 cabin in cruise mode at 36,000 feet mercifully replaced the human wall of judgment.

I was able to quickly don my pinafore in peace and repositioned myself on the half-inch foam mattress that barely cushioned the steel floor. I gazed longingly at the three "real" bunks on either side of me.

I'd snagged a second blanket to cover my body, the Glook still safely wrapped and hidden under my arm.

In order of their hierarchy, and without apology, cabin crew members stepped on or over me as they leaped or stretched to reach the remaining bunks.

I might have become immune by the time the final set of feet squished my legs on their trip to the last bunk. Sheer exhaustion and the Glook, perchance one more than the other, pulled me into oblivion from this reality...

...And in that space between wakefulness and deep sleep before my dream began, I felt a prickle of dread. What if all I received was bad news?

FLASH!

I hover above her, outside looking in.

The blond girl is supple and limber and full of vitality as she gazes at the scarlet double-decker buses that look ready to topple over on every corner. We marvel at high billboards sporting different colored signs screaming: *Joseph! Annie! The Pirates!* The scents of urine, flowers blooming in a garden around a statue, exhaust fumes, and horse excrement create an olfactory cacophony. But all the smells are trumped by anticipation that fills the air around me. I am giddy with glee.

She's popular. Everyone seeks her favor, her smile, her approval. She takes care never to disappoint. She lugs a pink plastic handbag the size of a small car. A mini Mini Minor on a strap holding all her worldly goods.

I'm nervous as she goes into a building. I stay outside for some reason. When she comes out, she is sobbing. Hopelessness follows us to a phone booth the same color as the big buses. She has a sixpence glued to a tatty piece of overused string. She stands outside the phone booth, considers things, then pockets the sixpence, and a desperate sadness overwhelms her.

She walks briskly to a station. She knows her way around. She's looking for something. We rush to a platform just in time to see the train engine pulling in. On the side of each carriage is a word encased under a sizable glass case. D – E – V... It shoots past us ten times before the train slows and stops in front of us. Devon.

Susan jumps aboard, I am right with her. Agitated, we bound from one carriage to the next, expending our energy and attempting to walk off our anxiety.

The train blazes through the countryside, stopping at stations. People get on and off. She pays no attention to them, but they look at us. She's vital and vibrant even in her depressed state. Disappointed to the nth degree is she, but her confidence never wavers.

Just when I think we must be going to Sweden, we get off the train and onto the platform. I see 'Welcome to Devon' painted on a wide wooden board dangling from the rafters. It's swinging in the flurry of passengers and the trains huffing and puffing. We've arrived. She fumbles inside the pink bag and pulls out what looks like an address with numbers at the end. We make a series of wrong turns, she asks a lot of people for directions, and at last, we enter a modest block of flats.

We take the lift up to the fourth floor. Whoa! She's lost her confidence. She's infused with trepidation and a hefty dose of fear.

We knock on a bright green door.

A disheveled-looking man opens the door. We step back. Unsure.

"I'm looking for Steven Smith from South Africa."

He nods, perplexed. "Who are you?"

"I'm Susan Smith. I'm your niece. Narelle's daughter."

He smiles a dynamic smile that entirely changes his face. Tears well in his eyes, and he grabs us, hugs us.

"Let's walk," says Steve. And we do. The traffic is very busy and noisy, so I'm having a tough time hearing them. I leave Susan and hover between the two to make out what they're saying.

Susan is trying to convince Steve of something. "You must understand, though you and Mom are at odds, fifteen years is a long, long time to hold a grudge. She won't make the effort. Will you?"

He shakes his head in denial. "I can't hear you," says Steve, his hand cupping an ear.

She grabs his hands in both of hers to make him stop.

She must convince him. This is the only win she has left. The one reason for coming to London—because dancing in the West End is never going to happen. She is jolted by that reality, but she pushes it out of her mind.

She jumps off the narrow pavement so she can look into Uncle Steve's eyes now that she has his rapt attention.

She begins "Uncle Steve, you must come home. We nee...
Whoosh!

A blow so hard, it throws us up six feet or more into the air.

I watch Susan defy gravity and fly up and up and up. Stop. Then, floppy as a rag doll, she floats down in slow motion, limbs akimbo before she smashes down with a deadly sound— like a mallet on a thick piece of steak, onto the hood of the delivery truck.

I smell the responses around me before I hear them or see them. Fear. Horror. Fright. All have their own aroma. Burned rubber from screeching tires.

Pedestrians' knees buckle. Horns bellow. And I can hear Susan through her shock and pain crying out in anguish, "My legs, my legs, my dancer's legs." And I know it is only I who can hear her.

Susan has slipped off the bonnet of the truck and lies broken on the cobbled street. Her lovely legs are twisted at odd angles.

Steve screams, as tears streak down his cheeks. He shouts. "It's my niece. Call an ambulance. NOW!"

Then his features change to anger and he shouts and runs after a man in a hoodie carrying our big pink plastic handbag. But he can't. He can't. He slips, falls, drops his head in his hands as he sobs, and we watch hopelessly, helplessly, as the thief and Susan's bright pink bag disappear around the corner at full speed.

BACK!

I shot up from the middle bunk on the floor of the crew rest, excruciating pain in my legs, my heart beating a million miles a minute.

I pushed on the winder of my watch, and a dull light came on: 2:16 a.m. South African Standard Time. I had an hour and a quarter of sleep left, but there was no way I was lying in this position a moment longer.

I got up and eased my way through the curtain, keeping the Glook tucked under my arm in his blanket.

Once I was refreshed and back in my skirt with pinafore over it, I sought out Stephanie, blanket, Glook and all. I had no intention of squeezing past Mr. Masturbation, but the man seated in front of Stephanie had vacated his seat, and the Japanese woman sitting on the aisle of that row was so tiny, I could squeeze past her knees. I positioned myself backwards on the seat in front of Stephanie. With cabin shoes hanging over the edge of the seat cushion, I leaned over the high seat back and gently touched Stephanie's knee.

She jerked awake; eyes wide. "What? What?"

"Stephanie, I don't really know what this means or if it's relevant in any way..."

"I don't care. I have nothing. Not one thing. Anything at all you can tell me, even if it doesn't pan out, will give me a place to start. Please, Lucky."

I handed her the Glook, and she unwrapped it reverently, like she was about to unveil the Dead Sea Scrolls and not the big, googly eyes and the shock of pink hair that was her sister's comfort.

"I've never been to London before. This is my first overseas flight." I smiled. "But I saw a sign that said 'Piccadilly,' and close by were theaters and billboards that boasted about *Annie* and *Joseph* and *Pirates*. I have no idea what that means."

Stephanie's face lit up. "I do!" she cried, and the guy two seats across opened his eyes so she continued in a loud whisper. "They're West End shows. *Annie* is about little orphan Annie. *Joseph and The Amazing Technicolor Dreamcoat* is a big show. Susan got down to the fourth audition but didn't get in. She also auditioned for *Pirates of Penzance*. Didn't get in, but she got to shake hands with Tim Curry."

"Wow. Tim Curry from *Rocky Horror Picture Show?*" I allowed myself to relish my crush when she nodded.

Then I said, "You know all about your sister's life. You two must be so close."

Tears filled her eyes. "We are."

I took a deep breath, hoping to heaven I was giving her even a smidgeon of information that would help her. "Once you've talked to her dancing friends in the West End, and she had—has many, I would get on a train to Devon. I don't know where it is, but it's quite a trek from London."

She nodded, and I prayed I was not giving her false hope. "Does the name Steve mean anything to you?"

She thought for a really long time, and my stomach began to knot.

Her expression changed from perplexity to recognition. "Uncle Steve," she exclaimed, her voice loud in the quiet cabin. The guy on the end gave us a dirty look, and we woke up the tiny lady on my aisle.

I smiled at Stephanie and put a finger to my lips.

She leaned in and whispered, "He's my mom's brother. Haven't seen him for years and years. They had a falling out. We never knew why. Susan and I always loved him as little girls, and we knew our mom did too, deep down. We thought he lived somewhere in England, but mom wasn't interested in reacquainting."

How would I begin?

"I think you should look for Steve in Devon to get answers. If you can't find him, ask the hospitals around Devon." I was so tempted to tell her everything, but the devastating news that her sister had been hit by a fast-moving something-or-other and her legs were damaged? No way. And I didn't know the outcome—if Susan was dead or alive—nor, for that matter, the veracity of my crew rest, Glook-generated trip to Devon.

I figured, if nothing else, perhaps she would see her long-lost uncle.

"Please know, Stephanie, I have no expertise whatsoever. Sometimes I am able to see things, but honestly, I'm really not sure that any of this will be helpful to you. So please don't do anything hasty. If what you find out from the dancers in the

West End indicates you go elsewhere, go. If not, start in Devon."

I guessed even in the dim light of the cabin my face was easy to read. Fear of disappointing Stephanie loomed large, and my face probably screamed, *I am not sure of anything!*

"Lucky, you don't understand. I had nothing. Nothing. Now at least I have something to go on, even if it means I reacquaint with Uncle Steve and we find Susan together. I won't be alone."

She hugged me... Well, she crushed me to her, and I saw the galley's lights turn from a night-light encouraging passengers to sleep to a full brightness that screamed, "Wake UP!" A warning that breakfast was being prepared so pax might start queueing for the bathrooms to ease the rush when big food trolleys usurped the aisles. *Wow, I've been here for half the second crew's rest time.*

I wished Stephanie well, meaning it with all my heart, and left to do my job.

There was no time to talk with Stephanie again. Our dance cards were filled with handing out hot towels with tongs; serving a full breakfast; double tea and coffee services; collecting headsets; handing out immigration and customs paperwork; and running up and down our own aisles, seeing to passengers' many needs.

When at last we touched down in London, passengers retrieved hand luggage from overhead bins and stood in the aisle while we still taxied to our gate, in spite of the senior air hostesses' dire warnings of safety. I was trapped just in front of the galley where my jump seat was positioned. I could see the whole section of our cabin, but there was no way I could get to Stephanie in the thick of bodies.

Luckily, I was tall and taller still in my stilettos, since I was back in full uniform, and could keep an eye on Stephanie.

Before wending her way to the open cabin door, she paused, caught my eye, and smiled her thanks.

I put my hand over my heart, smiled at her and sent up a passionate but silent prayer for Uncle Steve to be found—and another, with even more fervor.

Please let Susan be alive.

And it was only then I realized I'd missed seeing London Bridge from the air.

CHAPTER 25

A few months later, I had just returned from nine fun-filled days in sunny Perth, Australia, with a shuttle to Sydney and a fabulous night stop on the gorgeous island of Mauritius.

I couldn't wait to rush home and tell Alana all about it. I had one whole day with her before she winged her way to somewhere else in the world.

I was checking in my heavy first aid kit when Oom Faan, the chief scheduler for overseas crew who was as wide as he was high and didn't take crap from anybody, shouted, "Van Niekerk!"

Nothing could prepare a crew member for the exhaustion of an overseas flight. Fatigue seeped into your bones. I needed my own bed. *What now?*

As I appeared in his line of vision, he barked, "To Mr. Oost-huizen's office. Chop-chop!"

My heart dropped. What would the head of the whole of cabin services want with me? Last time I had seen him, he'd pinned wings onto my uniform after *ab initio* training.

I hadn't done anything untoward. My motto was to fly way under the radar at all times. So why?

I clean forgot my aching fatigue and hightailed it to his office, a corner suite overlooking the runways. His secretary looked at me like I'd crawled out of a piece of cheese. I straightened my jacket and pulled my lips together in an attempt to get what remained of my red lipstick evenly distributed.

"Sit," the secretary said.

I did, and I waited. And waited. I considered trying to tidy myself up a couple of times but fatigue won. But when the face of wicked Miss Venter loomed large her imaginary finger wagging too close to my nose, I whipped out my compact and resurrected my face. I didn't want to give that horrid woman a reason to say, "I told you so." Finally, the secretary ushered me into the plush office.

"Good morning, sir," I said respectfully.

"Sit," he barked.

I did.

What the hell had I done? It was at times like these I wished I had a sixth sense. I smiled at the thought.

"Miss Van Niekerk. You are invited here today not for a commendation, so you can wipe that smile right off your face."

Oh, boy.

He was right. Praise from a passenger was never delivered personally. I'd received my first one not long ago. An SAA letter-sized envelope dropped into our cabin services mailbox. Inside, a pristine, unlined summary of the letter of praise the passenger had written was paraphrased by some civil servant. It ended: *Thank you for your exemplary service. We are proud to have you as a member of South African Airways.* Instead of a signature, a rubber stamp wet by a blue ink pad masqueraded as Mr. Oosthuizen himself, and the kudos were signed and sealed.

So, this is what happened when there was a complaint. But why didn't I remember an irate passenger?

Alas, Mr. Oosthuizen picked up five pages of flimsy white paper with two fold-lines. I could see a flowing cursive handwriting in blue ink, but reading backwards was harder than I thought.

"Do you remember your flight to London on 7th September of this year?"

"Yes, sir. Vividly. It was my first international flight."

"I will read you just the last few paragraphs of this very lengthy letter." He glared at me.

I swallowed.

He pushed his glasses farther down his nose and read over the top: "It was because of Lucky Van Niekerk's intuition and foresight that I was able to find my sister in Devon. Please let her know that though Susan will not dance professionally again, her legs were so superbly reset by the exceptional doctors there, she may one day become a dance teacher. For now, it's one step at a time."

I was grinning from ear to ear when he looked up from the letter.

His face was pure thunder.

Oh, Shitzville.

"This is your first and final warning, missy. There will be absolutely no hocus pocus, witch doctor nonsense or spooky stuff on board any of our fleet of aircraft at any time, for any reason, whatsoever. No fortune-telling baloney, no sixth sense twaddle, no voodoo poppycock. Have I made myself clear?"

"Yes, sir."

"I am telling you, Miss Van Niekerk, if there is a mere whiff of any gibberish or gobbledygook that involves you, a passenger or crew member, I, myself, personally, will strip your wings off that nice blue jacket!"

He waggled his finger toward my left boob. "And I will make sure you won't even get a job at the drive-in restaurant in Brakpan. Do we understand each other?"

"Yes, sir."

"Now get out of my office. And close the door."

I shot out of there like a bat out of hell.

Well, that was that. I would have to do with my gifts what I had done with my invisible friends. I would lock away my instincts and block my nose. I had no choice if I wanted to continue in my dream job.

And then I thought of Susan and Stephanie and Uncle Steve. I grinned. It was so worth it.

Later in the crew bus, I sobered. I could never, ever do that again, no matter how dire the circumstances.

MY JEEP WAS STOPPED in traffic as we got closer to Hull. It was fortunate because concentration was interrupted by a stab deep in my heart that turned to pure anger.

"That bloody Mr. Oosthuizen made me lock up my gift so tightly, I was rendered absolutely useless to the person who needed me most." Tula looked at me anxiously. "I'm all right, Tula, but I'll never recover from being unable to find Alana. I worked so hard at not being empathetic to keep my dream job, that it robbed me of being able to find my best friend."

Tula stretched to lick my hand resting on the console and I stroked his fluffy neck.

Thank God nobody knew about my dream of dreams in that very same crew rest. The one where I met my Roy Moreno-Reyes the first time in *this* life. I'd kept quiet about that for nearly three decades, such was the impact of Mr. Oosthuizen's wrath. Silly. But at the time I had no idea of the ramifications of that dream...

I literally shook myself. *No time for regrets.*

I managed not to jump this time the phone rang, and answered right away with, "Chaps?"

Andy was excited. "Damned if we didn't find a Saint Christopher's medal in a compost of a decade's worth of leaves. If you hadn't insisted, we would have given up long ago. It was much heavier than the chain and a whole lot deeper."

"Poor Janice, so brave..." My voice trailed off as I saw the image of Janice ripping off the brute's necklace with her left hand.

Suddenly, though my windows were closed, my car wafted with the odor of stagnant water I'd smelled when I first saw Janice and her sparkler. It was followed by the distinctive smell of metal at high heat being forged into a talisman, the Saint Christopher. But what of that bastard's essence and the aroma I had yet to identify? Something with religious connotations...

"Wait!" Though we were stopped I pressed even harder on the brake and the jeep gave a lurch.

"Where're both here," Andy's voice was tinny with a hint of an echo so I knew I was on speaker phone.

"Guys, there are too many niggling clues for me to keep this to myself. I said 'Moses in the bullrushes.' Where did that come from? I'm not a church goer. And a Saint Christopher?"

They gave me the silence I needed and I let my mind go. The missing part of the essence had a sweet aroma. "There's a rapturous merge of fragrances...myrrh, frankincense...a Catholic maybe?"

"It's a lead we've never had before. We're on it, Lucky."

"Also, Janice thought she'd seen him before, it was a vague recollection. But he had been watching her. It wasn't a random killing. He told her she'd looked at him once. Somebody in that small town knows this guy, Boys."

The silence between us was filled with thoughts mulling through my head, and no doubt those of the agents as well.

As the cars in front of me started to move I said, "Over and out, chaps. I am in the middle of a reverie, call if you have anything new."

I clicked off the phone and glanced at Tula. "Things are moving fast for Janice. Hopefully, she'll soon be able to rest in peace with both her parents and her unborn child. And just imagine the joy of the Watkins Glen no-kill cat lady when she gets that cash injection. Good for her and her kitties."

I smiled at him, but he was quite rude and disinterested. News of cats getting a big break did not impress Tula at all.

We passed the famous Nantasket Beach with restaurants old and new. "Hey, look! We're nearly home. Home, my fellow. No more reminiscing. When we get there, we have to clean, clean, clean." I looked at my watch. "Holy moly! It's nearly 5 p.m., and we're both bushed. I hate bloody vacuuming. Do you think I can get away with a quick sweep and just make the beds? Maybe I should set up a bar on the counter—thank heavens we already bought the booze. Okay, I'll clean the bathrooms. All right, I'll make a dish for the first day. You're such a taskmaster, Tula!" As we pulled into Reunion Street and then finally into my driveway, I warned: "But just don't make me use the vacuum."

Tula nodded.

I rolled my shoulders to ease the tension. There was nothing else I could do for Janice...at least not at the moment.

And I said a little prayer that somewhere, somehow, Susan Smith was teaching dancing with all the passion she once had for her art and that she, Stephanie, Steve, and Narelle were living happily.

CHAPTER 26

I looked at the vacuum cleaner.

Not for long, but I acknowledged its presence, then moved on to the bedrooms to bedeck them in clean linen and good intentions.

I hadn't really considered how I was going to accommodate all of us when there was only one king-sized bed and two single beds in the house. But making them get hotel rooms wasn't an option. The only way this would work is if we were in close proximity.

I caught sight of myself while cleaning my bathroom. Beads of sweat trickled between my boobs, staining my CK final clearance sweatshirt, which was an inch too short for me. I had to hike up the sweats above my navel to avoid a midriff freeze, creating a most unattractive, uncomfortable camel toe.

The shirt was intended to show off a twenty-something's cute navel and nonexistent tummy, not the belly of a women in her... *Oh, to hell with it. At least I'm not chilly, and Tula loves me and couldn't care less what I look like.*

Then it struck me. Truth was, I *did* want someone to care

what I looked like. As grateful as I was for my Tula, I wanted a man's attention.

Eyes on the rainbow prize the universe promised, Lucky.

And I scrubbed the shower floor more vigorously.

I thought fleetingly of the little vibe I had with Andy. Truthfully though, if I was going to have a man in my life, I needed him to be present. Appearance didn't matter; it was all about the feelings he evoked. I needed a wholesome essence, and I certainly couldn't live without funny, smart, innovative, unselfish and interesting.

My friend Linda maintained one would recognize one's soulmate immediately. Linda had studied under Brian Weiss, the pragmatic psychiatrist who'd inadvertently discovered the power of the soul's ability to hold onto baggage over many lifetimes. Linda had worked with Dr. Weiss when he delved into the very real probability of soulmates who reconnected over and over again in many incarnations.

The doctor was convinced that every time we were reincarnated, we came with our people—those we'd been born to or given birth to; loved deeply; struggled with; fought alongside and adored in various lifetimes since the dawn of time. We also returned with those we hadn't managed to make peace with. A second chance to right a wrong.

Frankly, I felt shortchanged. My soulmate, my beloved parents, and my best friend were all gone—my people—were gone. My kin consisted a very small handful of good friends scattered around the world. No one here. No one close.

Lucky for me, I still had Kitty. And even though she was eight-thousand miles away I still could smell her kindness and her croquettes and now she was just a WhatsApp call away. Sadly, busy lives stopped us talking as often as we'd like.

C'est la vie.

I didn't imagine finding kin in this huddle, but it was promised we had a better shot together on this soulmate quest. I sure hoped I hadn't misheard, otherwise I was adding all this angst to my world for no reason at all.

My nerves! I had no idea of their expectations or how this collaboration would work. But I promised myself, if this group effort failed us all, I'd finally allow myself to give up on the ghost of the past, and start doing some real living. Enough is enough.

I'd have to compromise. But my heart felt as heavy as the last rock I saw the bastard lay on Janice, the one that immersed her under the water.

Compromise. What a terrible thought.

"Tula," I called. He'd been gone a while. I heard him blast through the doggy door and seconds later he bounded up to me, decidedly pleased with himself.

"Oh, Tula, you bloody stink to high heaven! Did you piss off the skunk next door again?" He was wearing the stench like a boy with his first splash of aftershave.

He had the grace to look sheepish, but just for a moment, as I stomped to the kitchen. "Sure, we have plenty of time to take care of your dalliance with the smelly neighbor, you big oaf," I chided, as I reached for two large cans of tomato juice, bought for this very purpose. Fool me once, and all that. I banged cupboard doors as I pulled out ingredients and popped the giant cans, boxes, and bottles into a bucket I'd intended to use for mopping the kitchen floor.

I led a reluctant Tula by the collar down the stairs to the hall bathroom I'd just cleaned. "Sometimes you're just a dog!" I complained and he gave me a mournful look.

With a sigh, I stripped down, moved the shower dial to the

right temperature and pulled Tula's fluffy, foul-smelling, reluctant butt inside the stall with me, and closed the glass door.

"I know. It's an old wives' tale but it worked fine last time. I can't have the hosties telling me my dog stinks. I'd have to throw *them* out because *you're* not going anywhere."

Naked as the day I was born, I stood just short of the showerhead's strong downpour, hoping the aquatic onslaught would wash away some of Tula's skunk-stink. With the grace of a mad scientist, I concocted a potion in the bucket: dish soap, baking soda, and thick tomato juice. Bubble. Bubble. Toil and trouble.

Tula was grinning as he turned this way and that through the needles of water like he was having a spa experience

"You little shit. I swear you enjoy this." I wielded the wooden spoon as if it were a magic wand, stirring my brew that would—oh please angels and ancestors—banish the stench.

"Yooooohooooo," I thought I heard, and wondered idly if my mom was popping in again from the other side, to give me strength for my upcoming social ordeal.

Alas, no spectral presence appeared and I began dousing giant spoonful's of tomato-infused gunk onto Tula's back and tummy. "And you, mister, could be more considerate. It's mere hours before the hosties huddle, and you know we have a ton to do before we can hit the sack. Now this!"

"Yoohoooooooo!"

The sound grew louder, there were no bangles jingling but I figured it must be mom threatening to scale the veil to scold me for giving Tula what for! I come from a long lineage of dog lovers.

"Eeeeeeeeeeehhhhhhhhhhhhhh!"

Shock and surprise caused my squeal, and Tula joined in with a chorus of annoyed barks. Both of us were trapped behind the closed shower door. Ridiculous as it was, I tried to cover my private parts.

"What have we here?" A voice spoke from the mist caused by the shower, which then parted dramatically to reveal a crown hovering at about five-feet-four. The voice of a queen, apparently. I blinked, my bewilderment intensified by Tula's barks, which were decidedly pissed off rather than welcoming.

A crown? What the f...? The mist cleared, revealing no specter at all, rather a solid body under the head adornment. "Who are you and why are you wearing a crown?" I spluttered, rinsing one hand at a time so I could cover my coochie and nins without looking like I was bleeding out courtesy of the tomato juice.

"Oh, don't bother covering yourself, Dahling. Even if I was so inclined, I wouldn't be tempted," the queen remarked with a dismissive wave.

"Yip" said Tula. Even he was offended.

I was furious and found myself looking down my body and up again. "You mean thing! I don't look *that* bad! Who the hell are you and why are you in my house?" I addressed her as I would any spirit wandering in unannounced.

The queen grinned, unfazed by my confusion. "Carry on doing what you were doing, dears, don't let *me* interrupt." She disappeared into the hallway only to reappear with a fan surely inherited from a Spanish dancer. Tassels, lace and all. She closed the loo lid and sat down, elegantly crossing her legs.

I was too flabbergasted to speak. The gall!

My house. My toilet. My dignity—meant nothing to this regal intruder.

"Oh, to hell with it," I muttered. Maybe if I ignored her, she'd go away. I found myself fuming as I gripped the wooden spoon and resumed my tomato juice baptism of Tula with renewed vigor.

As I massaged the de-stink potion into my pup's thick fur, I tried again, this time in staccato bursts from my exertion, "Who the hell are you?" I had a darn good notion, but I was determined to force this intruder to announce herself. Tula, annoyed by the forceful scrubbing, gave me a reproachful look.

"Sorry," I apologized to my four-legged friend then slowed down and glared at the woman on the loo, who was no spirit at all. Rather an elegant-looking woman, Katharine Hepburn-esque, who was perfectly at home sitting on the toilet seat wearing a crown.

I stood tall, hand on hip, ready to give her what she didn't want. I barked. "I can see you're the queen, but you better be from a country bigger than England because you've got balls coming into my house uninvited and watching me de-skunk my dog whilst sitting four-foot away, fanning yourself!"

The queen looked up and one eyebrow lifted half way up her forehead. "Well, it's just as well you're doing what you're doing, because your reputation as one who can sniff out the missing and the dead would surely be ruined if your pooch ponged. If those old bitches come in looking like they stepped out of an old Vogue magazine, and you and your dog are stinking to high heaven, your semi-celebrity status will go straight down the drain."

"Oh, to hell with you." I childishly flicked fingers of water at the shower door in the queen's direction. "And what do you know about my reputation anyway?"

"Well, you found Johnny Fatal. That he was dead sort of tarnished the whole happily ever after thing, but you found him all the same. No-one my age or even twenty years younger who lived in South Africa will ever forget that sensational story."

I was taken aback. That was decades ago. But the cheek of her. Annoyance replaced perplexity. "So my reputation was what prompted you to just waltz into my home like you own the place?"

"The door was unlocked. I rang the bell. I opened the door a crack and heard all sorts of commotion. Thought I would make sure you were okay."

The queen examined her short, unpainted fingernails while fanning herself with the other hand. Stumbling in on a naked woman washing her dog in tomato juice seemed like an everyday occurrence to this stranger.

"I got an earlier flight. I considered a hotel but then I thought, 'She's likely prepping for the influx of women. Maybe I can offer my superior hostess skills.'"

"Hostess skills? Your legend is scary as hell. Fear is what you left behind, Missy. Terror and a slew of Shakespearian insults. If your intention is to help, why the hell are you wearing a crown and fanning yourself while I work my fingers to the bone?" I cooled down the water temperature and snatched the hand-held shower off its stand, holding it close to Tula's body to get off all the gunk.

Then I turned off the shower and scooched and squeezed as much water as I could from his once-fluffy neck, back, tummy, and legs. When I finally tried to stand up straight, my back threatened to pop six vertebrae and I placed a hand on the shower stall glass door waiting for my spine to align and join me for the next move.

I saw movement and glanced up. The queen rose with leisurely grace, placed her fan on the back of the toilet and tossed me two towels. Both landed on the top of the shower door. A perfect throw. "Never say I don't help the naked, stinky and downtrodden." She said sitting down again like a monarch on a velvet-lined throne.

In my state of tomato-tinted fury, I made my 'thank you' as inaudible as possible and attacked Tula with the towel, still naked, still wet, and still thoroughly exasperated.

———————

CHAPTER 27

"I'll take the room with the single beds," the queen announced.

I could feel smoke still coming out of my ears from the unexpected and humiliating intrusion.

"And I'll clean the bathroom I'll be using," my unwelcome early guest added.

My reply was automatic, "You don't need to do that. It's my house." I may have emphasized the *my*.

"Happy to," came the reply I least expected, and the queen put down her crown and her fan, pushed up her sleeves and got busy. It was my turn to raise an eyebrow, albeit theoretically since my brows are anything but dexterous.

Tula and I dashed upstairs and began laying out liquor on the section of granite countertop I thought was best for a help-yourself pub.

I pushed gently on a wall separating the half bathroom from the polite world in the open living area. The hidden doorway sprang free, and I admired once again the architect's commitment to his avant-garde concept. The clean lines were too important to him to be disrupted by a lavatory.

As a result, unless it was pointed out by the owner, you'd have to possess a sixth sense to find the loo. The thought of someone, legs crossed, frantically searching for the bathroom made me giggle and Tula smiled up at me.

I freshened the bathroom.

"We're close to done, Tula. Oh, hell, I haven't washed the floors. Oh, well. They'll have to do. It's already ten p.m." Since his lustrous, fluffy tail had been lobbed off soon after he was born, he wagged his entire bum enthusiastically. Losing your fluffy parts was one of the disadvantages of being a pedigree. I grinned at him, pleased I was a mongrel and that we'd found each other in spite of his recent fall from grace.

"Oh my! It's time, isn't it?" I reached inside the fridge for the little bottle of opaque liquid and filled a small syringe. "You know the drill."

Tula obediently sat, watching me with resigned eyes. My sweet boy didn't stir while I gave him his shot. When I was done, he paid me in kisses, and I rewarded his bravery with the least offensive-smelling treat on the market.

"And you know, Tula? When this little soiree is over, and if the universe doesn't produce the goods, instead of having one-night stands, or rushing the issue with Andy, I think I'll investigate devices designed to fill such a void. You never know, it might be better than a compromise. I think you can actually buy them online now. Remember the one we sent Debbie? With the funky purple parts? We wrapped that thing in layers and layers of paper lest someone peeked. She said it perked her up no end after her husband left her, and she should've traded flesh for rubber years sooner." I chuckled.

"I have a funky purple one too. It delights me quite nicely thank you!" The cheery voice came from a few feet away. Damn the queen. I was hoping she was overcome by jet lag and had gone straight off to the bed *she'd* chosen.

Tula gave her a quick sniff then went around rubbing his face on the couch, chair, and loveseat, trying to find his pre-skunk smell so he could avoid an identity crisis.

Be nice, Lucky. She is your guest. You invited her for gosh sakes. So, she came a bit early and embarrassed you. Get over it. Deep breath, and then I turned and put out my hand. "Let's do this again, shall we?"

"I thought the first time was perfectly acceptable, but okay, I'm BJ."

"BJ. Glad you've put your crown somewhere safe. You're nothing like I imagined. Well, physically that is. Your attitude and presumption are exactly what I dreaded..." I tried to swallow the last few words I didn't mean to come out. "Well, come in and see the gathering area of my home."

She looked around. "A bitch to paint I'll bet with these high ceilings."

"Never worried about that," I said, knowing I would now. "Sit, please" I channeled my mother. She was indeed a fine hostess.

I watched as BJ assessed which seat had the best view.

I thought I'd help. "The very best place is lying that way on the couch looking into the mirror above the mantel, and taking in the whole of Boston lighting up our world."

"It's a gorgeous place, Lucky. Thank you for having me." Wow! She'd clearly strayed, but once she must have had a gracious mother too.

She was indeed the spitting image of Katharine Hepburn,

with elegantly swept up, wispy hair in half a dozen soft colors. Instead of mere pins, little yellow, and black bees held up escaping tendrils. The bees hinted at her complexity as well as her vulnerability and, somehow, that cracked a chink in my armor.

I'd smelled her Chanel No. 5 in the hallway after the shower incident. One had to be confident, understated and timeless to wear Chanel No. 5.

She was down on the floor, holding Tula's cheeks in both hands. "You're a sight for sore eyes. What's your name?" she asked Tula, and got a tilted head and a little yelp of appreciation for her sincere attention. He turned a little circle and went in for another kiss.

"Tula," I said on his behalf.

He looked all bashful with her attention. Score two for the queen. She had a way with dogs. I didn't give out that badge of honor easily.

"What can I get you to drink? I could rustle up a sandwich," I offered, though lackluster seemed to push its way through.

"No thanks, I brought my own drinks and I ate at the airport, so all good. But tell me more about the purple dildo you're thinking of investing in."

Shocker! It was like falling wildly into bed on a blind date without the dinner as foreplay. Boy! When I looked at her, relief washed over me as I realized I didn't say it aloud. Who knew how she'd twist it.

Her genuine expression stopped me from crafting a snarky reply. I took a big risk and said, "I lost my soulmate years ago. After all these years of partial abstinence, I think I should stop being a prude. Perchance I'll invest in something like that."

She lay on the couch as I'd suggested and looked into the mirror. "Wow. That's truly spectacular. What a night scape. And like the rest of your views, ever changing."

I warmed a notch. "Yes, it's pure bliss here. I don't need pictures on the walls. I have windows with moving pictures." I was pleased she didn't linger on my dildo confession.

"Smart not to have it all curtained or blinded up. Just leaving them naked shows you are something of an exhibitionist." She turned and grinned at me, "But we knew that already."

She chuckled when my face flushed recalling my brazen bathroom stance.

I smiled. "Ahh, you give me way too much credit as a liberal hip chick. I am actually a prude; my windows are one-way glass. No-one can see in." I almost boasted.

"Back to the purple toy," she said solemnly.

Shit.

And then she continued: "You don't have to cruise the aisles of an off-road, X-rated superstore any more. No chance of bumping into the mailman or the Cumberland Farms clerk there. The internet has incredible resources." She shifted her attention from her fingernails to me, grinning widely.

I felt the need to downgrade my prudishness and show her how cool I really was. "I've been a scarlet woman, a witch, and perchance I was the Queen of Sheba in the last couple of past lives I've glimpsed, so I have some experience in not being a prig."

"Well! That makes you a LOT more interesting." She smiled a smile so genuine I followed suit, then willfully pulled my cheeks back down. I didn't want her to think she knew me. Not yet.

"Sure I can't get you anything? I am going to have a glass of wine." I guess practicing with one guest before the onslaught might be helpful. I didn't plan for any others to me see me bent down butt naked.

"I'll get mine," BJ said and disappeared.

My phone trilled, startling me and I moved to the far window in the kitchen. "Hi, chaps," I said, feigning cheerfulness.

"How did you know it was us?" Jim asked. "Oh, I forgot. You're psychic!"

"Original, Jim! You two need a break from each other. You're both smart-arses now! I can usually count on you *not* to be one," I ragged.

"See? That's what I love," exclaimed Jim. "We say 'smart-Ah-sses.' You say 'smart-ARRRSES.'"

"A rose by any other name," I said.

"So," Andy cut in, "we checked out all the Catholic churches."

"Four in Springfield and one down the drag in Fiske," reported Jim.

"Of course, we had to investigate four out of five before we hit the luck."

"And?" I was excited.

I could hear the smile in Jim's voice. "The priest is an old-timer. Been there for forty-five years. Sharp as a tack. He remembers Janice. Who wouldn't when such an awful thing happens to a young girl in your small town? He said in the month before she disappeared, he'd seen her sitting quietly in one of the pews after work a couple of times a week. She didn't come to a service. Seemed to like to do her own thing. She attended confession a handful of times, but if he remembered what she confessed, he wasn't telling."

Andy took over. "We asked if a tall, youngish man with dark eyes, dark hair and very pale skin came to mind. He didn't hesitate. A seminarian by the name of Donald Cox."

The minute he said the name, teenage-boy-room smells, along with aromatic frankincense and myrrh, infused the air around me 'til it was thick and suffocating. I gagged and ran a higgledy-piggledy line to the sliding glass door in the dining room. I collapsed on the decking outside, coughing, and coughing, and when it stopped, I exhaled the last of Donald Cox's vile odor as Tula stood over me protectively.

"It's okay, boy. Thank you, Tula. You saved me, as always."

"Lucky?" Andy's voice was far away and tentative, like an uninvited visitor checking if it was okay to pop in. I stumbled back to where I'd dropped the phone.

"Sorry, chaps. Just had to rid myself of Donald Cox's root ugliness. I can tell you you've found your killer."

"I fukinhell knew it! We'll make the bastard pay. *When* we find him, not if." Andy's anger vibrated through the phone.

Jim said, "You're an amazing team member, Lucky. He sure sounds like the killer. Cox was spending part of the summer as the pastoral intern. Priest said he was an odd sort and left just before the priest heard about Janice. He only remembered because Cox's departure was so close to the town's shakeup of a beautiful girl gone missing. He believed Cox had high tailed it off to a Catholic church somewhere in Ohio for a particular course they were offering. But that was twelve years ago."

"Shitzville!" I was getting cold outside in my short-sleeved shirt. I ambled in, closing the door behind me.

"The Springfield priest didn't know which church, but he'd heard Cox's name mentioned not long ago. Good news. It means he's still in the Catholic system. He promised to make some hush-hush calls to find Donald Cox's current where-abouts." I could hear hope quivering in his voice.

"Holy cow! That's amazing, chaps."

"We warned the priest. We can't afford to make any waves to tip Cox off. He's not even allowed to cause a little ripple until we nab the swine and get him inside an interview room." Andy's voice was determined.

"He's not a swine 'til you know for sure he is," I said, just in case, though every heightened sense in my arsenal was on fire. "I desperately hope I'm right for Janice's sake and all the people who still care about her, but there's always a first time. Keep me posted," I asked before ending the call.

"Up to your old tricks, I see." I jumped. Janice was so preva-lent I'd forgotten the queen in my living room.

"You caught me," I said for want of anything else.

"Good for you, making a living with your gift. It's admirable."

I glanced at her to see if she was joshing me. Her sincerity was evident and I felt ridiculously shy. "Why do you know so much about my 'gift'?"

"There was a check hostess on your first flight. Unbe-knownst to you she was watching you the whole time to eval-uate your first flight. When the girl you helped was disembarking, the check, in her civvies so no-one would know she was from cabin services, joined the girl on the exit ramp. I was friends with that check hostess, she was on *ab initio* with me. She shared that the girl mentioned you were psychic, giving her strength to locate her missing sister.

I was shocked.

Before I could find the words to respond she asked, "Did you ever hear what happened to Susan and Stephanie?"

"Wow! You remember their names after all this time?"

"Yeah. What you did made a huge impression on me. It's the reason I'm here."

"I was called into Oosthuizen's office. He had a letter from Stephanie. She told him thanks to me she found her sister where I'd told her to look. Despite nearly losing leg function in the accident, Susan received timely surgery and her doctors' worked wonders. She would walk again and hopefully teach dance. Oosthuizen told me that if I was ever caught doing any voodoo or psychic poppycock in the airline again, he would personally ensure I would not even be allowed to serve hamburgers at the Brakpan road house."

BJ shrieked with laughter. She laughed so loud and so hard I had to join in. When we quieted down, she said, "That's exactly what that old toss would have said. Thank God, he didn't stop you completely. I remembered the Susan Smith story and your name is hard to forget, so it blew me away when it was you who found the body of Johnny Fatal."

"That was years and years later. But Oosthuizen screwed me up for ages. Because of him, I couldn't find my gift when I needed it most." I felt my heart clench again as I thought of Alana.

When I glanced up, BJ was looking at me with genuine kindness. Instead of pushing me she said, "I, on the other hand, turned my magnificent South African Airways years serving in first class, meeting movie stars and influential politicians into a most lucrative business."

"Good for you," I said, meaning it as I snuggled into the loveseat with Tula next to me, ready for a good story. I had a feeling she had more tales to tell than most.

"Indeed-ee. I hosted the most successful sex toy parties in

the greater Durban area for five years. I had loads of titillating toys to whet the appetites of ladies young and old. And those very toys made me rich."

My hand flew over my mouth. "What the hell?" I managed.

"I had parties five times a week. People's homes were stuffed with women ages eighteen to eighty. I had them playing games and drawing penises on their heads with pencils and paper I provided. The closest rendition of the real thing would earn discounts to my sexy loot displayed in the host's bedroom. Many of the ladies framed their works of art.

"After that I'd have a question-and-answer session and some Doctor Ruth frank sex-talk. Then I would invite them to meet me one-on one in the bedroom where all the goodies were displayed. I'd help them choose an item or two that would be of most value to them. I was the Vanna White of dildos. I could present them like no other." Her fan made an appearance and did its work.

"No wonder you knew about the purple thingy I was discussing with my dog!"

"Purple, green, black, pink, flesh colored, I was a specialist in them all. Imagine all those women in Podunk South African towns with an offer to host a party—and a sex party at that—with all their girlfriends. It was riotous. Squealing and squeaking and giggling were the sounds of hard cash paid by women who grew up with censorship, like we all did. No *Lady Chatterley's Lover*. No *Deep Throat*. No *Kama Sutra*. These women were wild on the inside until they banded together, then it became a jungle boogie. Worse than cloistered convent girls on the loose."

I laughed so hard it released all the tension that had built since Tula flew through his doggy door hours before.

As we prepared for bed, BJ was in "her" now-spotless, tomato-juice-free bathroom cleaning her teeth when I wandered out of my bathroom and asked, "Were you a flying mattress in the airline?"

BJ choked on her toothpaste. Then she laughed so hard she slid down the door frame slowly, till her night gown was around her neck and her granny panties were exposed. And she laughed some more. By that time, I was lying on the carpet in the hallway in hysterics.

Tula was most concerned. He'd never seen me in this state. Sitting wagging his fluffy stub for a minute, he'd get up and circle me, then sit down again. He kept glancing at BJ with a quick wag but his eyes were seldom off me.

When at last we sobered I turned onto my stomach and kicked up my legs behind me. I watched BJ as she rinsed her mouth, and sat back on the loo which had no resemblance to a throne. "I went through a mattress every year and I was in the airline for well over a decade. Nicely packed, plump, well-made mattresses they were. But, alas, they were threadbare all too soon. I never lost an opportunity to develop my worldliness or make good use of my flying mattress." Her smile was wicked.

Oh! How we laughed.

CHAPTER 28

Another sleepless night, anxious about curses for my visitors' wasted time, money and hopes. Then I leapt up and frantically deboned a chicken for the only meal I intended to prepare for them.

I also attempted to display the South African delectables I'd ordered from Canada. I stepped back and acknowledged it was a pitiful effort, but time had not been on my side.

BJ ambled up, much to Tula's delight, and she greeted him like a long-lost lover, which he really appreciated.

Back at the Crock-Pot, I added mushrooms, cream and a hefty dose of white wine and BJ's voice startled me with a, "Shall I add some pizzaz to these goodies?"

"Please. I'd love to see your 'superior' hostess skills in action," I challenged with a hint of sarcasm.

She grinned mischievously and began cupboard-diving. Somehow, she found some gold ribbon, twirled it brilliantly with a knife and, all of a sudden, we had a festival on my countertop.

Not only did I marvel at her artistry, I amazed myself. I didn't feel she'd invaded my space. WOW!

I took another look. "Okay, okay," I conceded. "Your hostess skills are indeed superior." And I applauded as Tula bounded around with glee.

When BJ went downstairs to tidy up, all my fears came trudging back. I paced up and down the living area with Tula in tow, nervous as a reluctant groom.

Oh, the aromas they'd bring with them!

They'd be here in ten minutes or at least that's what their text had just threatened. My stomach lurched.

I breathed deeply and concentrated on sunrise's early gift coming through the south windows from floor to ceiling on either side of the fireplace, washing the living room in shades of indigo and orange. I turned my head towards the dining room, delighting in the delivery of the morning gift of violet and amber hues. My divine paradise. I took another deep breath to calm my churning spirit.

"How does it look, Tula?" His head tilted like mine—left, then right. "I want it to look lived in. Modest. Comfortable. Unpretentious."

Tula lost interest, and my string of low-key superlatives tapered off.

Then the phone rang. I looked at my watch. Four minutes to nine.

Shitzville. Not now.

"Hello, chaps." I paced, attempting to walk off the adrenaline coursing through my veins.

"Just reporting in, Lucky," Jim said, but I imagined him smiling.

"What'cha got, Jim?"

"Well, we had a whole lotta dead ends courtesy of Mr. Cox." Andy sniffed. "But we think we found the son of a bitch. In Kansas City."

"Did you guys get any sleep? I hope you had your minions do all the research for you. When do you leave?"

I didn't hear his answer because the doorbell chimed.

The sensation I felt was akin to takeoff in the cabin of a 747, while holding a three-hundred-pound steel trolley, unstowed, twenty feet from your jump seat, and the nose of the massive 747 Boeing rears up...

I clutched one hand to my throat, the other splayed over my pounding heart as I gripped the phone 'twix ear and shoulder.

Tula huffed, yipped, and took off downstairs in a flash of mottled fur.

"Be safe, you two. Gotta go, but keep me posted." I clicked off the phone and flew down the stairs.

I snuck a look in the hall mirror to make sure my best friend, Ruby Woo, was taking enough attention from my nose and the new wrinkles, lumps, and bumps.

WOW! My physical insecurities lost no time in coming back, thirty years after they'd nearly ruined my life. Intimidated by just the thought of seeing these former air hostesses, who were no doubt better looking than I.

I was shocked at the thought. How quickly a woman can lose her depth, her sense of self-worth. What kind of fragile state had I been in during my days in the airline?

Tula amped up the noise to a deafening level. I choked out a hoarse, "Coming."

What have I done?

Then I cleared my throat and pasted on what I hoped looked like a genuine smile.

I glanced back to look for BJ but the door to the guest room was closed. I could have used some backup.

Hand on the brass doorknob, I fought against the tsunami of doubt threatening to flood my world. One hostie, four hours spent together was one thing. I tightened my grip around the orb, forced a deep breath and held it in ... one, two, *three* more on the doorstep. My air escaped and I had to start again. One, two, three, *four altogether... shit ... breathe, breathe...* five, *six long, dastardly days...*

I swear I would have fainted if the banging on the door hadn't begun. *Banging? On MY door?*

What have you made me do, Miss Universe? I looked up and cursed.

There was a good chance my life would never be the same again.

CHAPTER 29

Seconds before I yanked the door wide open like a Band-Aid on an open wound, excited voices filtered through the tiny open crack.

A girlish giggle. "Maybe this is all a hoax, and an axe murder has invited us here for six days of torture."

"Yeah, maybe not so Lucky after all..." came a vaguely familiar voice.

Oh-so-fake smile in place and I was in business as I gently opened the door to the huddle of hosties.

There on the stoop stood three middle-aged women.

For a moment, I was shocked. I'd been expecting girls. Then I remembered my own reflection, and my Ruby Woo smile grew wider and my welcome warmer than I expected.

The second thing that hit me was their perfumes. Wham! Whack! Wallop! My head swam. I refrained from ducking and slamming the door to shield myself from their overwhelming fragrance, as powerful as an H-bomb.

Tula, on the other hand, was ecstatic with this barrage of

bodies. For his sake, I quickly sniffed my wrist to free it from the onslaught, and concentrated on one woman at a time.

"Come in, come in, please." I waved my arms and headed up the stairs talking to them over my shoulder: "It's so crowded on this little porch with your bags and all, let's go upstairs where Tulu and I can smell you...ahh...meet and greet you properly."

On the landing to the bedrooms, I turned and watched them schlepping up their bags. "Oh, BJ arrived early," I slung out casually.

All three stopped quite still on the step on which they'd landed, their expressions displayed varying degrees of apprehension as they looked up at me.

I understood.

BJ. The queen.

But I was unprepared for the little stab of tenderness I felt for her royal self.

When the three were clustered in the wide hallway to the bedrooms, my Aussie did a whirl of glee knowing he could at last fulfill his calling as a herder.

"This is Tula. My bestie."

"Nice doggy," said the prettiest face, with perfect, untainted, pore-free skin; below-shoulder-length, perfectly streaked blond hair; and a smile that turned night to day, winter to summer.

Brie?

She was different but the same. She was five foot two-ish and wore her fluffiness well, perfectly groomed in a pair of peach-colored designer jeans, a loose-fitting, pearl-colored, satin camisole, and an eggshell shawl with gold flecks. Dangly golden chain earrings would occasionally peek out from under her hair.

Her off-white Versace sneakers shimmered with a gold hue. A bottle and a half of the *Creed Aventus for Her* dabbed on her wrists could pay off my Jeep.

She drew back and air-patted Tula, who stood a foot below her. Hmm, he had his work cut out for him convincing her he was huggable. "He's bigger than I'm used to," she said with a semi-apologetic smile, but I didn't have time to puzzle over her words. She put out her hands and clutched mine in both of hers. It was an intimate gesture without being too familiar. I respected that. It had been a long, long time. "I remember you, Lucky. You did it. You got to fly. I knew you would."

I gave a shy smile. "It took me two tries," my cheeks burned. I'd never confessed that to anyone. But my mouth wouldn't quit. "And you were instrumental in making me believe I was good enough."

"I'm so glad. Otherwise, I wouldn't be here." She laughed quietly. Her sincerity hit me like a soft pillow at a pajama party. Sweet. Oddly innocent. No hidden agenda here.

"This place is divine," came a deep, melodic voice behind Brie, her voice cracking twice in the delivery. It was the kind of interesting vocal instrument country artists would kill for.

"I'm Chantelle," she said as she took my hand in hers. "We did a Lisbon night stop together. I thought you were ballsy when you chastised the cockpit for drinking a bucket of Portuguese liqueurs while we hosties had a glass of house wine each, and they wanted to split the bill."

"Bastards!" I exclaimed, and we smiled into each other's eyes.

She was tall. A dazzling smile showed off teeth bright enough to guide you to your seat in a dark movie theater.

"Your voice, the light you generate. Your name wasn't

familiar but you are," I said, feeling warm. Why hadn't I spent more time with this striking girl on that trip? I just couldn't remember.

"You went off with Madame Callas and his crew to the Algarve, I did something else." She'd read my mind.

"Wow, what a memory you've got!" I was impressed.

She gave me a quick hug, and Aerin Mediterranean Honeysuckle titillated my nostrils. A perfect scent that accented her tanned complexion and aristocratic bone structure. She was a force of nature and could have risen from the azure sea and landed on a sun-drenched beach while losing her tail and gaining a pair of long legs. She wafted all things sensual, rich and magical.

"Helloooo, Tula. I'm Chantelle." Her grin etched its way into her crackle, so even if your eyes were closed, you'd have known she was smiling. She shoved her face into Tula's for kisses, and when he was done, she held him still, looked into his eyes and said, "My name means *song,* and I shall sing to you, my handsome boy." He had the grace to look coy.

Chantelle wore a pair of jeans and a black peasant top that showed off a narrow waist. Hoop earrings peeked out between dark curls, and she sported sneakers that had been around the block a few hundred times. This one didn't strive to impress. Chantelle was simply born this way. Lucky thing. I wanted her to stay close for a bit to complete the lineup of complex ingredients of her perfume. But she left me with a hint of amber and tonka bean.

"I hope you live up to your name so you can entertain us," I teased.

Chantelle turned, and her smile dazzled as she fluffed her dark, wild bob. I watched, fascinated. This wasn't a gesture; it was a procedure. With palms facing front and starting at the back of her head, she fanned her hair out to the sides, as if mosquitoes nibbled behind her ears and she had to shoo them away. Chantelle followed the elaborate fluff with a quick head-shake, which was more like a head-shiver.

Then, after all that, as if no time had passed since the procedure began, she smiled and nodded, making direct eye contact. "I intend to," she rasped then grinned, and at least two-and-a-half of my taut muscles relaxed.

The tiniest one was as cute as a rare button. I'd watched her push past everyone and take her place behind me up the steps. No question she'd prefer to be in front of me. She turned around, let go of her suitcase and threw her arms around my waist—likely because she couldn't reach my neck. I couldn't decide if I was thrilled or overwhelmed. My senses were overpowered by cattleyas, jasmine, freesias, roses, patchouli, and vanilla. Flower Bomb. Was she as easy to read as the ingredients of her perfume?

"Moxie," she said.

"Do you have it?" I asked, keeping eye contact. It was a trick question since I'd remembered her in action in *ab initio*'s deportment class.

Laughing easily, she said, "Yep. I suppose I do. I was named Esme for an hour or two, then I may have bossed around the wet nurse because I became Moxie pretty quickly."

Forthright she was. I approved. Cute face, cute legs, cute smile. Moxie wore khaki shorts above her knees, expensive flip flops designed for long walks, minimal but artfully applied makeup, and a short, flattering pixie cut with an ombre effect, blond on top and darkening its way down to the straight cut at the base of her head. A sexy 'do that added an inch of height to her diminutive frame. She had on a no-fuss, cheesecloth top with creases made by an iron, a tool I avoided like the plague. The whole outfit had a hard time being modest. Her figure wouldn't let it. But how the hell she'd stretched to make the SAA minimum hostie height requirement of five foot one, I couldn't fathom.

The guest room door opened with a whoosh, and out swept the queen, crown and all.

A chill of apprehension swept over the three around me like a thick fog. I was suddenly very glad I'd had four hours with BJ sans crown. I was much more afraid now of four people's smells and strong personalities taking over my home than the legendary terror that was BJ.

"I remember you," Moxie said to BJ. "We flew to Buenos Aires together." She did have moxie.

"I was first class, *dahling*. Who the plebeians were back there was all very beneath me," BJ drawled.

I laughed a little too heartily. "There wasn't a soul in the airline who wasn't scared of you, Queen,"

"I know," BJ drawled with a poker face before she chuckled.

Moxie giggled. "Yeah, you scared the shit out of me. I found you in first class to report there were plastic utensils on the dinner trays instead of silverware. You looked at me like I had just blown in through the window once we passed the 20,000 feet mark, and you said, 'Didn't you learn about this happenstance during your extensive training? B.A. flights are the only ones on which we serve all meals in economy with plastic cutlery.'"

BJ winked. "I remember you, too. Spunky little thing as you proved in our recent email chats. You were too bloody cute to forget, and you're still bloody cute now. Pisses me off, frankly.

Sometimes you can't forget what you ache to and can't remember what you must."

Moxie's eyes widened, and she looked like a cornered wildcat. She didn't seem to hear the compliments, only the harshly delivered tone. Hmmm. It was too early for conflict. And, like my mother, I wanted to do my utmost to fill any silence before it could become awkward.

"Well, BJ, that was the best backhanded compliment I've heard in a while. Way to go, Moxie. You made an impression on The Queen!" I said, a little too loud.

This was going to be exhausting.

"It's silly to believe such stereotypes, but I can't remember if the knives, forks, and spoons were plastic because it was believed all Argentina's countrymen were prone to kleptomania, or if people from Buenos Aires had a reputation for killing with cutlery in enclosed spaces," said Chantelle in that sexy, musical way.

We all chuckled, though I felt it was more of an exhalation after holding our breath for so long. I silently blessed Chantelle for helping to ease the tension.

Moxie asked, "You *do* have booze, don't you?" Real fear that it might be a dry six days nipped at the corners of Moxie's cute mouth.

"Lots," I said. "And there's a bottle store a couple of miles across on the mainland."

Moxie relaxed, beaming.

Now I knew how she'd defied the strict height minimum of the airline's creed. This Little General grew an extra inch on spunk alone, and her bossiness I'd witnessed in deportment did nothing to dimmish her worth as far as the airline was

concerned. Coming from this little body, assertion was a memorable asset. She had IT.

My! A queen and a general in one house for six days? Spare
my overcrowded soul!

I was just relieved there was no animosity lingering between
the queen and the pixie after their bitchy email slinging. And
rightly so. We were all women. Women on a mission. We had
something in common.

Whoa! Look how socially accepting I turned out to be.

*Don't get ahead of yourself, Lucky, and no back patting. You
know where that gets you!*

"Let's get you settled. Downstairs is all yours, pick a
sleeping spot." I extended my arms out to the side to show the
bedrooms.

"Never only do half an emergency demonstration," Brie
said in a monotone. And exactly as we were taught in training,
she lifted her arms, index, and middle fingers together, thumb
in she pointed forward then she bent and lifted up her elbows.
With practiced precision her fingers pointed behind her.
Between us—my contribution was unconscious—Brie and I
had completed a portion of the airplane safety procedures.

"Okay," said BJ. "Now we know where the exits are and
you've just proved you're one of us, I'm BJ. You can call me
Queen."

"Do I have to?" Brie asked, then started to giggle.

Silence like a monarch's heavy coat, covered our four heads.

I stood stock still and scared shitless. I didn't know how to
fix this. I felt Tula looking at me, begging me to take the
atmosphere down a hefty notch.

Tula made me do it. I said "I met the queen last night.
Frankly, I didn't love her. Then she put down her crown. And

to my great delight, BJ arrived, rolled up her sleeves, cleaned my bathroom and turned my dull display upstairs into a work of art."

Chantelle's eyes were big. "The queen cleaned the bathroom?"

"No!" I said with a touch too much emphasis. "That was BJ. The queen sat on the loo seat with her crown on, fanning herself while I was washing my dog in the shower, naked of course. I wasn't exactly expecting guests. There she sat on the lid of the john, body erect, crown glinting and disdainfully announced that even if she was a lesbian, she *would not* be buying *my* body.

"But afterwards, thank God, BJ turned up. I was entirely unprepared for you girls and BJ helped me so much. I had a lovely fun time with her." I looked pointedly at the queen.

She reached for her crown, took it off, looked at the three new arrivals and warned, "Don't think this means the queen won't pop in when she needs to."

"We'd be disappointed if she didn't." Chantelle's smile dazzled, and the atmospheric cloak went up in smoke.

Tula did a little dance.

"Which one's mine?" Moxie asked briskly as she assessed the two rooms on that floor with quick, birdlike glances.

My bedroom had a king-size bed and a fancy ensuite with a Jacuzzi tub and separate shower. The guest bedroom smaller and already inhabited by a very big personality.

Moxie made up her mind and pointed at Chantelle and Brie. "You two can sleep together because you're so noisy. I'll sleep on the other twin bed," she barked.

Now *that* was a surprise. Moxie taking the bull by the horns. The queen by the crown?

"I sleep naked," announced Moxie, then looked pointedly at BJ. "And I'm fabulous naked. Even at my age." Sarcasm dripped as she referred to their sparring via email.

BJ shrugged nonchalantly. "Just don't flaunt your little 'fabulous' nude self around unnecessarily."

If Moxie intended to shock the queen, did I have news for her!

"And you, Lucky?" Brie asked me sincerely, her lovely face creased in concern.

"You're safe. I wear pajamas," I promised, and grinning I answered Brie's question. "Tula and I will sleep on the couch upstairs. There's a loo up there, so I'll only come down to shower in the big shower. See you girls upstairs." With a sense of relief, I leapt up the stairs, desperate for a moment to regroup as they settled in.

Upstairs, Tula and I plonked ourselves on the big chair. He was squished beside me. I loved having him close. *Together, just us two. Quiet. Breathe. Just breathe. No smells except our own. Take this moment of peace and pretend it's an hour.*

CHAPTER 30

BJ was first to surface to the top floor and plonked herself down on my sofa. Sprawled out, head on the armrest, she looked into the humongous mirror. "Good sodden-witted Lord! Here is Boston at her best. The harbor. The cosmopolitan city. Day vistas. Nightscapes. There's never nothing to look at."

"She talks funny," exclaimed Moxie, making an appearance from below and twirling towards us like she'd just entered stage left and a balletic leap would follow.

Behind her, Chantelle growled in *that* voice, "BJ used to scare the shit out of the crew with her Shakespearean insults."

"I hear that's a thing now, isn't it?" I asked.

"It's always been *my* thing." BJ was still view-gazing at Boston. "Somebody stole the idea from me and ran with it. Made pots of money. Books. Websites. The You-tube-thingy. Bastards! Well, I suppose I stole the insults from Shakespeare, so easy come, easy go."

Chantelle exclaimed musically, "Oh look, is that green space right next door?"

"I think it's too swampy to build on but the town calls it a nature preserve," I said casually, though I was thrilled it was there, except when my dog provoked the neighbors. The coastal flora, fauna, and airborne inhabitants flowered, scurried, sang and showed off nature's wild bounty from dawn to well beyond dusk.

Soon all four were touring my home, and I watched with pride as these former hosties did the rounds from window to window to sliding glass doors, gazing out at the bay of Hull. They angled to catch glimpses of crashing waves to the southeast between modest Cape Cod homes and smaller colonials hugging the rugged cliff edge like barnacles.

The hosties couldn't help but be amazed by the breathtaking views of the Gut of Hull. The channel marks the peninsula's edge, and close by the pier extends over a wide beach.

Well, no matter how it panned out from here, my Frank Lloyd Wright-ish abode elicited the appreciation I'd hoped for.

"We'll go to breakfast over there." I joined them and pointed to a large structure with umbrellas near the pier. "They serve the best breakfasts in the whole of Massachusetts."

"Today?" Moxie asked, wide-eyed.

"Sometime," I offered vaguely.

"We're not here to visit the local eating spots," BJ chided.

"We have important things to accomplish," Chantelle said huskily, and my stomach lurched. WTF were these girls expecting from me? From this soiree?

To distract myself from myself I joined them at the north eastern window where, in the distance, the stoic Coast Guard station seemed to salute the vast ocean. Inside, America's best sailors, swimmers, and frogmen waited for disasters. All around, the bay was a haven to recreational powerboats, sailboats, and rowboats until low tide, when little islands and sand bars suddenly appeared. The Coast Guard had their work cut out for them.

"I think we should schedule a tour of the Coast Guard station," drawled BJ, who'd slipped back to her horizontal position on the couch.

I joined her. "You're into all things nautical?" I asked, truly interested.

"I'm attracted to the cut of hunky, naughty sailors," she said, grinning before her face fell. "Damn, then I remember I have lumbago and sagging skin," she said so softly, I barely heard her.

I whispered, "You're still fabulous, Queen. Any seafarer would be lucky to have you." I smiled, though her well-hidden vulnerability tugged at my heart.

"I love it here," said Brie.

"Me too. It's divine." Chantelle's voice raised up into her "head voice." What a range. I tingled with the thrill of anticipation. Oh, to hear that voice in song!

"Me three," Moxie said, twirling around like a Dervish exercising her daily rites.

"What the hell's with you, child? Round and round like a top." BJ gave Moxie a long look.

"Just be glad *I'm* your roommate and not these two giggling Gerties." It seemed that Moxie was completely unaware of her strange need to constantly rotate.

"I think I'll move in and stay forever," BJ stated, and nobody argued, though I desperately hoped she wasn't serious. Tula's tail wagged even more vigorously.

Fickle little bugger.

The muscles in my neck and shoulders relaxed a smidgeon

more. If my guests were disappointed or disgruntled or demeaned during their stay, at least they'd remember my cool pad.

"Oh goody, goody," Moxie declared, as she admired the impromptu wet bar: two bottles of tequila, one bottle of Veuve Clicquot, four of Moet Brut, a liter of orange juice, Zing Zang Bloody Mary Mix, a liter of vodka and four little bottles of tonic water, with lemon wedges, celery sticks, and a salt cellar all standing at attention. The latter were BJ's additions.

"There's more in the fridge," I announced. "Except for the fancy champagne. I thought I might pretend I was posh, but one bottle was all I could handle, so the plebeian champers will have to do when the fancy one's finished."

"Ahhhh, just for me," exclaimed the lovely Brie when she spied the coffee maker. It was piping hot and wafting Dunkin Donuts. Brie studied the accouterments—coconut palm sugar and half and half. Her eyes lit up. She'd found the South African treats: Romany Creams and Eet-Sum-More biscuits, Jelly Tots in a little bowl and Cadbury's Flakes lined up in their purple and yellow jackets. Tastes of home.

"BJ made it all look beautiful. I just plonked it on the counter," I confessed.

"Well, she *was* a first-class hostess for as long as Methuselah lived," Moxie threw out, then clamped a hand over her mouth. She was childlike in so many ways.

BJ studied her fingernails. "I have five more good years left. I turned 964 this year. Better believe I'm going to make the most of them." She looked up and grinned.

"She's quick. I like her," Moxie announced, and sat on one of the two chairs.

I stood so they could all choose their preferred spots. BJ had moved to the love seat and Brie and Chantelle claimed the couch.

"I have an announcement." Best I set the tone early and alleviate any domestic expectations. "I've done my best to prepare for you four, but I really have zilch post-airline experience as a hostess. So don't judge me. I love my life as a hermit, and Tula is my preferred company, so this..."—I waved my hand over them as if casting a spell, "...is a one-time-in-my-life thing. If you can't sleep because the sheets aren't ironed, you're shit out of luck, because I don't own one of those hot, heavy things. If you're bothered by dust or dog hair, wipe it, vacuum it or do whatever your little hearts' desire in the cleaning department. I won't resist. If what you want isn't here, we'll pop down to the shops and pick up what you fancy. No fuss from me. I warned you in my email."

Brie said, "Oh, it's too lovely. Thank you. So happy to be here." And she absently touched the small gold trinket that hung around her neck, as if she was sharing her joy with somebody or making sure they knew she'd not forgotten them.

Hmmm, there is much to delve into.

Chantelle fanned out her bob while chasing those mosquitoes from behind her ears, shivered and said, "Me too!"

Moxie did the darndest thing. She jumped up and spun in a figure eight. I wondered if she was getting ready to do a breakdance to take us back to the eighties. Then she flew off to the kitchen with a, "No one dare steal my place," making a beeline for the booze. She didn't ask; she merely assumed we all drank mimosas and filled five glasses with juice and bubbly, then called on Brie and Chantelle to help her distribute the liquid courage.

Moxie was both officious and in touch with a girl's basic

needs. She was odd and constantly moving. She'd taken over my precious space without permission.

I felt my cheeks on fire. I hated this feeling of having no say and no control in my own home.

Tula, who'd been flirting with BJ and Chantelle, came dashing back to me. He jumped up, back legs on the floor and front legs either side of my thighs. He forced his fluffy head into my line of vision. I looked into his light blue, earnest eyes, and I saw my truth. *Let go, let the universe. 'Tis she who put you here. Trust the process. This is the means to an end that includes Roy.*

Man, he was so very smart. I put my arms around my beloved fellow and hugged him.

There was a shriek from Brie followed by Chantelle's loud shout, then her husky laugh.

"Turbulence! Holy shit, who am I trying to fool. I didn't see the step!" Brie peeked into her mug and the glass of bubbly and they were still full, not a drop spilled. Such was her delight, she beamed as if she'd won America's Got Talent.

I had a flashback to Brie tripping on, well, *nothing* as she made her way to my booth at Kitty's that rainy morning so many years before.

Chantelle gave a throaty laugh, "I remember on our flight you tripped over everything. One of the stewards said, as he watched you oops down the aisle, 'That chick's a trip.'"

"I've always been ungraceful. Once I started flying, I found a valid excuse. Whenever I tripped, I said 'Turbulence!'"

"Better than being DIS-graceful," BJ said with a mischievous look in her eye.

"Listen Brie," I said. "With a face like yours, you're permitted to trip over anything, anywhere, anytime. Just don't break your neck. I have very limited liability insurance."

"It's okay," BJ drawled, "we're South African-bred. We believe in karma, not lawsuits."

Brie placed a glass down in front of me and, with her free hand, patted her backside. "No chance of any breakages. I'm padded like those tubes you pull behind power boats."

"All the more to love," Chantelle said without a hint of sarcasm.

Brie carefully placed her mug on the coffee table. "Holy Shit, Chantelle, you never felt like a stranger, and how could I forget our time together? Now I remember! We had that Cape Town night stop. People called you 'Chants" back then. Well, that's my excuse. We had so much fun. You were fun. I met your brother. What a hunk! I batted my eyelashes at him, but that didn't work. I'm so happy to see you again." Brie smiled beautifully, and I noticed Chantelle's face was tinged with instant color. By the time she leaned over to place the drink in front of BJ, it was gone.

Yet another mystery. This is going to be v-e-r-y interesting.

The queen gave Chantelle a palm of rejection.

"What in the world is the matter with you, BJ? You don't drink?" Moxie was incredulous.

"I brought my own," BJ said and flounced downstairs, leaving a wake of Chanel No. 5.

Just the same way as she'd exited, straight-backed and booty-swinging, BJ made an entrance with a six-pack of Diet Cokes in both hands and a strap over her shoulder from which hung a guitar.

"I wondered what was in your cabin bag marked with a big duct tape 'X' in our room. It had an odd shape." Moxie noted.

"That all came in that little case?" Brie asked incredulously.

I'd gone down to fetch my Ruby Woo lipstick from the

bowl at the front door and heard the giggling earlier. I saw the two sharing my room collectively hoisting up Brie's humongous leopard-skin case onto my bed. It took them longer than it should because Chantelle had passed wind in the process. The two laughed so hard they'd collapsed on the floor. Now the vision of Brie's mammoth suitcase taking up three-quarters of my bed gave me heart palpitations. *Breathe Lucky, Breathe.*

"This thing folds up like a jackknife, see?" BJ expertly reduced the guitar to a third of its size.

"Wow," we said collectively.

"What kind of music do you play, BJ?" My interest was genuine.

"I play all sorts of things, but I gig with two guys and we play bluegrass." Her face was animated and she looked like a very young Katharine H.

"BJ, your case isn't big enough for anything else but sodas and a fold up guitar." Moxie poked the bear.

"They do sell Diet Cokes here too you know." I winked at BJ.

BJ, completely out of queen-mode, strummed a few chords just to tease us, then threw back her head and chugged down her soda—in what my mother would call a "most unladylike manner"—then burped unroyally in Moxie's direction.

And I heard my mother turn in her grave.

"Clothes are the least of my must-haves. I'm wearing what I need. I have a toothbrush, hairbrush and five clean pairs of brooks—panties, in case any of you've lived abroad so long you've forgotten. The multitude of brooks was in case Lucky's place didn't have a washing machine. Oh, I did pack another blouse. I assumed Lucky here would have a jersey I can borrow or maybe a coat if it gets unduly cold."

Talk about low-maintenance. I was suddenly sad. I should have let her wear her crown for as long as she cared to.

"You need to play for us and I'll sing," Chantelle demanded.

"Just a second," Moxie stood up, all five-foot nothing of her and did a slow pirouette. "You girls do know why we're here, right? This is not to rekindle Woodstock. We are here to find our soulmates."

"Woodstock? You were but a babe in arms in '69." BJ didn't smile, but Moxie did.

"We can always interject some music into our serious business," Moxie conceded.

"Why thank you, Moxie." Chantelle's retort was laden with sarcasm. "Don't think I don't remember your airline name, Little General."

Oh, boy!

Tula, sensitive to any conflict, started showing off in front of each of the four girls, going into a real downward dog position before moving on to the next. It delighted them so all tenuous vibes were quickly forgotten.

My dog was a much better host than I.

I watched BJ as she watched Tula. She wore...well, I couldn't concentrate on her clothing because the enigmatic aura surrounding her was so colorful and complex, it hid her worldly sheath. I caught a glimpse of at least a hundred smells underneath the Chanel No. 5. BJ's soul was the oldest in the room. It was even older than mine.

I found clothes so often spoke to the essence of who we are, so I had a better check them out. BJ had on no-fuss sneakers, or takkies as we called them back home; a pair of jeans; and a blue and green blouse she wore with the collar up. The three-quarter sleeves hid most of the age spots similar to the ones I was seeing pop up on my own fair skin.

"BJ, you're full of surprises. Crowns, guitars, bluegrass, Diet Coke, burps. You're an enigma." I grinned at her.

Then I asked them all, "How easy was it for you three to find each other at the Hertz counter at Logan?" How quickly I'd slipped back into the habit of calling cities by their airports' names.

"I looked like I was hiding a strangulation attempt," Moxie said dryly. "Wouldn't be the first time, but those were consensual." She smiled smugly but her eyes were inscrutable. I looked at the others, none of us knew if she was serious.

"We looked like three old biddies from the eighties," Chantelle said huskily.

"Speak for yourself," retorted Moxie with a wink this time. "But we sure looked bloody ridiculous." Then she pointed to Brie and pouted, "Except her! She's always pretty."

Brie blushed. *Didn't she know how gorgeous she was?*

Brie touched the gold pendent that lay at the base of her throat. It fairly bulged with trapped secrets.

"We waited for you," Brie said to BJ. "But a Hertz guy came out holding a piece of paper and said 'BJ said she arrived early so you should carry on without her.'"

"Well, the objective of the scarves was for you to recognize each other at the Hertz counter. There was unlikely to be two other women with scarves tied around their necks in the whole of the airport." I smiled and took a hefty sip of my mimosa.

"It's amazing that out of all the crew members in SAA, we five interacted with one or two in this tight circle. There were, what, two thousand ever-changing crew members? Every trip was a new adventure with new people, most of them nice,"

Chantelle began, her face glowing and her raspy voice bubbling with joy. Perhaps she *was* a famous country western singer.

"Except me," said BJ. "I've never been nice." She smiled that Mona Lisa smile. The truth would out.

Moxie raised her hand. "I can attest to that."

BJ lifted her glass to Moxie and said, "Hey, I'll make it up to you, roommate!"

I needed to distract myself from myself, and not worry so much about who was doing what or saying what to whom, so I asked, "Where do you girls call home?"

"I still live in South Africa. Rosebank," Brie started.

"Australia's sheep country." *How the hell does Chantelle make three words sound like a yodel?*

So much for my country singer notion. Those were made in America. Well, except for Keith Urban.

"I recently moved to Melbourne, Florida," said Moxie, and she spun around once. Yep. Here was a story itching to come out. I wonder how many lifetimes she'd lived with the turns and constant motion. It was time to find the source so we could pull it from its hiding place and stub it out for good! She was making me dizzy.

"Watkins Glen, upstate New York, on Seneca Lake," said BJ. "How long have you been here, Lucky?"

Watkins Glen. There was a cat shelter there about to get some big bucks. What a coincidence. Who am I kidding. There's no such thing. "In the States, fifteen years. I moved to Chicago for work, then here to Hull two years ago."

Then a thought struck me, and I said, "Wait BJ, I remember you were even more exotic than anyone else in the airline because you were born and lived in America. We revered all things American. When did you come to South Africa and when did you leave?"

"We moved there when I was nine. My father was an American ambassador to South Africa. I left after I'd made enough of my own money—in the enterprise I told you about Lucky, and came back to the States on my own terms."

I felt Brie's eyes on me. "Are you...involved?" she asked shyly. It was clear no man's fingerprints were etched into my abode.

"Only with Tula," I replied, and they all laughed easily.

"Best kind of boyfriend," said BJ as she stroked his back, and his eyes went all dreamy. Typical male. Attention from another woman and he drifted away, sans conscience.

"You, Brie?" I asked.

"I've been married since I was twenty-four."

"To the same man?" BJ asked in mock horror. We laughed heartily more at her abnormally high eyebrow than the rhetorical question.

"I'm guessing you haven't been married?" I looked at BJ.

"Hell, yes. Three times. And by the cold-blooded, dizzy-eyed bull's pizzle I do declare, third time is not the charm!" BJ said, straight-faced, and threw her head back to take another long glug of Diet Coke. I noticed the elastic band around the can. Once she was done, I'd seen her roll the band off her wrist and onto the new can. The only reason was that her hand couldn't be relied upon to hold onto the slippery can. Arthritis. I felt a pang of pity. Her coke intake was astonishing. Just as well it was the much less harmful liquid coke, otherwise she'd be as high as a kite.

I realized this thirsty-sailor-sworn-off-the-hard-stuff-routine was BJ's drum roll, and the burps, the symbol crash that followed punch lines. It was likely also a shield for whatever it was she was hiding.

"Ready for number four?" asked Chantelle.

BJ took another swig, poker-faced. We all waited in eager anticipation. Then she drawled: "Welllllll, we'll see."

"Oh, so interesting," Moxie cooed, and I was pleased BJ had a love interest. She oozed sex appeal. A partner was essential.

"You, Moxie?" I asked.

"One down, one potentially coming up."

"In what sense?" Brie asked naively.

We belly-laughed at that one.

"Chantelle?" I asked, steering the conversation so my turn would never come.

"Once and only once." Chantelle chortled; her perfect teeth white against olive skin.

"And you're a lesbian?" Moxie asked me.

I threw my head back and laughed my arse off. It was unexpected laughter. I had been called many things, but never a lesbian. Though God knows my life might have been easier with such inclinations.

"What kind of six days did YOU think I had in mind, Moxie?"

She shrugged. "Hey, in for a penny..."

"Keep your dirty little purse closed and your pennies inside." I laughed. "I only like men, but my story is sad and true and I will tell you when it's my turn during these six days together..." I realized I sounded sorry for myself so quickly added "I've had many *affaires*..."

"You sound so fancy...affairs with a French twist." Brie giggled.

"Well, they weren't all fancy, Brie, and certainly only one

was French. But I was young, enthusiastic and undemanding. I am a spinster, and it's been so long I think I may have become a virgin again." I was shocked to hear my own naked truth being publicly aired.

What had come over me? Why was I sharing all this private information with people I barely knew?

Have I just settled for my own company because there's been nobody who really wanted to be in my world? Have I intentionally blocked people from my life? Have I loudly called myself a hermit because it's easier than opening up my heart and being rejected?

What have I missed all these years?

CHAPTER 31

We talked airline talk for a while, eventually landing on the topic of Oom Faan, our overseas cabin crew scheduler. He told you where you'd fly, and you flew. No excuses. If you were on standby, you'd better turn up packed for ten days away in both northern and southern hemispheres. You never knew if it'd be passengers bound for Paris or Perth you'd be called upon to serve aboard the 747s waiting on the tarmac.

"I offered Oom Faan everything from a dinner at Linger Longer to a blow job to let me go to Madrid once a month," BJ blurted.

For a second, there was stunned silence before shrieks followed.

"Which did he choose?" I asked.

"Neither," BJ muttered, then shook her head like a really, really disappointed Katharine Hepburn.

We all collapsed. The mental picture of 395-pound Oom Faan turning down either of BJ's propositions was hysterical.

Brie yelped, "I have to pee NOW," and she shot off like one

of BJ's husbands, no doubt. Brie's eyes were wild as she looked around frantically. "Where the hell is it?" Voice desperate, face pinched in discomfort, Brie stood in her expensive clothes looking like a Nordstrom's advertisement, holding her crotch with both hands.

I flew up the step, followed by Tula, and touched the secret wall. It opened achingly slowly, as if showing off for the gals.

"Where?" she squeaked, a frightened child lost in the OK Bazaars, hopping from foot to foot. She looked at me in utter desperation, as if wondering why I'd chosen this frantic time for a magic trick.

"Cool," hummed Chantelle, and her gravelly voice made it sound even cooler than the magic door actually was.

"Do it again. Do it again!" Moxie clapped her hands.

Brie pushed past me, not waiting for the architect's *piece de resistance* to open in full. Her fly was open, jeans pulled low on her hips. She didn't care that the door was still open when she hit the john in the nick of time.

When the door had finished showing off, I pushed it closed to allow the girl some modesty. I would have bet Tula's next treat that Brie would rather die than be heard—let alone seen—doing her ablutions.

"How the hell would you know it was there if you weren't told?" BJ asked.

"You wouldn't. It makes the hostess essential on the guest's first visit. I strive to be essential," I declared, suddenly realizing how true that was. I quickly changed the subject. "BJ, what was in Madrid?"

"A Spanish Adonis. A human male specimen created by God on a Sunday in His best mood."

Moxie, in the throes of sipping her drink, snorted her delight and inhaled her mimosa.

While slapping her on the back, Chantelle announced in a voice suitable for a 747 cabin intercom system, "Moxie, through the mouth, not the nose," which increased Moxie's choking and sent BJ off to the loo. Brie had left the door open so as not to tease the next one in. The discreetly little hidden loo had well and truly come out of the closet. I'd put money on it being the most popular spot in the house.

When we were all back and recovered, I tried again. "And what became of this virile Spaniard?"

Moxie, still clearing her throat, leaned so far forward to hear BJ's response, she nearly fell out of her chair.

"I wore him out. After every ten-day Madrid night-stop, he resembled Wee Willie Winkie. He recuperated quickly. Oom Faan would not fan my obsession. I had to get my Madrid's the old-fashioned way. Luck."

"How many years did this fling last?" Brie asked earnestly.

"Five. Six. But I only saw him ten or so times a year. Bloody Oom Faan. I would have turned my Spaniard into a husk in half the time if the old bastard had co-operated."

"No doubt," I said dryly.

"How old were you when you quit flying?" Chantelle sang.

"Thirty-four. An old bag of mammoth proportion, airline-style. But I didn't quit. I was told by the check hostess more than once that I should consider transferring to the ground crew at my age."

There was a collective gasp of horror and I said, "Wait, you girls. Have you forgotten how ridiculously politically incorrect it all was? How downtrodden we women were? It's scandalous in this century. In 70s and 80s it was all we knew."

Four heads nodded sagely.

"I challenged them," BJ continued. "I said, 'My weight's well under the limit, my face is made up, my uniform is clean. What the hell do you want from me?' There wasn't a beat before one said, 'You're too old, BJ. This game is for fresh young faces. You're no longer fresh. Face it.'"

Variations of "Oh, my God," followed as we all stared slack-jawed at The Queen.

Sweet Brie looked especially horrified. "What did you do?"

"I told her to fuck herself because nobody else would. And that was the end of my airline career."

Chantelle shook her head in awe and slapped her thigh. "What a way to go."

"Those old bitches were the gatekeepers of our looks and our youth. How dare they do that to you?" Moxie rose, turned twice and threw herself back onto the chair so hard, its big self slid two inches forward. And she hadn't finished: "They got the job because they were bitter has-beens, those instructors and check hostesses. Brass knew they would be harder on us than anyone else."

Nobody knew this better than I did. I shivered and sniffed my wrist. Mercifully, my Opium calmed me.

I wondered what they'd done to Moxie to elicit such a strong opinion.

"Our airline was sexist and anti-feminist and degrading of women. Its doctrine defined all the inequalities women have been fighting to correct since the dawn of ages," BJ said. "But we had to be what they wanted us to be, otherwise we were out of the most coveted, most glamorous job our country had to offer. A job which we all know was *only* glam when we strutted through airports and lived it up in lovely hotels around the world. We had no unions. Nobody who'd fight for equity or fairness or against discrimination."

"You're right, BJ," I said. "We had no voice. Good for you, for leaving on your own terms." I smiled at her, and she looked away, almost shy.

"But we had an amazing chance to see the world. No one else I knew could ever have afforded to do so on their own—at least safely," said Brie.

"I remember girls our age going off on a one-way ticket to backpack through Europe in the seventies and eighties." Chantelle shivered. "I can't imagine roughing it around Europe."

"I know. There was no slumming for us. How lucky we experienced the world with wallets weighed down with hefty stipends to spend in each location. There we were in safe, fancy rooms all to ourselves on top floors of five-star hotels," I said.

Not to be outdone, Moxie jumped up, grinning from ear to ear. "I had a one-night stand with *Playgirl's* Mr. July on the last night of a New York night stop."

"I thought you looked familiar. It was *you!*" Brie's eyes were wide, as she looked crossly at Moxie. "I'd never seen you before, and you accosted me right after briefing and before a New York trip. You made me do the unthinkable."

"Oh, my, now I remember." Moxie giggled. "It was YOU! You were beautiful *and* kind. I was in search of both attributes —someone who was soft enough to do anyone a huge favor, *and* who could *wow* the customs chaps on home entry. A rare combo. But you appeared before me like an answer to a prayer."

"I was so shocked when you told me what you wanted me to do," Brie said, blushing a golden hue. "But I was oddly flat-tered you thought me up for the job. You scared the shit out of me. I'd been in the airline longer than you, too. Not only did you have—well, the moxie to bed a playmate, but the brash to ask a stranger to risk her wings to help you!" Brie's face took on a darker shade of gold. She had *that* kind of face, the kind that gets better in dire circumstances while others are stricken scarlet.

Brie shook her head ever so slightly as her fingers found the gold talisman. Though she smiled, I'd have bet my next glass of bubbly she'd beaten herself up about being a pushover—albeit subconsciously—'til now. Now she was pissed.

"What the hell...?" Chantelle asked, hands on either side of her face like the *Home Alone* kid. "Tell us, tell us," she chanted, her voice breaking delightfully.

Moxie hogged the limelight and stood to continue her performance. "Well, I knew Mr. July wouldn't recognize me again if my taxi ran over his foot. And frankly, he was more into his own body than he was into mine, so I knew where I stood, or where I lay. But still, he was *Mr. July*! I had to get hold of a *Playgirl* to show my future grandchildren, but alas, there was no time. I was late to the crew bus because I'd rolled from Mr. July's bed minutes before pickup."

She took a breath quickly so nobody could chime in. "Yeah, I'll admit he didn't have far to look for his quick pomp." She'd reverted to the coarse Afrikaans. "I was lingering and lusting after him from the moment I spotted him in our hotel lobby— where he was also staying. Once I saw him, I knew I had to have him. So we snogged in the lift—do you still call it that, Lucky, or is it 'elevator' to you now?"

"For God's sake, child. Get on with the sex part," BJ demanded.

She glared at BJ. "Well, since you are so demanding, can you guess the foreplay?" BJ raised her hands, and Moxie glanced at us, like a bird awaiting a worm.

Chantelle took a stab. "Lift, catch and feel?"

Pleased somebody was playing her game, Moxie grinned and shook her head and kept us waiting for five more seconds, though by this time BJ was feigning filing her nails. "He flipped open the *Playgirl* to the centerfold."

"Was it enough?" I asked.

"Girl! It was no holds—or is it holes?—barred!"

We fell about with mirth.

"You concupiscible, leaden-footed coxcomb," BJ shrieked.

"Determined little monkey, aren't you?" I said, smiling at her.

She grinned unabashedly. "Yip. I usually get what I want. Well, except in marriage, it seems—so far, anyway. So, after a very innovative romp and eleven winks of sleep, I dashed to my room, flew into the shower, fled to the transport laden with crew with my wet hair and a love bite so big, my scarf couldn't hide it. The crew had no sympathy for me at all, even after I'd bragged about Mr. July, and they wouldn't let me stop at a magazine stand during our collective traipse through JFK concourse."

I was imagining this cute little spunk, flaunting her night with a celebrity in crew transport. International celebrities were a huge deal when you came from our politically disgraced country, where no famous face would be seen dead, so you'd better believe Moxie was proud of her hickey and pissing off the crew wholesale—most envious, a couple disgusted with her promiscuity.

Moxie leaned forward and lowered her voice. "When we got back to base, I saw this gorgeous, sweet, smiley blonde walk out of a New York briefing room. Now I know it was Brie! I accosted her to bring a July *Playgirl* home for me. It was the twenty-seventh of July. Oom Faan wouldn't change my roster to send me back to New York, and my Mr. July would be lining exotic bird cages in trendy lofts on Park Avenue in a few short days."

Chantelle was hooting and hollering and rasping and stood rolling from one foot to the other. She took the conversational pause to run awkwardly up the one step, shouting, "Not one more word more until I get back."

It was an agonizing three minutes. We were all seated once more and Brie told her side. "I was so nervous. I was sure one of the crew members would see me buying a *Playgirl*, and my reputation would be in tatters. God knows I'd worked hard at creating a new one for years." She lowered her voice to whisper. I wondered if it that last declaration came out by accident. Brie recovered quickly and beamed like a naughty girl. "To make it feel like was scoring something from the nerve-wracking ordeal, I read the articles."

"Naturally," I grinned.

"Informative, were they?" BJ asked, lifting that Olympic-gold-medal-worthy eyebrow.

Brie nodded vigorously. "I have to say, the articles encouraged a study of July myself, and Holy Shit, I got quite carried away." Brie's blush burnished as we roared. "Then I loosened the staples in the center of the magazine very, very gently, because God forbid, I should disfigure him. She is small, but she is fierce." She stared at Moxie, who pointed to herself in mock shock. Brie continued, "Then I had to plan my reentry past our narrow-minded customs patrol. After some thought, I lined my first aid bag with him—he fitted perfectly—then I covered him up with that molded foam rubber with the prefabricated dents in it for aspirin and EpiPens, bandages, all the stuff we carried, and voila! Mr. July made it into Moxie's box at cabin services without incident."

"The poor prissy lamb could have been arrested. Did you appreciate Brie's great risk?" BJ asked Moxie.

"You know, I was sick after that flight and off work for another two weeks."

"You probably had the Mr. July pox," declared Chantelle, to an onslaught of guffaws.

Moxie continued. "It's very likely. The late seventies and eighties were ripe with free love, baby. We thought The Pill could keep us from all evil. Ha! When I got back from my sick bed and found him in my box, he was but a faded memory with holes in his most outstanding parts."

"Rubbish!" Brie was passionate. "I took great care, but those staples were badly placed, I'll admit. But Moxie? Take his broken parts up with *Playgirl*. It wasn't my fault."

"You little bugger," I said to Moxie, laughing up a storm. "Did you remember to at least thank Brie for the great caper she dared to attempt on your behalf—someone she'd never seen in her life but who wore the same uniform? She would have been kicked out of the airline had she been caught."

Moxie had the grace to look sheepish. "Well, quite honestly, I had no idea what Brie's name was, let alone her surname. She didn't add a note when she dropped the hot bod into my mailbox. He was lying there sedately, naked and holey."

I jumped up, holding out my hand Vanna-White-style, and presented Brie to Moxie.

There was nothing slow about Moxie.

Much to Tula's confusion, she fell to her knees and knee-walked to Brie's side of the couch. "Oh, Brie, thank you for risking your career, your *life* for me and Mr. July. And I forgive you for scarring the poor man so severely. As you may recall, even though his face was simply divine, it wasn't his biggest asset."

"Oh, I *do* remember," Brie said straight-faced before she burst out laughing.

We joined in with gusto, and then it was my turn to run knock-kneed up the step. As I loped off I informed everyone, "There are two more loos down below if you need them."

Before returning to my interesting guests, I called, "Come, boy," and Tula and I shared some love before I poked his rump with a needle and gave him a hug.

I dreaded the question—What's the plan to find our soul-mates? It was inevitably coming up. Sure, it's why they were here, but I'd not yet wrapped my head around how best to present my alternative modus operandi. I was getting to like them. I didn't want them to flee too soon.

CHAPTER 32

The early-afternoon sun washed the bamboo floors with light as, through the windows, those tall white birch trees showed off their dexterity, waving this way and that in the unseasonal winds. The outside urged that basking and drinking be done inside. I found we were excelling at both.

Birch trees. Paper. Letters. Roy. He was seldom from my conscious thought.

I considered for a moment if, without the alcohol, I'd be equally at ease with Moxie mixing and delivering drinks from *my* kitchen, with other people's feet on *my* furniture, with foreign toothbrushes balancing on *my* bathroom vanity, and visiting soaps and shampoos in *my* shower.

I decided I might be okay with it all but I was buzzing, so it was perfectly possible it was entirely the alcohol that strangely didn't make these strangers feel like strangers.

"I think we should eat," I proposed. "We had a liquid breakfast, and it's way past lunchtime. Cooking is not my forte, but I managed a Chicken à la King for your pleasure." I presented the warm Crock-Pot I'd had on low since the morning. It was a length down from the booze corner, with plates, napkins and cutlery arranged next to a bowl of fluffy white rice. I hoped the girls had low expectations.

Once our plates were loaded, Chantelle said "*Bon appétit*," which, because of her timbre and the smile in her voice, sounded more like an invitation to an exotic bed partner than a wish for each of us to enjoy our meal.

I asked Alexa to play some seventies and eighties rock to take us back. Uriah Heep then the Moody Blues serenaded us as we tucked in, diluting the alcohol in our bloodstreams.

"Look at us," I said after a sip of wine. "We all eat with a fork in our left hand and knife in our right. Our colonial upbringing is still evident, no matter where in the world we live now, or how long we've been away."

There was a full-mouthed consensus and I was delighted that the only meal I cooked flawlessly was hitting the spot. Or perhaps I'd deprived them of food and had plied them with enough alcohol that they would have enjoyed Hull sand. I was on a sudden quest to buoy my self-love, so I chose to eliminate the second option.

We chatted and teased each other easily between bites and enjoyed chilled Spier Chenin Blanc and a Neethlingshof Sauvignon Blanc, South African wines that did my chicken a favor. Or was it a flavor?

It was Chantelle who addressed the African elephant in the room. "So, Lucky. I am thrilled to bits to be here. Loving every minute. But what did you have in mind with that cryptic Facebook post?"

'Here's Johnny.' Who was I kidding. The question was even more scary than Jack Nicholson in 'The Shining.'

Oh, how I wished I hadn't diluted the alcohol with food. I took a deep breath and concentrated on Chantelle. "You know, I've asked myself that a hundred times since I posted that invitation on Facebook." I knew my features were earnest. I tried to smile, but it came out wonky. "All I know is, my life changed when I slept in the only middle bunk on 747 Zulu Sierra 216, and I wondered if anyone else's life was drastically altered because of a dream on that plane or any other. I know you all were affected, otherwise you wouldn't be here."

They all stared, not at me, but through me, lost in their own thoughts and memories. I was surprised. Did they realize the words they'd heard weren't really mine? Their expressions told me it didn't matter. I'd lost them at that jumbo's license number. It was enough to take them back in time.

I let them stay in that state for a while before I broke the silence. "I call you 'girls' because in the few short hours we've been together, I've lost years and years. I'm back in the airline in my twenties, and damned if I don't love it. Anyone have a problem being a girl for six days?" I asked.

"Hell, no," was the general reply.

Suddenly I was confident because I knew I had the divine help I needed to get this done. "Here's what I think we should do." They watched me earnestly, and I focused on looking each in the eyes so they knew I was making a commitment. "We all get one day to spill the beans about our dreams; then to hear if we found that soulmate we dreamed about or if we're still looking for him. We needed to spend much of today getting to know each other. But nobody will be shortchanged. We'll start this afternoon and go until we've unraveled the mysteries for each person as best we can." I looked around. So far, so good. Whew! "Then I have an idea which I hope you'll go along with." Now came the hard part. Their body language told me they were all in. But they'd not yet heard me out.

I was suddenly nervous again. Tula's paws were on my lap. I whispered in his ear, "It's okay, boy. I am all right, Tula." He gave me a quick lick and hopped off.

I skipped the deep breath I needed to calm myself because I didn't want to upset my very sensitive fellow, so I just blundered on. "I want to try and find the missing parts to those dreams, the ones our subconscious won't let us remember because of how damaging they were. 'Tis those parts that we haven't faced, that haunt us and mess us up in this life. Once we find the bruised and broken parts, we'll face them, thank them for their lessons, and send them on their way because they no longer serve us. Acknowledgment is all they need. I believe we come to each life to learn. If we've never learned from that which hurts too much to remember from a past life, then we can't move forward. We're stuck like a broken record, coming back to learn the same things, over and over.

"This way, we can clean the soul's cobwebs and get rid of any baggage we've schlepped with us into this century. This life. Our goal will be to get to a freeing place, where we can look forward to living our very best lives in the Now. And then we'll be in a healthy mental and spiritual state to move on with conviction. To earnestly attract those soulmates we all found on ZS 216 and were torn from abruptly; or if we've already found them, the exercise will help us make the most of our second chances with them in this life. Dammit, life's too short *not* to have it all."

When I was done, I was depleted. I'd just trusted that the right words would come from somewhere when I needed them. And they had.

I forced myself to look at the women—girls. They were leaning forward in rapture. Or was it horror? Moxie and Brie's mouths were open. Chantelle's eyes were so big, she looked like a nagapie—a bushbaby—sensing a threat, but when I looked at BJ, my wildly beating heart subsided. She wore a slight smile and nodded slowly, sagely.

At least now I knew the plan.

I braced myself for a mass exodus. I thought BJ would stay.

Brie broke the silence, said, "Holy shit!" and clutched the gold charm at her neck with both hands. Chantelle fluffed her hair, palms back to front, ending with a quick headshake. BJ threw her head back, chugged her Diet Coke and burped. Moxie rocked her body back and forth, her arms hugging herself, while perfectly cute legs folded under her own ass, like an eager little girl watching Punch and Judy.

I gave a long wink to Brie, acknowledging I'd heard her, then marched onward towards our crusade, still not sure who was in and who wasn't. "How would you describe your experience in ZS 216 crew rest, Chantelle?" I asked.

Chantelle was upending her glass of bubbly orange as I called on her, and she spilled the last sip down her neck and blouse. Unfazed, she grabbed a napkin and swatted at the sticky mess, saying, "Hell's bells. 'An experience?' I'd call it a bloody miracle! But until your Facebook post, I thought I was the only one it happened to." Her South African accent was, like all of ours, very pronounced, likely more so now that we of the same ilk were gathered.

She grinned, raising her empty glass to Moxie, the bartender.

"What would you call it, Brie?" I asked. Best to start with the easy ones.

Brie answered quickly. "Like you, Chants, I had no idea others were affected. I was afraid to say anything to another crew member in case they'd think me quite mad." She twittered nervously. "But as bizarre as it sounds, I've always believed that dream gave me the chance to complete a life I never got to live with my soulmate last time."

My heart gave a little leap of joy.

"Wow," said Chantelle. "That's deep." She gazed up at the high ceilings for a long minute, and we all waited patiently. When she looked at us again, she was bright-eyed. "I reckon I could say the same."

"Whoooooooah." Moxie returned from her booze trip. The girl knew what we needed when we needed it. It was surprising all she could carry in one fell swoop: a liter of Stoli, the neon green Bloody Mary mix, five celery straws and salt and pepper cellars under her armpits.

Into the empty long-stemmed mimosa glasses, she poured half vodka, half Zing Zang, and garnished each with a celery stick. She proudly pushed her works of art and the salt and pepper closer to those of us who were exceedingly thirsty.

"You'd make a helluva air hostess," I told her, and she nodded her thanks.

The mimosa-filled glass in front of Brie was still filled to the brim. I saw Chantelle eyeing it and after Brie's quick nod, Chantelle downed it, making way for the Bloody Mary which would, no doubt, be enjoyed by one of the others, but not Brie.

"Brie, these piss-cats hijacked your glass. Do you *want* a Bloody Mary?" I asked.

Brie smiled pure sunshine, shook her head and said, "I'll get a cup of coffee."

Moxie huffed in disappointment. Apparently, she only served alcohol.

I peered at BJ the Enigma. "Your thoughts on the crew rest on ZS 216?"

"It's proof of reincarnation. No doubt. Absolutely none." Her words hung in midair as she grabbed the diminishing Stoli and poured a healthy dollop into her Coke can.

We took another glug of our respective drinks when Brie came back.

"What would you call it, Lucky?" Brie asked, steaming mug in hand.

I stared slowly at them, one by one. "Very interesting," I said.

Moxie leaped up and Tula stood at attention. Then, to our great alarm, she jumped up and down like a spoiled child. Tula followed, dancing on hind legs. He'd never seen such behavior, and boy, he liked it!

If Moxie wasn't so cute, it wouldn't have been at all funny, but it was, and made all the more so because she was dead serious.

Perhaps Moxie was unable to verbalize her feelings quickly enough, so she'd found a way to use her bouncing body to distract the listener until she found her words.

And when those words came, she stood stock still. "Interesting? My butterfly garden is *interesting*. What we potentially all experienced"—she glanced around, daring anyone to come out as a fraud, "is supernatural. Mind-bending. Mind-blowing."

Then she sat down with aplomb—like an entertainer dropping the mic.

"You're right. It's all of that. I put my S.O.S. on Facebook because I too wondered if it was only me. I met my soulmate in a bizarre emergency landing on an island. I knew him to be the soulmate from my crew rest dream. I've been waiting for him ever since. But for gosh sakes, girls, here I am, fifty-freakin-something on a good day, and still searching for him in *his* country of origin because my soul won't allow me to be complacent or to accept second best. All because of what that dream promised me."

What was Moxie serving us? Truth serum?

I had to know. "Which bunk were you in when it happened?" I asked Chantelle.

"Middle."

"Me too," said Brie, Moxie, and BJ at once, and we all looked at each other. The coincidence was profound.

"So, only that bunk," I said, shaking my head at such impossible odds.

"Did only the four of us respond?" BJ wanted to know.

I nodded.

"The phenomenon or whatever we call it *must* have happened to more crew, but either they refuse to admit it, or they're too skeptical to believe what happened afterwards was destiny," said BJ.

"Or they don't do Facebook. Or they're dead," Brie said soberly.

"That lumpish, nook-shotten middle bunk was our portal!" said BJ, and we nodded.

"But why?" I asked, hungry to unearth the reason for a simple mattress becoming something otherworldly.

"Maybe it was cursed by a witch who sewed the cloth that covered the mattress." That was Moxie.

"Maybe when the cabin of the 747 was being designed, the

crew rest happened to be aligned with some magnetic field that opened up a vortex," Chantelle offered.

"I believe I was there when the portal was created," BJ said softly.

Four out of five of us exclaimed, whined and begged. But BJ shook her head. "Not yet. I want to hear what all of you encountered before I share."

"Bitch!" Moxie cried, then grinned to dilute any ill intent.

"When do we start?" Brie asked.

I put hands out, palms up. "Now?"

Chantelle squealed with delight and ended with a yodel-like rasp.

"Who's first?" Moxie asked, eyes wild.

"I think we should draw straws," Chantelle said.

I hurried to the kitchen, fiddled till I found them, tore the paper straws into unequal portions and held all the ends in my closed hand so four little paper piggies peeped out evenly.

All the while, I marveled at how easy this was.

But Lucky, it's the first day. And there's lots of booze.

That sobered my joyful delirium.

As I offered the straws, I said, "I go last, okay?"

"Your idea, your privilege," said BJ.

Little did she know that I couldn't have a turn before the others who'd traveled from far and wide, because who knew how long this exercise would take for each of them? And I had promised not to cut their experiences short. If I didn't get to have a turn, I could work on myself with what I would learn from them. That wouldn't be at all as much fun, but I would have done what I was instructed to do, so I could look forward to my soulmate, my Roy, landing in my lap sooner than later.

"Pick one. Smallest goes first," I said, offering four equal-looking straws. Tension quivered like newly made Jell-o out of its mold. We were all sober as judges. I was pleased they took this as seriously as I'd intended.

All of them held their straws like they were holding a matchstick end to end—at eye level and away from their bodies —while they sized up everyone else's.

Chantelle announced in her hoarse voice, "You're it, Brie. You are it," then squealed again with delight. "I'm soooo glad it's not me! I'm second. That's scary enough but at least it's not first."

Moxie was on her feet offering her straw to Brie. "Here, I'll swap. I wanna go first."

Brie childishly hid her short straw behind her back.

These girls cracked me up. There was no pretense in my house. No wonder I was so enthralled. No airs, no graces, no false modesty... Hell, no fake anything...well, since the crown had been shelved.

The ruckus subsided and Brie's torso kind of elongated. With straight back, shoulders down, and chin up she said, "I'm ready." Then she lifted her hefty coffee mug to her lips like she held a delicate China cup and was having tea at a palace. "I can't wait to share with you. I've only ever told Ryan and he didn't believe me."

There was absolute quiet in the room as we all watched Brie in her semi-trance brought on by long-ago memories. It was a companionable silence and not one I felt the need to fill which I usually did with a foot in my mouth.

"Start whenever, however you want to, Brie. No pressure. Share what you will. No judgment here." I looked around the room, and heads nodded in unison.

Brie began as if in a dream. "Remember how we had our

own airline language so the passengers wouldn't understand us? Remember 'Hilda' was horrible and 'Grizelda' was even worse than that?"

Brie never heard our shouts of agreement. Her beautiful face showed us she'd already slipped back to 1983, on board flight 907 to Madrid on Jumbo 747 with aircraft ID number ZS 216.

Then my cell phone trilled, shocking us all into the present. I shot the women glaring at me an apologetic smile, scooped up my phone, rose, and walked a short distance down the stairs before answering the call. Behind me, Moxie was calling out airline lingo, and the others shouted out the meaning, as if they were in a game show. I turned my back to them and pressed a hand over my free ear.

"Hello, chaps?"

"Are we the only ones who call you?" asked Andy.

"Have you heard of a contact list? Your names come up together 'cause you're joined at the hip," I smiled. "News. I need it like the air I breathe." I dangerously skipped down the last step to the bedroom level still feeling like a girl. My trusty canine followed. "But don't tell me till I get to where I need to be."

But when I got down there, I had nowhere to go. There were suitcases wherever I thought to sit.

Had I not been on the phone, I would probably have had a moment of panic brought on by this massive takeover of my space all over again.

Instead, Tula and I planted our rears on the top steps of those going down to the front door.

"Spill," I finally said, draping my arm around Tula's neck.

"We found evidence of Donald Cox's sorry ass in Kansas

City. And Lucky, you did it again. A scary-looking dude with puffy lips," Andy said.

"That's him!" I hissed, shuddering at the memory. "Janice was fascinated by his lips and his uneven top teeth."

"You're unfukingcanny, Lucky," Andy muttered.

"Watch the language, Andrew." Jim—always my advocate.

"Wait! You said you found 'evidence' of him. Does that mean you did *not* find Donald Cox himself?"

"You are too quick," Andy complained. "Yes, he's gone from here. Left in a hurry, immediately after we started making inquiries about him on the phone. The priest swears he was not overheard by anyone during our conversations. But something happened because the son of a bitch is MIA, and we hopped a jet the minute we confirmed he was in Kansas."

"That was less than twenty-four hours ago," I noted. "He's a slippery bastard, isn't he?"

"Yes, and we need to trace his steps from when he left Massachusetts twelve years ago as a seminary to his present commission in Kansas City. Must check to see if any women went missing in any of those places while he was there." Jim said.

"Wow! That's a mammoth task." The enormity of the investigation took my breath away.

"Or perhaps Janice was a one-time kill," Andy said.

But something still niggled. "How did you know about the big lips?" I asked.

"There's a picture of him and the choir boys on the wall. We're looking at it right now," Jim said.

I shivered involuntarily. "I am so damn glad I can't see it." I shivered. Tula moved closer. "What position does he hold now?"

Jim asked. "That's curious. After twelve years he's just an acolyte?"

"What's that?"

"This Catholic Church ministry still operates under the old-fashioned order which imposes a number of steps between seminary and priest. An acolyte is just an attendant, a follower. Usually, he is entrusted with no more important tasks than lighting the altar candles."

"Twelve years is a long time to still be an underling I would think, in any institution."

Jim's tone held disgust. "You're right, Lucky. There must be a story behind that, too."

"We must assume he knows we are after him, which makes our jobs so much harder," Andy said with a sigh.

"As you know, I have a houseful of girls with me for six days. I can't go anywhere, but I am here for you via phone if that helps." I almost felt bad I couldn't be an active part of the team. But only for a minute.

"Thank you, Lucky. We might just might have to call on you. Good to know you'll be available," Jim said.

"If you're not too drunk and disorderly," Andy said, and I recognized he was smiling.

"It's not that kind of reunion," I sort of lied as I heard a flurry above me on the stairs. I looked up, and a bevy of old beauties looked down on me, most of them a little drunk, all of them full of fun, and I could smell an avalanche of anticipation emitting from four essences.

"We're miiiiiising you, Lucky" they shouted in unison and at the top of their lungs, ending in a gaggle of giggles.

I sighed a happy sigh, hugged my phone between shoulder and ear and put two thumbs up in the air.

Andy's voice had an edge. "I thought it was not *that* kind of reunion."

Envious? Naaah. But a hint of possessiveness. I'll think about that later.

"Until next time, chaps. And wish me luck. I have six days to find five soulmates."

"Soulmates?" Now Andy's voice had a distinct edge. A beat, then his tone was softer, "And if you have no luck, please, let me know. I will do all I can to help you find him. That's how much I like you."

I heard Jim say softly, "Let it go, Andy," but not softly enough for me not to catch it. I realized Jim thought Andy was hitting on me when he was instead, offering to do me the favor I never had the courage to ask him for. Who was the psychic one...

"Luck, Lucky," Jim said.

"Thanks, Jim, and you two go safely, please." I clicked off the phone and consciously clicked off my association with Donald Cox. He could not get in the way. I had an important job to do with four friends.

Friends?

Yes! My friends!

Excitement welled inside me.

Life was way too short. I was going to do everything I knew to do to help these girls find their soulmates, or make their lives easier if they'd already found them.

Brie's dream was waiting, and her post-dream trauma would unearth all manner of secrets. An excitement I hadn't felt for years bubbled through me. This was new territory for me... Wait! Not really, I'd been conducting forays into hundreds of my own past lives for as long as I could remember.

Maybe, doing it for others was old hat for my old soul, and I would remember in this incarnation.

Perhaps all my soul had needed, was the universe to remind me to help others to help myself.

I shouted up, "Clear the skies for us to fly in, girls. I have your wings!" and Tula and I took the stairs two at a time to join my friends.

AFTERWORD

I do hope you enjoyed my first in the *Time Flies* Series. It was important to me that I introduced you to Lucky and her complexities, as well as explained the reason for this gathering of hosties. Knowing Lucky is imperative to the series, what better way than her very beginnings?

If you enjoyed *Timeless Beginnings*, it would really mean the world to me if you went onto BookBub, Goodreads, or your favorite reading site, and left a review.

Your positivity keeps me writing.

Look for *Timeless Pirouette*—the second book in the *Timeless Beginnings* Series—and start collecting all six books! Be sure to join my newsletter for release dates, shop discounts and more. Sign up at **jillwallace.com**. I value my readers so highly, and my goal is to consistently delight you.

At my website, you can go behind the scenes and read my musings, listen to audio clips and get firsthand news of coming events. You'll also find interviews, media resources, the inside scoop on my books and my Books & Goodies Shoppe.

My Books & Goodies Shoppe has all manner of fun stuff,

including South African lucky packets and signed books. I'm always adding cool things I think you might enjoy.

Join me on Facebook and together, let's contemplate, cogitate and celebrate as we strive to make life as fabulous as it can be https://www.facebook.com/jillwallaceauthor/.

I *love* to hear from my readers, so please never be shy to email me: jillwallaceauthor@gmail.com. It would be my great joy to see your name in my inbox!

Rest assured, your reviews of my books are the ultimate gift to me. Thank you, in anticipation, for taking your precious time to write them.

If you enjoyed your soiree into my South African world, I think you'll be moved by the epic saga of love conquering all odds in the multi-award-winning, *War Serenade*.

Those who love action, adventure and coming-of-age stories about the complexity of friendship will surely enjoy *Zebra*, an Amazon #1 new release.

Both *War Serenade* and *Zebra* are inspired by true stories. Read on for more details.

Look forward to BOOK 2 in the *Time Flies* series:

TIMELESS PIROUETTE

If anyone cared to look into her life, they'd deduce Brie Lenz has it all. She's beautiful, well off, and married to a talented man she adores. So what if she's gained a few pounds over her long marriage?

But Brie has a heavy secret she's kept bottled up for so long, it can never be uncorked, and it's eating at her, one agonizing bite at a time.

A Facebook post from a long-lost acquaintance becomes an S.O.S. to her own soul when Brie reads: *If you had a weird dream in the crew rest of a 747 that changed your life, or still haunts you, email me.*

At once Brie realizes she's staring into a chasm in her world that she'd convinced herself was merely a crack, and she immediately sends off the email that will change her life forever.

In just one week Brie finds herself 9,000 miles away from home, in a house full of odd characters who are all former 1980s South African Air hostesses.

The hostess for this soulmate-search-shindig is Lucky, a psychic for the FBI who uses her gifts to whisk Brie away to the first Swan Lake auditions at the Bolshoi Theater in Moscow in 1887.

There, as Polina the ballerina, Brie meets Mikhail, the one-legged beggar who changes her life by teaching her to believe in herself. More than that, he makes her believe she has the ability to reach the stars.

Mikhail and Polina share an otherworldly bond that is undeniable. The invisible cord that binds the ballerina and the beggar crackles with electricity. Where once ballet was Polina's true love, Mikhail has become her entire world.

But as the curtain falls on this ethereal romance, and Brie is back in the present, she's left with the age-old question: At what cost comes true happiness?

With stakes higher than the stars Mikhail made Polina reach for, Brie must summon the courage to venture back more than a century into the mists of time, where pain, disappointment and regret linger like ghosts in the wings, and the promise of a better future and a clear conscience hangs in the balance.

Timeless Pirouette promises a pas de deux with destiny like no other. It will leave you breathless and begging for an encore.

WAR SERENADE

When bon vivant Italian opera star-turned-pilot Pietro is shot down during World War II, he nearly loses his life. Worse, he's lost his passion for music and is close to losing his sanity in a soul-crushing prisoner-of-war camp in South Africa when he meets Iris. He has a vision of a love worth dying for-worth living for-and realizes he must find his voice if he ever hopes to find her again.

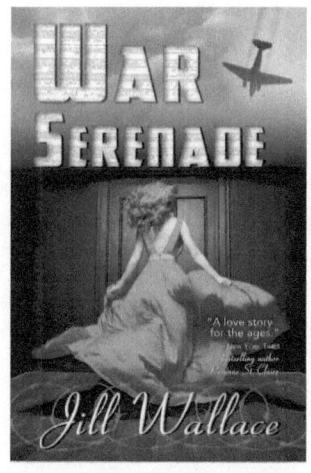

Iris's dreams are at stake when she meets Pietro. All she wants is for her brother to come home alive from the war and to fulfill her destiny as a costume designer in Hollywood. But this spirited redhead's life turns upside down as her eyes meet Pietro's through the cage of his prison. The world may be at stake, but so is her heart.

Their secretive and daring courtship raises the suspicions of the bully who runs the camp, a scarred and damaged tyrant who once dated Iris. Consummating the couple's almost mystical connection will mean crossing the barbed wire, risking the deadly charge of treason and confronting their worst fears.

Inspired by a true story, *War Serenade* is compelling, heart-wrenching, sometimes funny and always dramatic as it celebrates the endurance of the human spirit, the evolution of rich friendships, and love's triumph against impossible odds.

ZEBRA

A young white boy and a Zulu teen grow up together, building an extraordinary friendship as they explore the rugged Drakensberg mountains around a remote South African hotel during the apartheid era.

Jock and Papin forge an indelible bond while learning to love and appreciate each other's cultures. Despite whispers from intolerant guests, the boys are oblivious to the consequences of their friendship. "There goes the zebra," guests remark, claiming they can't tell where the white boy ends and the black boy begins.

But the boys' friendship is strong enough to conquer all—until society's impossible expectations wrench them apart, leaving bitter disappointment and soul-deep wounds that will not heal.

A decade later, these long-lost friends converge on opposite sides of a harrowing battlefield, one a reluctant soldier, the other a passionate freedom fighter. Their intimate knowledge of the other's way of life could be the very tools that save them...or destroy them. And an unimaginable choice will put Jock and Papin's once unbreakable bond to the ultimate test.

Jill Wallace, author of the multi-award-winning World War II novel *War Serenade,* brings together a fascinating coming-of-age story with a compelling tale of human connection in *Zebra*.

ACKNOWLEDGMENTS

When I started my Kickstarter campaign, I was as clueless as a cat at a dog show. This brave new world of marketing was introduced by none other than the illustrious author Pauline Baird Jones.

It all went down during one of our electrifying, informative, and downright entertaining GetMyBookOutThere meetings always masterfully orchestrated and hosted by the inimitable business maverick Narelle Todd. Narelle played a crucial role in helping me craft my campaign and nudged me to think outside the box. She's really, really good at that.

My heartfelt gratitude goes out to lovely Renee Massey, the extraordinary Valkyrie Psychic, who joined in with boundless enthusiasm; and Bev Wilcocks, dear friend, and kick-ass baker, who was quick to whip up quirky videos after a notably sober lunch to boost my Kickstarter debut.

I owe a HUGE thank you to author extraordinaire and Kickstarter guru Kyndra Hatch for her wisdom and unwavering support, and also to Tonya Spitler who brought her trademark grace to the table.

Brilliant Megan Fuentes deserves a mammoth shout-out for translating my visions into captivating videos and helping me with the entire presentation palette. I tip my hat to the graphically talented Trescina Bell, who carried my Kickstarter campaign to social media, and my sincere thanks to Keiti Pierce, who channeled the Kickstarter noise to my website.

How lucky I am to have all of you in my world.

And last but by no means least, a colossal THANK YOU to my marvelous Kickstarter Backers. Whether you backed me because you believe in my work and expected no reward, or you bought a token just to let me know I have your support, words fail me in trying to express my gratitude to you for participating. You gave me unadulterated utter joy watching my goal being not only met, but exceeded beyond my wildest expectations. Sincere thanks to all of you wonderful souls.

I have an overflowing well of gratitude for so many people who've played a part in bringing my series "Time Flies" to life.

A special acknowledgement to author phenomenon Kristen Painter, she who's sold a bazillion books but still took the time to brainstorm with me at an author's conference nearly three years ago. I dare not tell a lie; it took me a long time for everything to click for an entire series but my debt to Kristen for the concept of *Time Flies* is bottomless.

I give gracious thanks to my marvelous Chris Kridler (aka popular author Lucy Lakestone). It's entirely improbable that I would ever have written a book without you, dear Chris. You were paramount in gently guiding me to do my best in *War Serenade* and *Zebra* and then, as my editor, you not only made me better than I was, you made me believe my words were worthy of being read. I am sublimely grateful for your wisdom, your continued support and your friendship. Chris was my first

Timeless Beginnings developmental editor, my sounding board, my guide, and my formatter.

Amazing international author S.E. Susan Smith deserves so *many* of my thanks. Susan, when I was flailing in the dark pit of writer insecurity, as busy as you were and without any prompting, you reached out your hand and pulled me out of that literary mire. You shone your bright light on me and gave me ideas and made me find the core of my characters and held my hand until I could write all on my own. I am ever grateful to you for your patience, your foresight, your inspiration, and your brilliance. If I shine at all, it's in large part because of you.

And OMG my faithful friend, acclaimed writer, and literally poster girl for National Airlines, Debbie Shannon, is always ready to read my stuff again and again with divine enthusiasm. Then she makes brilliant suggestions while living inside my characters' heads. How blessed am I to have Deb as a sage mentor, developmental editor, and cheerleader. It's Debbie who hounded me to give you more Roy, and I obliged. I simply cannot find the words to thank you enough, Deb, for your generosity, your time, your quick responses to my S.O.S.'s and your years of friendship.

Megan Fuentes, you are a veritable treasure trove, and it is indeed a blessing to have you in my corner.

Thanks to my brilliant author friends who listened and guided, advised and encouraged until I must have bored them to death but they never showed it:

Kerry Evelyn, TJ Logan, Brenna Ash, and Lila Ferrari. You are awesome!

Unicorn Andrea Paine, you helped me in a pinch, and 'tis you I leaned on to tell me how the very last incarnation of *Time-*

less Beginnings made you *feel*. You're blessed with an eagle eye and I am very grateful to you.

I would love to thank all my willing Beta Readers. Your precious time and your feedback are imperative to my literary growth. Thank you to: Alana McIntosh, Kitty Low, Veronica de Kleyn, Isabella Jo Baines, Joni O'Connell, Betsy Galbraith, Brenda Morcom, Debby Clark, Gillian King, Darlene Hughes, Lorena Spensley, Mallena Urban.

Quite honestly, the seed of this book would never have been germinated without Debbie Sekula, my long-lost sister. Debbie awakened my psychic inclinations by accident, and the divine Sister Circle she created for like-minded women has fueled my hunger for new thoughts from one month to the next. Debbie is pure sunshine. Many of the words in this book—like the prayer of protection—are taken verbatim from Debbie. It is she who encouraged the inner child work which became the essence of *Timeless Beginnings*. I am so deeply grateful for you, my Deb.

Thank you to all my Sister Circle Sisters: Deb, Sands, Audra, Karen, Norah, Sheri, and Renee. How lucky I am to know and love you all.

My true and gracious thanks to Ann McIntosh who stepped in as my editor for version II of *Timeless Beginnings*. Ann, who supported my Kickstarter campaign and earned herself a printed copy of the first edition, bravely and oh, so kindly pointed out some issues with the book and made recommendations for making the read stronger. This was only a display of author-friendship; Ann in no way set out to garner an editing gig. She is a traditionally published author with scores of popular books under her belt and a plethora of doting fans. But lucky for me, I managed to convince her to take me on as her client. I am sublimely grateful for and to Ann, and trust she will see me through all six books to keep the girls performing at their optimum—whatever that may be!

To the women who inspired the four protagonists in this series: Beth, Brendie, Debby, and Bets, a huge thank you. My very first American friends, you took me under your wings, funny accent and all, and since then you've inspired me in so many ways. Best of all, we spent one week a year together for twenty-five years. I know you all so well. You will recognize yourselves under your *Time Flies* pseudonyms. Please forgive me for exaggerating your quirks, but boy, was it fun! I will love you four, always.

And my beloved, Athol Roy Wallace, you continue to be my conspirator, my bestie, my love and yes, my soulmate. How lucky I am!

Books by Jill Wallace

War Serenade

Zebra

Sunshine's War in
Festive Fates: 11 Spirited Holiday Tales

Timeless Beginnings

Coming Soon

Timeless Pirouette

Sunshine's War (The Novella)

ABOUT THE AUTHOR

Jill Wallace is a storyteller. Born and bred in South Africa, she's lived half her life in America. Just as it's hard to tell the roots from the branches of a baobab tree, Jill no longer knows where the South African ends and the American begins. Her stories will always be rooted in her birth country but may have branches elsewhere in the world. Her wish is that readers will remember her characters long after 'The End.' She married her soulmate, helped raise two heart-children and lives too far from her granddaughters. Jill writes happily from home in the Space Coast of Florida, which she shares with her husband and two fiercely opinionated Aussie Shepherds.

What makes Jill tick? Well, buckle up! Long-lasting friendships, unwavering loyalty, the unconditional love of dogs, the power of kindness, and the magic of chocolate and imagination, served in any order you please. And let's not forget her affinity for creatures great and small—they all find a place in Jill's world of wonder and whimsy. So, grab a bar of chocolate, cuddle up with a furry friend, and as Lucky told the old airhostesses who've just become her new friends, "Clear the skies for us to fly in. I have your wings."

Learn more and sign up for Jill's newsletter at JillWallace.com.

facebook.com/jwallaceauthor

x.com/jwallaceauthor

instagram.com/jwallaceauthor

amazon.com/Jill-Wallace/e/B079ZBFZC3

pinterest.com/jillwallaceauthor

bookbub.com/authors/jill-wallace